VOID

Book 3
Crocodile Dreaming Series

Novel by
Graham Wilson

2

Copyright

Void

Graham Wilson

Copyright Graham Wilson 2023

ISBN 9780645588712

5

CONTENTS

Part 2 : Escape from an Empty Place   211

8

Acknowledgements

Thank you to the many people who have had input into this revised edition of Book 3 in the Crocodile Dreaming Series, now called *Void*. As its name suggests, this is the darkest book in the series, and some find it too much so. It is a story of two empty places, one inside the mind of a person with no hope, and the other a real, remote place with no roads or people and almost nothing required for survival. For both, the word void seems fitting. In these empty places, I attempt to add an element of hope, the hope of escape for both body and mind.

In improving this book, the work of my editors was critical. I give particular thanks to Candra Hodge and Kathryn Moore for their contributions. Along with this, the input of a large number of readers and reviewers on sites where this book was distributed in its previous editions was also very important. Many sent me comments and suggestions for improvement, all of which I have read and considered and many of which I have incorporated.

Thank you, all!

10

Reader Reviews

Review of past edition of this book:
5 stars Fantastic good read.

How can the author think up this stuff?? Almost unbelievable story of a young pregnant woman who confessed to a murder. Also a helicopter pilot who crashed into a cliff where it was inevitable he would die

After finishing this book I have changed my mind about the series being slow and am grateful. I have just pre-ordered the next book

Review of Book 1 in Series:
Five Stars- Just Visiting —Excellent!!!!!! -So good! So impressed w/this story, can't wait to read the whole series! This book has it all: romance, suspense danger, secrets, beauty, culture, family, friends, travel and so much more! The description of the country of Australia is wonderful.

Review of Book 2 of Series:
Dreamtime, hypnotic, great atmosphere. It's superb.

Reviews of Full Series:
I read this series one volume at a time, over the last two years. It's very entertaining, well-written and really makes you feel like you're there with the characters. I can't praise it highly enough!

Five stars – very good read. The entire series is well worth the time. This author knows how to write a story that is suspenseful enough to make you want to keep reading. You care about the characters. He knows how to bring the location to life. The descriptions of Australia make me feel as though I have visited there.

A compelling story, told with sincerity. It would make a good plot for a television mini-series! The first book sets up an intriguing situation that is played out at length in the subsequent four books. Vivid descriptions of Australia's remote places are a definite highlight.

I've read all the books in this series and can highly recommend them. A storyline that begs to be read and characters you'll never forget. The wonderful Australian backdrop is the icing on the cake.

12

Authors Note

This book is set in the Northern Territory of Australia, a place which covers a sixth of the Australian Continent, the top centre part of a map of Australia. It lies in the tropics. Its capital, Darwin, is closer to Indonesia and other Asian cities than to the rest of Australia.

Deserts lie to the south, centred around the town of Alice Springs. Large rivers run to the north, full of a wealth of wildlife. Most famed is the fearsome saltwater crocodile, the world's largest reptile. Crocodiles can grow longer and heavier than a car and are able to drag other large animals, like a bull buffalo, into the water to kill. They stalk below the water and capture in a silent, deadly ambush. The crocodile is of great totemic importance to the coastal Aboriginal tribes. In dreamtime stories, it is one of the earliest ancestral beings. The crocodile's totemic spirit plays a central role in this story. Crocodiles have killed many people across Australia's north. As a young man, I survived my own attack by a large crocodile, which is recounted in the memoir *Kaleidoscope*.

This book is a work of fiction, but some places and events are real, told from my experiences in the part of my life I lived here.

A central location in this book is the Fitzmaurice River, which flows into the Joseph Bonaparte Gulf, where the western Northern Territory coastline meets the Kimberley region of Western Australia. It is a very remote, rugged place. Here the tides rise and fall by up to ten metres. In a running tide, this river becomes a white-water gorge as it thunders through its constricted passage. Very few people come to this place, one of Earth's least occupied.

Even emptier is that void inside a person who has no hope.

14

15

PART 1

LOST IN A VOID

Chapter 1 – Pulled Two Ways

Anne was conflicted. It was all so bloody hard and was driving her crazy. She was here in Australia to support her best friend, to try and talk sense into her. But it was hopeless, neverendingly and continually hopeless. Susan was buried in a morass of self-absorption. She seemed totally bent on trashing her life. And she was doing a really good job of making a mess of other people's lives as well — David's, her parents, not to mention the havoc being played with Anne herself.

But Susan was her best friend, and yet... And yet Anne was slowly and inexorably being drawn towards Susan's fiancé. It wouldn't have been so bad if she'd been the only one with these feelings. She could have caught a plane back to London, put some distance between them. There was nothing more she could do to help Susan right now. But this same chemistry seemed to be working on David. And, with two magnets pulling towards each other, it was getting hard to keep the pieces apart.

So here she was, flying first class to Sydney early on Christmas morning, with David sitting beside her. He'd drifted off to sleep, seemingly pleased to have her company on the flight. They'd departed Darwin at one in the morning. Christmas Eve had ended and Christmas Day had begun. They would arrive in Sydney in time for breakfast.

Anne couldn't help but feel excitement at her first visit to this famous city. The circumstances were all wrong, the attraction was all wrong. And yet...

And yet she does enjoy the company of this man. They'd been thrown together by a collision of circumstances of Susan's making. So, now she was on the plane, and it was far past a time for having regrets. She'd make sure nothing came of the attraction; she was stronger than Susan that way, less impulsive. The idea of getting entangled with her best friend's fiancé, even if Susan and David's relationship was doomed, must stay right out of her mind. She couldn't let herself go there, but it didn't mean she couldn't enjoy the trip and his company, even if just as friends.

As she looked at David's tousled golden hair and his beautiful face as she slept in the seat next to her, she couldn't help but feel regret that they hadn't met at another time and place. She knew it would only take one little move from her to start something.

All in all, it had been a very strange day. First, they'd gone to have a cup of tea with Charlie, an old aboriginal man. They'd talked about an evil crocodile spirit and a crocodile stone Charlie had given Susan yesterday. It had sounded like mumbo jumbo, and neither she nor David really believed what he'd said. Susan's parents had encouraged them to have this meeting; they had located Charlie, somehow, and they had met with him, themselves, two days ago. This morning when she and David met Charlie, he'd told them of his visit to Susan yesterday. He'd told them how, after she took that stone in her hand, the bad spirit had gone away, and her mind had become clear.

They liked the old man but thought the story would turn out to be superstition. Yet when they'd visited Susan, it was the first time Anne had seen a resemblance of her old friend in the room. Susan's laugh, smile, and mental clarity had returned. The night in London when Susan had come to her for help was the last time, before yesterday, she felt like she knew Susan. Although Susan hadn't shown any sign of changing her mind about what to do, that was still just as hopeless, at least she seemed to see and understand the world around her. She smiled again and could hold an ordinary conversation.

With this sense of the return of the real Susan, she and David had felt great relief. But that created another problem. With her anxiety about Susan lowered, it had become more important to start dealing with the ongoing attraction between her and David that came from both physical desire and from spending so much time together.

Eighty percent of her waking hours over the three weeks since she'd arrived in Darwin had been spent in David's company. With Susan's unwillingness to talk to lawyers, she and David were Susan's de-facto legal team, both determined to try and gain an understanding of what had happened as a first step in marshalling evidence that could give Susan a way out.

She thought back to her first meeting with David and then to all the times since. The first night they met at a sort of unofficial engagement party for David and Susan in London. She and David were a bit awed by each other. Even though David was totally enraptured by Susan, a thing like a primal attraction had flashed between him and her in that first instant.

Anne had dressed to wow the party. It worked, judging by David's open mouth when he first saw her red hair, green dress and sparkling hazel green eyes. And she'd been equally awestruck by this gorgeous man, even though Susan had already told her he was seriously handsome. That night she'd asked Susan if he had a brother she could meet. The power of her physical attraction was so strong she'd only been half joking.

Of course, she'd been overjoyed for Susan that she'd met such a gorgeous man, but deep down, she was a little jealous as well, not that she would ever show it.

Anne remembered the awful phone call Susan had asked her to make to David after Susan was called into the police station. Susan had known she could no longer marry David, that despite the hurt it would cause him, she must end it.

But Susan couldn't bring herself to tell him it was finished, instead, all she did was run away. She'd asked Anne to be her emissary. Despite strong qualms, Anne had reluctantly agreed to call David and tell him his engagement with Susan was off.

There was shocked silence on the other end of the phone as she'd bumbled her way through Susan's message. Anger followed, a refusal to accept the words from anyone but Susan that the engagement was over, then a slowly dawning acceptance of Anne's message being real.

As they continued to talk and he began to grasp the loss and the futility of it all, his grief was apparent. In that minute, she'd felt devastated for both him and Susan. When she said she wished her message was otherwise, she truly meant it.

When he asked, Anne kept her promise to continue to ring him on a weekly basis to share first-hand news about the legal processes in England as they unfolded. It had taken great effort on her part to dissuade David from flying to England. She'd been blunt, saying Susan didn't want him there, didn't want photos of her jilted fiancé in the English tabloids. Susan had already made up her mind to return to Australia and face the charges.

As time and the weekly phone calls went on, and she saw him on the television a few times, she gained ever increasing respect for David's decency and his mental toughness. He refused to get into sordid speculation; he simply kept repeating a consistent line of knowing that Susan was a good person. He also briefed his family to say the same. He answered the journalists' reasonable questions with politeness, but there were times when a line was crossed, and she felt white fire coming from him. He wouldn't tolerate anyone saying offensive things about Susan's character or her family, and he made this very clear. Even the worst type of journalists now stepped back before this line was crossed.

When Susan was extradited to Darwin and Anne had cleared her work sufficiently to fly there for the committal hearing, David had booked her a business class seat and insisted he pay. He said Anne was trying to help his fiancée and her finding time to act as a friend was more than enough for her to cover. So, he'd paid for her flight and for her hotel accommodation ever since she arrived.

Anne understood he could afford it, but even so, it seemed exceptionally decent and kind, both to her and Susan. Anne wasn't poor, but her family were not nearly as well off as Susan's were. On her legal secretary's salary, she had limited money left over each month after she paid for her tiny London flat. So, while Anne would have found a way to come anyway, even if she'd to borrow the money, David's help had made her life much easier.

She'd been apprehensive about meeting David again in Darwin; she was the messenger of the train wreck that had come his way. As she disembarked, he was waiting for her. From that first minute, he'd been so polite and gracious, saying how he appreciated all she'd done and tried to do. "And I really value your kindness and honesty."

This meant a lot to her. The evil press speculation that enveloped everyone who knew Susan, their nasty commentary on Susan's unresponsive state, had been hard to deal with. It felt good that someone saw and valued her efforts.

Anne liked Susan's family, but they had more than enough troubles of their own dealing with their daughter, and they didn't seem to understand the emotional cost to Anne, whereas David seemed to understand this intuitively.

The day after Anne arrived in Darwin, David announced that despite Susan's lack of response, he was still totally committed to her as a person and to her gaining her freedom, no matter what happened with their relationship. He appointed himself as Susan's unofficial legal representative and asked Anne to help him in this task. Her work as a legal secretary came in useful, and the two of them set up an office in his hotel suite living room, along the passage from her own accommodation.

They'd worked long days for the three weeks since then, gathering any fragments of evidence they could find from the various parties and sources: the pathologist, police, prosecutors, witnesses. Despite their work having no official status, most people seemed to want to help. It was as if, despite the continuous horrible speculation about Susan that went on and on in the papers, there was a general sense the story circulating didn't make sense, and there must be more to it. It seemed a lot of people welcomed someone trying to get to the bottom of what had actually happened.

They were yet to talk to the initial investigation officer, Sergeant Alan Richards. They were told his work on the case was finished and that, since the committal hearing, he'd been assigned to other work and so wouldn't be able to help with their inquiries.

Anne knew his face from the English legal proceedings, and they had seen him briefly in court at the first Australian hearing, but despite making countless phone calls and leaving messages asking him to contact them, they'd been unable to talk to him.

Was he was hiding something? Perhaps his discomfort about the way the investigation had ended. She understood that, when he first found the head in the billabong, he could never have imagined his investigation would unfold in such an awful way. Susan had mentioned their strange friendship on the plane trip, and Anne felt he must still be searching for the truth, even if he seemed to be avoiding them.

As their investigation proceeded, the only things Anne hadn't told David about was the information from Susan on the night she'd first sought Anne's help. She kept to herself the existence of the man's diary and the holiday text exchange with Susan. Because of these things, Anne knew Susan had acted because she'd been in fear for her life. But she'd made a promise to Susan that she wouldn't share this information, and she planned to honour her promise. Susan needed one person in her corner she could fully trust. Even though David was on Susan's side too, telling him these things would betray that special trust.

In a way she understood Susan's dilemma. Susan had totally loved this man she was charged with murdering. Now she was also carrying his child. So she couldn't and wouldn't sully his reputation. As her best friend, Anne couldn't deliberately act contrary to Susan's wishes, which left her fighting for Susan with one hand tied behind her back.

It would have to be left to others to discover these secrets. She could only try to think of things that could point to the truth without requiring her collaboration. But as they gathered the evidence, Anne had to admit it looked bad for Susan, who was doing zero to help her own cause. Susan was like a diver caught in a sinking submarine without an escape hatch.

As she and David had worked side by side with a quiet desperation, trying to find something in Susan's favour, they moved beyond simple physical attraction to something much deeper, an intense liking for each other.

United by a common purpose, they it seemed they both started to notice each other ever more. Anne had always been very aware of her attraction to David, but she'd kept that part of her mind closed off; he was her best friend's fiancé. Even so, she'd find herself looking forward to his smile of greeting each morning, and she loved the way he did little things to improve her life in this unfamiliar country and did them with an easy, unconscious charm.

Each morning he would have a breakfast platter of coffee, croissants, pastries, and orange juice set up on his verandah, looking out across Darwin Harbour. He insisted they begin each new day with breakfast together. As the weeks went by, they started to chat about themselves and things beyond Susan. He always had lunch brought in when they were not out at meetings, and, despite long days of work, he insisted they go out to eat a proper meal each night in one of the local restaurants. Sometimes Susan's family dined with them, a couple times they were joined by other business acquaintances or legal people. Often, it was just her and David.

Something was happening between them that they both tried to deny, a deep sense of mutual attraction. Sometimes, when she turned to look at David unexpectedly, she caught him looking at her in a way that seemed more than just friendly, and he seemed embarrassed and looked away. He caught her doing the same. Occasionally, she felt an almost deliberate touch as his hand or body brushed past her, and it gave her a little thrill.

Each Sunday, they took a day off, and David took her sightseeing, first to the zoo, followed by a swim in the crystal clear natural pool at Berry Springs along with Susan's family. On another Sunday they went on a boat trip in the harbour with some of David's business friends.

When she saw David's bare body in his swimmers, the power of her physical attraction to him really hit her. She could tell he was noticing her in the same way when she wore skimpy tops, shorts or a bikini. The day at Berry Springs, she'd almost swum up to him without thinking and wrapped her arms around him. It was a thing she ached to do. But, once done, there'd be no undoing it. It was lucky Susan's family had been there too on that day.

Their rooms had a connection door that David had left unlocked so she could come into his apartment sitting room which was their temporary office. A couple times in the morning, she'd gone into his room when he was still in bed, and she'd had to fight an almost overpowering urge to climb in beside him; she could feel him willing her to do this. But there would be no way back if she did that either.

When he invited her to Sydney with him for Christmas, a private invitation for her only, it felt as if a line had been crossed, and they were heading down a path towards something more.

She hadn't immediately said yes, feeling uncomfortable about getting in deeper with him, but then he'd presented her with a return ticket to Sydney. "Please come. My family have invited you, and I'd love you to see the New Year's Eve celebrations in Sydney before we go back to Darwin."

Despite her nagging reservations, she'd agreed to go, while also feeling she should politely decline so as not to be disloyal to her friend, and yet there it was, this mutual attraction. It was drawing them together like a rubber band stretched tighter and tighter that one day must inevitably break. In that moment of saying yes, she knew a line had been crossed. As they descended into Sydney, even though nothing had happened between them, she felt as if she had stepped onto a roller coaster from which she couldn't disembark.

It saddened her to realise that after almost three weeks of her month in Australia gone and, despite all her effort, she'd done little to help Susan's cause. By the time they returned to Darwin after the New year, there'd only be four days left before she'd need to be on a flight back to London and a return to work. She had well and truly used up all her annual leave and the goodwill of her employer.

Part of her felt her loyalty to Susan should have seen her stay in Darwin with her over Christmas and New Year to keep trying to help her. But it would have been a miserable time in Darwin between now and the New Year, Susan in prison, she alone in a hotel room, her own family back in England, and all her other friends in other places.

If Susan's parents had stayed in Darwin, it would have been easier to stay too, but they were also flying to Sydney over the holiday to see Ruth and Jess, the Australian cousins. They planned to return to Darwin for a final fortnight after the New Year before they'd return to England too.

Anne didn't have enough money to take a side trip these holidays. If she'd extra money, she might have flown to Cairns to visit the Barrier Reef as, like Susan, she loved diving. But it wasn't financially possible.

Their week together in Sydney passed in a rapid, exhilarating blur. On arrival, they met Susan's cousin, Ruth, one of David's best friends. After a quick catch up over brunch, they drove David's sports car across the mountains to reach his home in time for Christmas dinner.

It was a traditional gathering with all the trimmings. The whole family made Anne feel welcome. She couldn't help but like them too. What a nice family Susan had come into when she met David. She was glad she'd now got to know them.

Over the next few days, there were driving trips out into the country along with endless visits by relatives, combined with uncounted cups of tea and slices of Christmas cake. It was a complete breath of fresh air after the last few months of Susan's legal challenges.

Occasionally, Anne felt guilty about Susan being locked up while she was enjoying herself, but she knew it was beyond her to help Susan at this time, and her unease soon passed. Two days before New Year, they said goodbye to David's extended family and returned to Sydney. David organised for her to stay in the spare room at Jess's place, perhaps sensing he should minimise temptation for them, and also avoid the risk of gossip.

On the drive back, he seemed quiet.

"Is everything okay?" she asked.

"I should have said something sooner. I won't be able to come back to Darwin with you after New Year. A bit of a red-hot issue has come up at work. I'll need to spend a couple of weeks in Sydney to sort it out."

When she didn't immediately reply he glanced at her and said, "I know you're booked on a flight back to Darwin on New Year's Day, but you actually could stay on here in Sydney if you preferred?"

Their relationship had become much more relaxed and honest since their time away together. Both were happy to enjoy doing things together. For now, each would park their desire for anything more.

"I'd much rather stay here with you because I've enjoyed this trip so much, but my first loyalty needs to be with Susan. There's only a week until my flight back to England. I want to spend as much of it as I can with her, see what I can do to get her feel comfortable telling the story of what really happened, unblock her fear of whatever this thing is she is hiding from."

David took her hand and squeezed it. "Thank you. You've been such a good friend to us both, and I've truly enjoyed my time with you too. But you're right. Susan needs to be the priority. I'll be back in Darwin about a week after you leave. Perhaps it's better if each of us meets and talks to her alone anyway. She might be more open on a one-on-one basis. I've noticed whenever people try and put pressure on her together, she feels like they are ganging up on her, then she gets defensive and closes up.

"I want you to come back as soon as you're able. Certainly, we both need to be with her for a week or two before the trial starts. Will you be able to get time away from work again?"

"You can count on it."

They spent New Year's Eve on a boat on the harbour with Ruth, her boyfriend, Steve, Jess and her partner Robbie, and a couple of other friends.

They hugged tight as they said goodbye next morning.

"I'll miss you," they both said together as they pulled apart.

The question about what they were really feeling for each other remained, but they both knew that now was not the time.

Chapter 2 – Helicopter X

Vic was flying low and fast, enjoying the physical thrill as he twisted his helicopter through the gorges of the Fitzmaurice River. He had done a job between Wyndham and Derby yesterday and needed to be at Timber Creek tomorrow, from where he was booked to do a scenic trip, taking well-heeled tourists out to see the country where the Victoria River cut through the ranges south of the town. It formed a series of spectacular gorges carved out by the river.

In the wet season, his regular work was quiet, so today he had a free day to kill. Nothing much happened in Timber Creek. It was just a sleepy little place on the Victoria River, barely more than a one-horse town.

He logged in with flight control on leaving Wyndham, putting in a flight path from Wyndham Airport direct to Timber Creek, but the idea of spending a whole day in this quiet backwater when he had full fuel tanks and a couple of spare jerry cans, giving plenty of flying time, was a little boring, so he made a diversion from his logged route, flying east then north east over the Joseph Bonaparte Gulf, a place of monumental tides. As he came out over the water, he noted the tide in its huge river estuaries was full but still running in. This fitted with the almost new moon he'd seen late yesterday evening.

He'd been avoiding reading the document Susan had given him on the tiny memory chip. He knew he needed to read it. He had bullied Susan into giving it to him, something he didn't feel proud about. He'd promised Mark he would take care of her, yet in his rage, he had slapped her up. He could still picture the shock and the red marks on her face from his backhander.

Now, even though he should still be mad with her, he just felt sorry for her. It had come to him with dawning clarity as she talked, that Mark had done something really, truly awful, and she had found out. Yes, she'd killed him, but in truth Mark was a wild, dangerous man, notwithstanding being a brother. He was a man always living at the edge and sometimes way past it. Vic had always sensed a dangerous spirit in Mark that sometimes drove him to do bad things.

Something bad must have happened between them, which had tipped Susan over the edge, and in the heat of it, Mark had ended up dead. Somehow, it seemed a fitting way for his mate to go, killed by a lover then given to the crocodiles, which were his other true love.

Vic knew the story of the bad part of Mark lay hidden in the diary Susan had given him. But he wanted to hold on, just for a little bit longer, to the good memories of his friend. That was the real reason he was avoiding reading it. He knew, once he read this story, his mind's image of his friend would inevitably be transformed for the worse, and he didn't want to go there.

At least not yet. So, in the meantime, Susan was carrying the can for this awful thing. He was sure Mark wouldn't want that, for her to suffer on his account.

So, Vic knew he had to bring himself to read and understand Mark's story, then decide what to do. For now, he was in avoidance mode, at least for another few days.

This helicopter thrill ride was a further part of this avoidance, just like the other things he'd done to fill his days since he'd found out about Mark's diary.

He justified it by telling himself that his laptop couldn't read the tiny memory card Susan had given him. He'd have to buy a Micro SD card holder that would fit into a regular memory card slot, but with Christmas and New Year, most shops were still closed. He would go into Katherine for a couple days after New Year's Day and buy one then.

In the meantime, he was flying over Fitzmaurice Gorge, one of the most beautiful remote places of The Territory. He'd only ferried over the top of it in his helicopter a couple times, and looking down, as he flew over, he marvelled at the massive cliffs that fringed this river, which was in the middle of nowhere. He'd always thought of this block of country as an empty place, and he'd heard other locals talk about it in that way too, the emptiest and most godforsaken part of the NT, hard to get to and almost completely uninhabited. Even the Daly Reserve blackfellas, his coastal cousins, rarely came out here, and he knew why. It was way too rough to walk through and, with the big tides and supersized crocs, only a madman would come here in a small boat, particularly a dugout canoe.

Today, he would take an up-close look. This morning, there was a fresh flow thundering down the gorge, the result of big storm rain up around the back of Pine Creek.

It was a blast flying up the gorge, skimming over a thundering white-water torrent, which ran hundreds of metres wide, with huge sheer cliffs rising alongside. It was sort of like a gulf river but even wilder. Wet season flows had combined with thundering tides to become just awesome.

It was hard to think of a more inaccessible place, particularly in the wet. It was around a hundred miles to the nearest trafficable road. There wasn't even a rough bush track within fifty miles. God help anyone who got stuck out here. No one would ever find them. It was hard to see any way to get out of a place like this on foot.

The helicopter engine was running like a dream. Such a steady and sweet thump came from the blades of his metal bird. He passed a big creek running in from his left side, swelling the river with its own huge flow.

There was a sharp turn to the right coming up, with the cliffs rising up straight up ahead. He would go with it using his reflexes and the engine's power to pull his chopper around the river bend before it hit those beetling cliffs. It would take full power to pull the old bird around this tight corner.

As the cliff came racing towards him, he held off on his turn, wanting the thrill of pushing the far limits of the machine. When he was barely a hundred yards to the cliff, closing in at seventy knots, he knew he must soon make a thirty-degree hard right hand turn to stay in the gorge. There was nowhere else to go. Even with his machine at full power, he couldn't pull a sharp enough climb to get out of the gorge.

At that last critical moment, when he knew he must respond immediately, he pulled the control stick hard right.

It wouldn't move, it felt jammed solid. He tried to flare up, but it was jammed that way too. He threw all his weight behind the stick to move it right. It was like steering a Mack truck without power steering. He managed to move it millimetres with huge effort, turning the metal bird to the side so the skids came up towards the cliff.

With sudden clarity, he knew it was too late to escape, there was nowhere for his helicopter to go but into the cliff.

This would be his date with destiny. He had a bare half second to turn off the power before the helicopter slammed into the cliff face, fifty feet above the raging river. He figured his speed was at least fifty knots in the split second before impact.

He felt a fleeting sense of his life passing before his eyes as the metal of the helicopter crumpled around him, trapping his body inside. Then, as full impact hit, he felt nothing.

The hawks, soaring overhead, watched as this strange metal bird first attached itself to the cliff with a crashing and grinding sound and then slowly fell away into the river below.

It was picked up by the raging white water and swept along with the current around the bend and on down the river. For a minute or two, it was partly visible on the surface as it bobbed along, then it vanished from view.

Chapter 3 – Missing

Buck got a strange phone call just as dusk was settling over Victoria River Downs station and he had sat down and opened a beer. It was from the publican, Jack, at Timber Creek. "Have you seen Vic, chopper pilot?" his voice boomed down the line. "Was expecting him midday, he's done a no show. Thought maybe you'd booked him for a job at short notice and he diverted down to VRD Station."

It was more puzzling than anxious, but with a strange and fearful feeling in this whole affair with Mark. He'd found out about it last week, and it made him uneasy, over and above this.

He'd missed all the papers and TV news at the time Mark was connected as the 'Crocodile Man'. Even if he'd listened to the news at the time, he was unsure whether he'd have paid heed. November and December were often the busiest months of the year, and this year was no exception. TV watching was lost in distant memory, and unread newspapers lay in a pile in the office. So when Vic turned up the week before Christmas to clean out the scrubbers from the top end of the station, where the river ran into the gorge country, he'd been none the wiser. From the moment he laid eyes on Vic, he could tell something was seriously wrong. It was no surprise. He and Mark had been like brothers for as long as Buck had known them. They'd done lots of jobs together and built an understanding of working as a team more seamlessly than any other pilot and contract musterer he knew.

That was why, despite having his own machines and plenty of others to pick from, he still regularly booked the two of them for tough jobs like rough country clean-ups, where in one critical minute, the wrong operator had the ability to lose every animal mustered, and Buck would be left with an empty yard and a big helicopter bill to pay.

He'd wanted to book Mark and Vic for the pre-Christmas clean-up but had been unable to run Mark to ground. He'd not been seen around these parts for two or three months, not since he'd come through with that pretty English lass, Susan, who'd helped Mark to bring some cattle up the Wickham Gorge. Buck hadn't thought much about it. Mark was like that. He sometimes dropped out for a couple months, then would reappear when he was ready.

In the end, he'd booked another contractor to work with Vic and clean up that pocket of country in the week before Christmas. He thought Vic might be able to shed some light on where Mark was. He expected a story like an unexpected trip to the Middle East. That had happened at least once before. But the moment he saw Vic's face, he knew there was more to this story. It was like a sixth sense spoke to him. They'd no time to talk until the mustering was done. It had gone well. Vic had lost none of his touch, and Billy, who had run the ground side of the operation, was good, if not quite the class act Mark was. He'd moved fifty-nine big scrub bulls into the yards and about the same number of cows and heifers. Three quarters were cleanskins now wearing the VRD brand, along with a scattering of young stock that would go into the paddocks. All in all, it was a good morning's work from which they'd all made real money.

But as they sat down for a cup of tea at the end of the job, Vic pulled him aside and asked him if he knew about Mark.

Buck's perplexity had been obvious. "Only that I've not been able to get in touch with him since August. That's why, a month ago, when I'd still not heard from him, I booked Billy to work with you. I hoped you could tell me where he was."

Vic was his usual direct self. "Yeah, wondered too where he'd gone, but I never really thought about it. Too busy. Now I know. We won't be seeing him anymore. He's dead. They say he was murdered by that British bitch he was travelling with."

The story had come tumbling out. Buck found it hard to believe, even now. Susan had seemed such a sweet girl, so it was hard to imagine her killing Mark or even that it was Mark's body they'd found. Vic had no doubt. He said something about an old bullet injury on Mark's arm that made him certain it was his body they'd found. When Vic explained about the two surnames used by Mark, it gradually became clear why the name Mark Bennet, mentioned on the radio news, had not connected. Buck knew him as Mark Butler, same as Vic.

Vic couldn't hide the cold, calculating rage bubbling inside him at the idea that someone would kill his best mate, whatever the reason. And that was only the half of what was odd. The last night he'd seen him, Mark had asked him to witness his will, right after dinner. The will was made in yet another name again, Vincent Mark Bassingham.

"It was my name as a kid," Mark had explained. "My father was a bad bastard. I ran away from home as soon as I was old enough. I kept the name Mark but changed the surname I used, though the other is still my legal name."

That seemed fair enough. What was really odd was that apart from a few minor gifts, the will gave all his possessions to that girl, Susan, who he was travelling with. "She knows nothing about this, probably wouldn't agree if she did," Mark told him.

Buck had only half read the will as he witnessed it. It was pretty short, there for all to see and not something he was likely to forget. Just a few lines of minor beneficiaries. He half saw his own name and Vic's there, though never bothered to read any detail of what was given, and then there were a couple pages of paper at the back that listed other assets. It seemed like quite a lot of stuff for a bloke who'd never shown any signs of owning more than himself and his vehicle, but again, he didn't give it more than a passing glance.

Truth be told, he didn't think it was likely anything would come of it. Mark was a super tough bastard. He'd watched him survive many close shaves, too many to count. Buck thought it was fanciful to believe anything would ever touch him.

When he'd questioned Mark as to whether he was sure about that bequest and why it was so important, Mark had admitted to Buck he was smitten with Susan. "I've had a bad feeling, sort of karma like that my nine lives are running out. And if I'm right and something bad happens, I'd prefer that the stuff I have that's worth real money goes to her instead of to the state or my mongrel father."

He'd said this with such quiet certainty that Buck didn't argue. He just signed the document and handed it back to Mark who took it and nodded his thanks.

Mark had laughed the whole thing off as superstition a moment later. "It must mean I'm getting old, seeing shadows dancing on my grave and all that. Still, it's what I want. Would you consider being an executor, should the need arise?"

Buck knew nothing about Marks affairs, but hell, Mark had been his mate, and they'd worked together on a lot of jobs over the last seven or eight years. What were mates for if not to see you right if something bad happened? That's why he'd said yes to being an executor. Now he wondered where the will was?

Since that day when Vic had told him Mark was dead, he'd been thinking about what his course of action should be. Should he talk to the police? Should he visit Susan?

He'd intended to discuss it with Vic when a chance came. On the night when he'd signed the will, he'd noted that Vic's name and signature sat alongside his own. But now Vic was missing.

"Like I said, he was due no later than mid-afternoon," Jack told Buck. "Asked me to hold a room for him. But the day's done, and there's still no sign of him. I've two tourists staying tonight who're booked for his scenic flight tomorrow. They want to confirm the flight and plan a route, so they're keen to know where he is too."

They were both perplexed. Vic was super reliable and always called flight control to cancel his flights. "I'll make a call to Darwin Flight Control," Buck assured Jack.

This call confirmed that nothing had been heard from Vic since this morning when he'd left Wyndham about nine o'clock. Flight Control hadn't initiated any action as it wasn't unusual for helicopter pilots to fail to cancel their flights and, with a massive storm over Darwin from early afternoon, radio reception had been terrible.

Now the storm had moved further south over Pine Creek and the Daly River, so the radio reception was still just as bad from down that way.

"The other thing you should know, if you haven't heard it on the radio, is there's a low-pressure system heading your way. It's been sitting in the Arafura Sea, north of Arnhem Land for the last couple of days. As of this afternoon, it became a cyclone, and it's now heading in a south westerly direction at ten kilometres an hour. It's still a hundred and fifty kilometres out to sea, but its current trajectory will bring it down over the western NT coast, crossing land somewhere between the mouth of the Daly River and the Joseph Bonaparte Gulf."

That meant it was headed right towards here, and the weather was likely to deteriorate badly tomorrow, particularly in the afternoon if the cyclone held its course. Of course, it could swing further to the south and clobber Darwin or break further to the west and hit the Kimberley coast.

But as things stood, the place Vic was flying through today was in direct line for this super storm, and that didn't improve the odds of finding him tomorrow should a search be required.

Of course, Vic could have landed somewhere and been unable to get his helicopter to start again. If this was the case, why hadn't he called in? He could have used a local frequency to let someone down this way know to ring Darwin if he couldn't get through, but not if he had a flat battery or radio problem.

Tomorrow, they needed to locate him early, or it would be time for a full-scale search for a missing helicopter. With bad weather forecast, they'd need to get cracking at first light.

Two helicopter pilots Buck had known had gone down during his decade in the industry up here, and this was something he didn't even like to think about.

They'd been awful affairs for all concerned. One pilot had burned to a crisp, so what remained was past resembling a person. Buck had been one of the first on the scene, and he still remembered that awful stink and the charred mess.

Anyway, that was for tomorrow. Nothing more he could do tonight bar call the other stations en route, Legune, Auverge and Bulloo River for starters, to see if anyone had sighted or heard from Vic. He'd have dinner first, then make the calls before he went to bed.

Chapter 4 – Christmas Alone

Susan sat in her cell. Christmas Day was almost over, the light outside fading. The day had a surreal, empty feeling. No presents, no visitors, no singing or laughing, just her and the crocodile stone for company.

Prison was a strange place. She'd overheard the warders talking about how overcrowded it was, but she had a cell to herself, and it seemed to be a bit away from the other cells, so there was no one next door to talk to. She was in the remand section, awaiting trial. At this stage, it seemed that despite lots of men being on remand, she was the only woman in maximum security facing a serious charge. It was just her in a block of several cells with its own visitors' room. She rarely saw or heard anyone else, other than in the far distance.

The cell was often hot and steamy with no fans or other cooling, although the visitor's room was lovely and cool with full air-conditioning. At night, she would pull a sheet over her head to keep the buzzing mosquitos away from her face. Last night, late in the night, there'd been a huge storm with endless flashes of lightning and rain banging down and, for a while afterwards, the air was cool. But today, there was an airless, hot steamy feel to the atmosphere, both inside and out of her cell.

Normally, she didn't mind solitude as she didn't want to talk to others about what she'd done, although this was the question they invariably wanted to ask. But solitude on Christmas day felt wrong. Where had all the laughter in her life gone?

Today she'd tried to pass the time by reading a cheap, trashy romance novel she'd taken from the visitors' room bookshelf. Now she was bored with it. It was not much of a story. Still, she persevered, making herself continue to read to help pass the time, sitting with her legs crossed on her bunk, with the crocodile stone in her lap.

A few times she'd put the stone aside and tried to pretend it was just superstition, not really influencing what was happening inside her head. But, each time, within a few minutes, she could feel the fog return, as if the malevolent crocodile spirit was insinuating itself back into her mind. Then, as her hand returned to touch the stone, clarity would instantly return.

She felt truly grateful for the visit yesterday from her mum, dad, Tim and Anne and David. They'd brought brightness into her life for a couple hours.

Then David had flown back to Sydney last night for a family Christmas. She knew he wanted Anne to go with him and sensed the spark there and was glad. If something happened between them, then she'd less guilty for her part in messing up his life.

She'd not formally broken off the engagement, but as soon as the New Year passed, she would. She suspected David and his family would be relieved.

Anne would be better for David than she was. She and David were impulse driven. Anne was steadier and would balance that part of David in a way she never could. Still, her intuition about them was all speculation, not based on anything more than a hunch. If she was right about them, she'd be glad. She wasn't jealous, just a little envious of the freedom they enjoyed. She wanted something good for them both. They were both true friends she deeply cared for.

She was thankful her mind had been clear enough to talk to her parents properly yesterday. It had been so hard before with the fog filling her head. Although they didn't have any deep and meaningful conversations, she sensed something approaching relief in them that their daughter's mind had returned.

She wasn't really free of the crocodile spirit, but at least she now had a way to keep it back. Thanks to the new clearness the stone gave her and Vic's words of confrontation about what she had done, it had come to her yesterday that she needed to plead guilty. She must stop this farce of pretence, saying she would neither confirm nor deny what she had done.

As soon as New Year passed, she'd tell the truth about killing Mark and dragging his body to the water. Her words would match the evidence they had, so it would be accepted. But she'd say no more than this.

More would lead down a path that would destroy Mark's reputation. Once her words were spoken their child would have to live with that story. There would be no going back. It was better the true story remained untold. Nothing could undo the past harm done. Nothing would be gained by opening the deep cesspit of Mark's bad actions.

She was determined to retain the good memories of him, held by her and his friends, not to let them be destroyed through a revelation by her, leading the media to spill out a different version of Mark across the airwaves.

That story would travel down the generations, guilt by association. Always after, people would ask whether the child of a psychopath would become like the father and turn into a monster. Since his death, Susan had come to understand the two sides of Mark, and she was prepared to live with this dual person, to love and honour the memory of the good part of him.

She wished he'd been open to a life with her after she uncovered the truth about him. They could have had more time together, raising their child. It wasn't much, but compared to the nothing she had now, it would have been enough. God, she hated the lost chance.

Had she done the right thing in handing over the memory card which held Mark's story to Vic? Either way, a promise was a promise, and so she must honour the one given by Mark, even if it caused more harm. Vic must shoulder responsibility for what he did with that knowledge.

Overall, she felt relieved she'd shared her burden. Vic could now also agonise over it like she had. She'd found herself more alive in Vic's presence than she'd been for months, even if it was partly to rise to the challenge of being slapped, which had cleared her mind.

It was good Vic cared about Mark and about what had happened to him, cared enough to rage at her for causing the loss of his best friend. She touched her face where a tender spot still remained. It was good pain, the most alive thing that had happened since she'd returned to Australia.

Now she wanted the trial over with. If she pled guilty, she'd end up with a long prison term, and she'd need to make arrangements for when her child was born. She would ask her parents to adopt the baby. That way she could see him, at least now and then, when they visited. She didn't know why, but she was sure the baby would be a boy. If her intuition proved true, his middle name would be Marco, a continuity of life and memory passing from father to son.

Imagining a future where her child would be an adult before she was released from prison wasn't much of a life to look forward to, but it was justice for the life she'd taken, and it would bring her closure. She would find useful things to keep herself sane while she served her term, and then make a new life when she was released.

The recent visits from the old man, Charlie, and Vic, had helped bring clarity back into her life. She was able to think and plan again. It was much better than sitting trapped in a fog all day. She hoped they would both visit her again soon. Their visits had lifted her out of despair. She sensed she would need more help from them both and then more help besides to stay sane in this place in a cage.

What really terrified her was the idea she'd become trapped in her mind again with only her and that awful crocodile spirit for company. She would eventually kill herself if she stayed in that place. There was a certain allure to escaping that way. Mark was in that place. But she would not dwell on such thoughts before her child was born.

Perhaps Charlie and Vic could help her to put that bad place behind her. She hoped so. There was hard steel in Vic. He'd know what to do. He could help her find a place beyond here, a place where her torment would cease. He'd honour Mark's memory, but he would help her too, that she knew.

As soon as the Christmas and New Year period was over, she'd ask to be put in touch with the lawyers for the public prosecutor so she could make an early guilty plea.

With that done, everyone who was hanging around in hope of a miracle would get on with their own lives, and she could get on with hers too, wherever it led. She felt a sliver of satisfaction that she could now see a way forward.

With her mind now clear again and the crocodile stone in her lap, she settled to read more of the book. It would help pass the rest of the day more quickly. She'd had her fill and more of Christmas alone and wanted tomorrow to come.

Chapter 5 – Michael Riley

Two days after Christmas, the warder announced to Susan she had another visitor. She'd been told visitors wouldn't be permitted until the New Year due to a skeleton staff, but people seemed to find ways around rules.

She was perplexed as to who it could be. David and Anne were in Sydney, as were her parents. She didn't imagine either Vic or Charlie would be back so soon and couldn't think of anyone else she knew. But a visitor was welcome to break up her day. She almost skipped out of her cell with a light heart.

As she walked down the passage into the visitor's room, she could see bright sunshine outside, just a few fluffy clouds, none of the big lightning and rains of the last day. Her mood lifted with the sunlight, even if just glimpsed through the window.

A weather-beaten old man wearing a cowboy hat sat at the table. She didn't recognise him. As she walked towards the table, he stood and doffed his hat in a polite greeting.

That's when recognition came to her. He was the bar tender from Top Springs, the man who'd made the strangely prophetic announcements about Mark and the crocodile spirit. Back then, before any of this had happened, he'd given her a cryptic warning that now made a sort of sense. She didn't remember his name and was unsure if Mark had even introduced him, despite them talking to him for two hours, so she was uncertain how to greet him, again a friend of Mark's.

She must have shown uncertainty in her face as he said, "Michael Riley, at your service, ma'am. Not sure if you remember the day you and that larrikin, Mark, stopped to tell stories at my bar at Top Springs." With that he gave her a broad toothy grin.

Susan couldn't help herself and smiled back in response. There was something mad and infectious in the mood she caught from him. She gestured. "Please, sit down, Mr Riley. Of course I remember. Who wouldn't. You and all your prophetic crocodile tales. I told Mark you were a bit fey. He said it was the spirit of the Johnny Walker talking."

The man shook his head. "Well, you'd think he'd get that one thing right, at least. Paddy's is the drop I always drink.

"Just before Christmas, I got word you'd set that crocodile spirit free, and they'd locked you up for it. Me, I thinks, I'm here in Darwin for my regular Christmas visit, perhaps I should pay you a visit so as to pay my regards, like.

"You see, me, I know what you've done, girl. I felt it on that day. A choice was coming. One of you had to go to be with the crocodiles, and one was to stay. It had to be him to go and you to stay, him having the crocodile spirit, like. It couldn't have been another way.

"He was not a bad man, all in, but he'd done bad things. His time had come to pay. Since your deed was done, his spirit has bin talking to me, telling me things. He says 'tis better this way. He wants for you and the child you share to be happy. He says his life will go on through the child. You must have no fear for the child. Don't try to protect the child from the truth. You must tell his story for all who would hear."

Susan found herself protesting. "But you can't know what it really is that you're asking of me. You can't expect me to tell the world what happened!"

Michael looked at her with a sad and perplexed expression, as if he couldn't see where to go from here. Then he shrugged and said, "That's his message for you. He said I must tell you." With that he nodded, stood and walked out.

Susan sat there alone, feeling mystified. What did it mean? Was she to tell her child only later, when they'd grown, who their father really was and what he'd done? Was she to tell the lawyers, her family, and the police about the Mark she knew and what she'd discovered?

She wasn't ready to do that and wouldn't reveal it, no matter what any supposed messengers said. Everyone always promised to help her, encouraged her to tell the truth, but none of them had to live with what followed—the consequences of the truth. She did. The truth could never be told, that she knew.

With that, she dismissed this meeting from her mind.

54

Chapter 6 – The Search

Buck was awake an hour before first light. He quickly ate breakfast and got on to Flight Control. There'd still been no fresh reports of Vic or his helicopter, and Buck's phone calls last night had also yielded nothing.

A search had been organised at first light, based out of Kununurra and Katherine, as the weather in Darwin was currently too bad. The cyclone was hovering out to sea, sitting about 150 kilometres north-west of Darwin, with its track still much the same though starting to bear more south. It had now intensified from a Category Three to a Category Four, with wind gusts at the centre rated at upwards of 200 kilometres per hour. Based on the current speed and trajectory, they'd have four to six hours of search time before the weather would force them to call it off.

Buck offered to send the fixed wing and two of the helicopters based at VRD station and to start searching the area just north of Timber Creek, while the Kununurra planes concentrated on the area between Western Australia, and the mouth of the Victoria River, and the Katherine planes concentrated on the rough and broken country on the east side of the Victoria River, and back north towards the Daly River, just in case Vic had decided to divert on to Katherine or even Darwin, for some reason.

Since Vic's take-off at about nine yesterday morning when he confirmed his destination and flight track and signed off just after take-off, there'd been nothing heard of him, and no sightings or other information to say where he might have gone. It was a huge area to search, over 500 kilometres east west and 300 north south, but they'd all do their best and hope luck was on Vic's side.

By lunch time, nothing had been found. They pushed on, each aircraft now searching an ever-widening sector, racing against the clock and the weather

Buck hadn't abandoned all hope. Vic had always struck him as a survivor, though he'd thought the same about Mark. But it was a bad time for a machine to crash. The hopes of even looking, let alone finding anything in the next three to four days, were extremely poor.

Just after lunch, he got the VRD plane to fly him north to Timber Creek and out across the swollen rivers, which burst out of the rough hills. He looked out at the flooding water and the grey scudding clouds sweeping in from the north with a growing sense of hopelessness. If Vic was alive, he would not die of thirst. But chances of ever finding him or his helicopter were becoming vanishingly small.

By two in the afternoon, the weather deteriorated such that the flying had to be abandoned, and Buck told the pilot to turn around, and they flew home, where they battened down for the heavy rain and the big wind coming their way. The cyclone was now stationary about 100 kilometres out to sea north-west of the mouth of the Daly River. It was still intensifying, and they knew huge rains and winds were coming their way. Already light rain had started at Timber Creek, and overnight, Pine Creek had received over a hundred millimetres from a large storm cell on its southern edge. This meant the Daly would be coming down, and soon all the rivers coming from further south would be running a banker too.

By nightfall, it was raining steadily at VRD, and over the next three days, they got three hundred millimetres while Timber Creek got five hundred.

Now every river west of Darwin was in flood. As expected, the cyclone had come down over the Joseph Bonaparte Gulf, and its residual low-pressure system was now somewhere down over the southern Tanami Desert west of Alice Springs and was expected to bring rains over a wide belt of inland Australia.

***

It was three days before the weather was good enough to fly again. Buck and more than a dozen other aircraft used the next four days of good weather to do a widespread search across the northern VRD and west Kimberley, but in the end, with absolutely nothing found, the search was abandoned.

In due course, there would be an official investigation. For now, the case was closed. Vic was missing presumed dead in a crash somewhere far out in that empty place, a wilderness void. To Buck, it felt like another pointless waste of a promising life.

He must now take carriage of the will Mark had entrusted to him. He'd visit the police and Susan. He was unsure whether anything was to be done for her, and she'd bigger problems than an inheritance where a will may or may not still exist. But he felt he needed to advise both her and the authorities of his piece of knowledge in this matter. Not that he expected her to know about the will, as Mark had said he wasn't going to tell her. It was his own little piece of the sad, unintelligible jigsaw he'd inherited.

A month later, a fishing trawler working off the coast west of Darwin sighted wreckage floating in the water. It was hauled aboard and taken to Darwin where experts determined it was a fuel tank from a Bell 47 helicopter, badly damaged, as if from a crash impact.

The official finding was that it was likely to be a part of the helicopter flown by Vikram Campbell on the morning of December 30th, and he'd most likely crashed somewhere in the lower reaches of the Victoria River, the helicopter wreck then washing out to sea.

Two days more were spent searching the area around the mouth of the Victoria River, but still nothing further was found, With his the search was officially ended and the files passed on to the coroner's office for its consideration.

Buck and a few friends held a wake in the Timber Creek Hotel one steamy afternoon in early February. A thunderstorm was turning the sky purple with its flashing and rumbling far out to the north, out near where the Victoria River met the sea. It seemed the Gods had joined in the ceremony, too.

"Vikram Campbell, helicopter pilot extraordinaire, RIP," they said as they downed their drinks in his memory.

Chapter 7 – Fragments of Investigation

Alan found it hard to return to work in Darwin in mid-January after being on holiday with Sandy since Christmas. She was staying on in Sydney until the end of the month to spend a little more time with her family and start planning for their end of year wedding.

Sydney was her home town and they'd flown there together on Christmas Eve and enjoyed a great couple of days with her extended family in and around the city before going to visit his family in country NSW, up past Scone in the Upper Hunter Valley. They'd both got on well with each other's families and had done lots of holiday things such as country driving, beach swimming, and eating meals in pubs.

New Year's Eve was spent in Sydney where they ate in a restaurant looking out toward the Harbour Bridge. Over dinner, he proposed to her. Despite thinking he was in control of this emotional stuff he'd never felt more nervous in his life.

He felt great elation when she said, "About bloody time, and before you change your mind, the answer is *yes*." He loved her directness. That night together was special.

For now, he'd left all the arrangements to her and was glad of it. Complicated family stuff was really not his thing. It was good they lived far away in the NT and escaped most of it.

It had been a wrench to say goodbye to her. He'd have loved to stay until the end of January and travel back together. Since returning, he'd missed her in his life each day, mainly little things like a mussy good morning smile, the way she arched her eyebrows or kicked him under the table when he talked crap, and most of all, the feel of her body next to his in bed.

But he had a stack of work to do, thanks mainly to neglecting other things while he was working on the Crocodile Man case before Christmas. No one did his other work while he was away, so it was piled up waiting for him.

His career was on the rise, his name becoming well known as the man who'd cracked this big case after all the work he'd done in tracing the leads in that case, and nobody seemed to have any doubt he'd got it right. Susan was definitely in the frame and she'd more or less admitted that hers was the hand that had struck the fatal blow.

The problem he had was not with what she had done but why. There was a whole other story that needed to be brought to light before any of this made sense. Loving girlfriends did not bash in the skulls of their lovers and feed them to crocodiles without a reason. But he seemed to be the only one who wanted to get to the bottom of this why question. The prosecution lawyers only seemed to care that the case against Susan was watertight. It clearly was that.

When he'd explained his concerns to his superiors, he was told they had all the evidence needed for the conviction, and the rest was window dressing. His immediate boss had given him permission to spend a couple of hours a week chasing up the loose end on the Crocodile Man case, but right now, he did need to get on with other work and that had to come first.

They'd just assigned him to a major role in the investigation of a criminal syndicate suspected of murder and drug smuggling around the NT's 6000 kilometre coastline. That was taking sixteen hours a day, leaving little time for anything else.

But he sensed a great injustice was rolling forward while he let the Croc Man case slide.

The weekend after his return, he went to the office on the Saturday to get his old paperwork up to date and look at all the stuff that was sitting in the less urgent piles. Even though it was an unpaid day, he beavered away all day, and by the end of the afternoon, he'd shrunk the pile from a foot high to two inches.

As he sorted through these things, he came across a scribbled note he'd left aside. It had got mixed up with this other stuff. It was the name Vic and a mobile number. He dug in his memory for the name. It soon came to him. Vic was the helicopter pilot he'd met in Katherine with Sandy that afternoon. It was the trace from the mobile phone record that had found him Vic. This link showed Mark used the name Butler as well as the name Bennet that was on his driver's license.

He remembered that day clearly now. The link they'd made to this pilot seemed to hold such promise and they'd rushed off to Katherine to meet him. After all, Vic had known their murder victim for ten years. They'd been sure he'd lead them to something that started to make sense. There was no doubt Vic knew Mark better than almost anyone else in the NT, but as to getting beyond that association and digging deeper, they'd again drawn a blank about who Mark really was.

The ephemeral Mark seemed to drift in and out of people's lives like a smoke ring, seen, gone, seen again. While at first Vic was open and told them what he knew, as the afternoon wore on, he seemed to harden inside. They could sense his tolerance for their questions was slipping, that he was holding things back. Whatever he'd been hiding had been a thing for another day.

Maybe Alan should arrange another chat. Then it would be time leave this pile of paper.

He had in mind a beer with Charlie, the catfish fisherman, before going back to the flat for a night on his own. Before he left he rang Vic's mobile number. It rang out, and he listened to the "sorry-leave a message" recording but decided not to. Less notice was likely to be better if he wanted to get useful ideas from this bloke. The element of surprise was more likely to dig out that hidden ten per cent.

He drove to Charlie's place and, as expected, Charlie was sitting outside on the verandah, no sign of anyone else in the house. Charlie told him Rosie was visiting relatives for a few days out in Kakadu country.

They got to chatting, and Charlie grinned broadly when Alan announced his upcoming wedding to Sandy. He winked. "Maybe catfish curry I give her when you meet her make her like you. So, now, you must marry her. That last time I get it for the marriage party of my Becky. Now, maybe, I get another big catfish for another marriage. We must have a big celebration party when Sandy comes back."

Alan nodded. "Nice, I like the idea."

The conversation moved on to the murder investigation. Because Alan trusted Charlie's judgement about people he asked him, "What do you reckon. Did she kill him?"

Charlie nodded, and there was silence for a few seconds before he added, "Bad crocodile spirit. It make her that kill man. Mark fellow, him very dangerous man. Him like crocodile. I think it's like he bite her then she hit him."

It was cryptic but made a sort of sense — attack and strike back. But if this was true, why was she hiding it?

Alan kept digging. "But why, Charlie? This man seemed to like her. All the witnesses who saw them say they were like love birds, like you and Rosie, like me and Sandy. So why would he attack her, and why would she hit back?"

Charlie gave one of his expansive shrugs. "Her I know. I visit her in prison just before Christmas. That day I give her crocodile stone to keep crocodile spirit away. She's not bad person, just frightened, so much frightened. But this man, Mark, I do not know. You must find someone who know this man, really know, not pretend know. Man is answer to why, not woman."

Alan nodded in return. "Yes, I know that too. Just before Christmas, I found a man, a helicopter pilot called Vic Campbell. He said he'd known Mark for about ten years and, even after all that time, he still didn't know why. But he was hiding something from me. Perhaps he only half knows something, a thing he's guessed or just glimpsed, but he doesn't want to say it. I need to find a way to get him to tell the truth for her sake.

"I tried to ring him before I came, but he didn't answer. I'll try him again tomorrow."

Charlie looked at him intensely. "What you say that helicopter pilot's name is?"

"Vic Campbell."

Charlie shuffled off and returned with a pile of newspapers.

He laid the papers on the table between them. "What, Mr Policeman, you not read newspapers?" Charlie moved them around and pulled one to the top. "Hope fades for the survival of missing helicopter pilot, Vikram Campbell" the headline read. It was dated two weeks ago.

Alan read the article. More than four days of searching had found no trace of Vic or his helicopter, both missing since December 30. The day after Vic had last been seen, a severe tropical cyclone, a Category Four system, had passed over the area where his helicopter had been recorded as flying, causing the search to be suspended. The search resumed on January 3rd and continued for four more days. As no trace of the pilot or his helicopter was found, the search was then suspended as officials considered hopes of his survival as very low.

Alan looked at the paper in shock, in part it was for the loss of this bright young pilot, in part for his most promising lead just being snuffed out.

Without any trace back to the real Mark from someone who knew him it seemed futile. He didn't have time in the next month to follow the other fragments of threads, yet he knew he wasn't going to let this beat him; too much was at stake. He racked his brain trying to think of some other way forward.

Charlie seemed to sense his consternation. He laid his hand on Alan's arm and said, "If you find one person who knew him, you can find more, friend of friend. Still this Vic will help you.

"You must find the people he worked with, this Vic, people who knew him. Some will know Mark too. It's always the way. Even if he hides his secrets real well, someone will know something. Tomorrow, I start to find out about this missing helicopter pilot. When I find someone who knows this Mark, I give you a name."

Alan spent the next day working through all the clues he had about Mark again, but nothing stood out. Then he remembered the barmaid from Timber Creek who'd given the evidence that Susan and Mark had left there together, despite Susan's claim they had separated and gone their different ways. She'd only known him as Mark B, just an initial and no second name, but still, she seemed to know him well by sight, well enough to watch what he did and where he went. He still had her statement somewhere, although he hadn't read it in more than a month. Perhaps they'd had a fling at some stage. something had motivated her to come forward and give evidence, something more than just being a responsible citizen. Perhaps she could give him some new leads. Then he remembered at the committal hearing in December that she was on her way home to Perth. Perhaps it was just for a Christmas break.

Alan rang the Timber Creek Hotel and talked to the publican, Jack. Tanya had left in December and wouldn't be returning. His only forwarding address was her mother's place in Perth. He didn't have a phone number. Alan knew he could run her to ground, but it might take a few days to get on to her.

The paper said Vic's intended destination on the night he disappeared was Timber Creek, so it was worth asking Jack about him. This could be a lead.

"Yes, I knew him well enough. Vic stopped here a few nights last year since I bought the hotel. I rang the manager of Victoria Downs Station, Buck Owens, that evening when Vic didn't arrive but was supposed to be staying here. I knew he did lots of work in the VRD and Buck was a good friend of his."

Friends of friends. Charlie was right.

He rang the VRD station number and got the station manager's wife, Beverly Owens. "I'm sorry, love. Buck's out and not expected back until about dark. I'll ask him to ring you tomorrow. He'll definitely be here then because he has a day of paperwork in the office." She paused before saying, "That is unless it's really urgent. Then I could call him on the two-way radio right now."

Alan could feel his impatience bubbling but said, "That's kind but tomorrow is fine."

About 9:30am the next morning, the call came through in a booming outback accent, sounding like someone used to yelling out across a set of cattle yards. Alan was conscious of needing to handle this carefully after Vic had become defensive.

"Thanks for calling Buck. I'm trying to find out about a good friend of Vic's, and I understand Vic did some work and was well known at VRD."

As he spoke the names of Vic and Mark, he could almost feel a reserve come down the line.

"Yes, I did know them both quite well. Are these questions something to do with Mark's murder?"

Alan hesitated. He didn't want to give too much away, but he needed this man's help and sensed any bullshit wouldn't wash. "Yes, that's right. I'm trying to find out who Mark was. He's a man nobody seems to know."

Another long silent pause ensued. Alan started to wonder if Buck was still there.

Then the voice came back, asking what Alan's movements were on Wednesday, as he'd be coming to Darwin.

Alan knew they were doing a night surveillance operation that night, which would begin with coming into the office at about 3 pm. His morning was free. "Officially off duty until 3 pm, but I'm happy to see you if you're up this way before then."

"If it's okay, I'd prefer to talk somewhere other than the police station. I'm driving up from Katherine, so could we make it for about ten o'clock, say for morning tea?"

They agreed to meet in a café at the local shopping centre, which they both knew. Buck's wariness was intriguing; it seemed there must be something here worth knowing.

Over the next two days, Alan barely had time to think any more of this. Full time planning for the surveillance operation was all consuming. But it was top of his list on Wednesday morning, so he arrived at the café early and treated himself to a big cooked breakfast. Buck was early too. Alan was just starting into his meal when a burly bloke came walking in and instantly spotted him. He strode over and held out his hand, all the while looking with admiration at Alan's plate of food. He ordered the same for himself. When Alan put the money down before Buck could pay, he was rewarded with a grin. "Anyone who buys me that sort of breakfast is worth talking to!"

Somehow, they each trusted the other from then. It seemed they both had a no-nonsense desire to make sense of this situation, so rather than a roundabout explanation, Alan just launched into his story and told Buck about the discovery of the body, the cover up at the billabong, the trail of Mark and Susan's movements to Timber Creek and then how they both vanished until she flew out of Darwin, alone, two days later.

He told Buck of Susan's total unwillingness to answer any questions about what happened after Timber Creek, the way she turned on them when they'd extracted the confession that she had been frightened. He even told Buck the story of the trip on the plane with this lovely girl and of her almost willing him to discover a truth which she could not reveal herself.

"I know there's more to this story. The evidence points to her killing Mark. She doesn't deny it, but none of it makes sense. I must find out what really happened, or she'll end up spending twenty plus years in jail. The only other clue I have is she's expecting Mark's baby. She told me that on the flight. She shows a strong loyalty to him as well as guilt for making a mistake."

Buck then told him of his long friendship with Mark and Vic, of Mark's strange request that he witness Mark's will, of his attempt to locate Mark after this. "I didn't hear of his death until just before Christmas when I met Vic. Now Vic's vanished too.

"As for Mark, I knew almost nothing about him, just that he was already working in The Territory when I took this job up at VRD. Before that, I was managing a station in Queensland. Mark was always quite private. Didn't seem to have any family or personal history. He'd drift in and out of work, but he still always seemed to have money. Occasionally, he'd disappear. One of those times, I know he travelled to the Middle East."

Buck went on to describe Mark's work skill and ability in so many things, and his fearlessness. "Had a rough, dangerous edge. It wasn't uncommon to see him travelling with different girls he was clearly being intimate with, but then a month later there'd be a different one with him and all he'd say was 'Easy come, easy go.'

"Susan seemed special to him though. When they left VRD after that day of cattle droving, I know they were heading to do a job that night on the Victoria River up near its mouth. Measuring the flow was all Mark told me. That and the money was good. They returned from the job okay the next morning.

"I did make some of my own inquiries. Their last known sighting was breakfast together the next morning at the Timber Creek Hotel. After they'd eaten, Susan stumbled out and climbed into the Toyota to sleep, looked exhausted, apparently. Mark followed her out and drove away with her still asleep. That was about an hour later. Mark told the barman they were off to have a sleep under a shady tree, as they'd barely slept the night before with a big night of work out on the river."

Buck told him how a barmaid called Tanya at the hotel had a bit of a crush on Mark. She'd been the one to report all this when Mark's identity was discovered, but he hadn't known this for months and had only found it out over Christmas.

"Mark mentioned that they intended a trip to Kakadu, and then he'd spend a final night with Susan in Darwin before she caught her plane home to England. So, it made sense for them to be heading that way. It's not really surprising no one saw them on that trip. Mark knew the place so well he often used back-roads. Plus, if they'd slept a few hours, it may have been late in the day when they travelled."

Buck knew something strange had happened because, from what Vic and Alan told him, the evidence said that, by the time Susan flew out, Mark was already dead, and she was now trying to hide his existence. "Quite peculiar really, as if she'd discovered something awful she wanted to hide. I can't explain it, anyway."

Buck told Alan about the day they both spent at VRD, helicopter mustering and horse riding "They both loved it, they were openly affectionate when they were together. It's no surprise to me how hooked Mark was by this Susan girl. She had an amazingly magnetic quality, and she was beautiful too.

"In my heart of hearts, it doesn't fit that she killed him in a cold-blooded way. She seemed to like him as equally as he liked her. And of course, Mark asked me to witness his will. Susan was the main beneficiary, but she didn't know anything about that.

"The only thing I can think of that may help you is I that I think I may know what his real name was. It wasn't Mark Bennet or Mark Butler. I'm ninety-nine per cent sure it was Vincent Mark Bassingham. That was the name on the will, and he told me it was his legal name.

"That same night, Mark told me he had a lot of money. He didn't say exactly how much, but it was clearly plenty, so somewhere, there must be a trail to that money. His will named me as an executor of his estate, but I haven't seen the will since then, and I have no clue as to where his money actually is.

"One thing I'm concerned about is his money could be used to explain a motive for his death. I don't believe for a minute Susan killed him for money though, because, as I said, Mark said he wouldn't tell her about the money or the will.

He said the will was only made in case something happened to him. It seemed he had some premonition. He was talking about it like he was the cat with nine lives, but they were all gone. He said the will was a precaution as he didn't want the state or his father to end up with his money. But if this comes out, some people may say the real reason he died was because Susan discovered the money, took it, and killed him, thinking no one would ever know. They'll say she has it and has hidden it away somewhere. But, if that is the case, why doesn't she say he attacked her? She could plead self-defence. The money will be of no use to her if she's locked up in prison."

Buck planned to talk to Susan in prison. He said he'd arranged to visit her that afternoon and he told Alan he'd ring him later if she gave him any more clues.

He finished by saying, "When Mark made me his executor and gave all his money to Susan, I felt he was saying to me he trusted me to look after her, no matter what. I don't know what she's done or why she's done it, but now Mark is clearly dead, I have this obligation, given as a promise to a good mate. I must honour it, so I'm going to see what I can do to help her. That's why I've told you all I know.

I trust you not to use what I've said in a way that would cause Susan further harm. You must judge what to say about the will. I don't know if it exists anymore and, unless it's found, I'm concerned that you telling anyone about it will only cause more harmful speculation by those who seek to find a motive for what's happened. If Vic was still here, I'd ask him, but he's vanished now too and I fear he'll never be found. It rests with you and me to try and find the truth for Mark's sake, for Vic's sake, and particularly for Susan and her child's sake."

Chapter 8 – A Month in a Cage

As January reached its end, Susan looked back on it as an endless month in a cage. It had three high spots when the great and good God, if such a being existed, decided to give a temporary respite.

It was funny how, for the month of December, when she was in this same place but fully enveloped in a mental fog, both the passage of time and her surroundings had barely seemed to matter. Now her mind was clearer time passed with excruciating slowness. A restless impatience continuously ate at her, and every day seemed so long.

Despite a clear mind, she found it very hard to read or otherwise distract herself. An underlying inability to concentrate on anything had infected her mind. Since she'd decided to plead guilty, it seemed like she'd lost all passion for anything, along with her will to fight. The only place where her mind had a clear focus and purpose was in her determination to say nothing about what really happened with Mark.

She could no longer see his face clearly. He seemed to have vanished along with the crocodile spirit's departure from her mind. Without some sense of him and having said goodbye to all her family and friends, she felt endlessly lonely. There was a vacuum about her. No one else seemed to have any interest in her or wanted to see her anymore. She had a premonition of the rest of her life of being within this place inside a total void, just herself alone, no one else in this space and nobody she cared for or who cared about her.

She cast her mind to those few days of visits. It was the day after New Year's Day when Anne came in, looking fresh and blooming. Her holiday had obviously agreed with her. Susan steered the conversation towards asking Anne about herself, but before long, they were talking about David. It was clear Anne was trying to skirt around this, but Susan was determined not to let that happen.

Susan burst the topic wide open by saying, "Anne, it's time for me to bring my engagement to a formal end. There's no longer a future for David and me as a couple. And before you say anything, I know he's pretty keen on you, and I know you feel the same way about him. I don't want my past relationship with him to have any bearing on what you and he do together.

"I should have been stronger and never let myself get involved with him knowing how this event could follow me. But it's a part of my history I can't change. What I am trying to say is, if something happens between you, I do hope it's really good and you don't rush it. Let it grow, if it will, in its own time."

She watched Anne closely as she spoke, and by the time she'd finished, Anne had tears in her eyes.

"Oh, Suze, am I that obvious? Yes, I really like him, and I think he feels the same, but it's mixed up by what has happened to you. I don't know if we can undo all those tangles. I won't see him for a couple months after I leave. I think it's a good thing to put some distance between us and all this. Maybe when we meet again, we'll have both moved on and it's no longer important. But thank you for your kindness. You have so many troubles without worrying about me."

With that, no more words were required, and they put their arms around each other and hugged for a long time.

Over the next three days, Anne visited her for as much time as she could. She brought little treats of chocolates and lollies, giving a big pile to the warders, who soon had a soft spot for Anne. She talked to them so politely and charmed them with a smile, and in return, they bent the rules as far as they could in allowing her to extend her visits.

Susan and Anne talked very little about the case, more about life and moments in the past they'd shared. One day Susan told of her decision to plead guilty.

At first Anne was inclined to try and talk her round, to find a way out. But Susan was so clear in her mind about what she was going to do that, in the end, Anne let it be and concentrated on being the best friend she could.

It didn't seem right to abandon Susan to this fate, but she was as trapped as Susan was by her knowledge.

They were both sad when the final day came, and it was time for Anne to say goodbye. She was flying back to London, leaving early the next morning. They held hands, talked, and hugged for a long time.

The following week, Susan's mum and dad visited her. Tim was back at university in Reading, but they'd stayed an extra week in Sydney, having been invited to visit David's parents.

Seeing them was also welcome but emotional. She told them of her decision to plead guilty. It had been hard to watch the shocked looks on their faces in response to her admission of what she'd done, and as they realised the consequences for her. She would likely spend a large part of her life in jail.

"But why?" they both asked.

"I'm sorry, but I can't tell you," she said, over and over.

Her mum had been in tears and her father not far away. But, as she explained, as slowly and rationally as she could, that she was facing up to the consequences of her actions, and for them to not ask her why anymore, they slowly accepted her choice.

"When David comes back next week, I plan to end my engagement to him. It's impossible for there to be any relationship between us from this place. He must move on with his own life. But I do so very much appreciate how good David and his family have been to me in these circumstances, and I'm glad you met and become friends with them. Once I've seen David, I'll write a letter to his parents thanking them for their support. And I hope David and me can remain friends, but that's all it can ever be between us now."

Her mum and dad could see the good sense of her choice. "I do think you've made the right choice about that in the circumstances," her mum said.

The last thing she wanted to share with them was the hardest thing. It was about the baby. She gently touched her stomach as she said, "I know I won't able to keep my baby in jail. So I wanted to ask if you'd take the baby when he's born and adopt him. Give him the good life he deserves that I can't give him. The only thing I ask is that I choose the name, and I hope you'll come and visit at least once a year so I can see him and watch him grow. I want him to know his mother loves him."

Now Susan's mother really was in tears, but it was agreed

Once they'd flown home, her final visitor was David. "I'd like this to be your last visit to me, at least for a few weeks. I need some time on my own to process everything. Right now, it's too painful being with you when my life is in tatters. I need to readjust my thinking.

"And we both need the time and separation to let our healing begin. I should tell you I've decided to plead guilty."

David was clearly stunned. He'd willed himself to believe that there was another explanation, that it was not really her, that yes, she'd had an affair with this man, but was not his killer. "You must be mistaken, false memory, stress. I know it's not who you are."

She remained calm and looked straight at him.

"David, I'm sorry, but it's true. I hit him on the head with a piece of wood and I killed him. Then I tried to cover up what I had done. I can't tell you why, so please don't ask. I can't and don't want to escape what flows from my actions, so I'll plead guilty and that's it. My decision won't change, so please spare me any more questions about it.

"Instead, I want you to get on with your own life. I want to hear your agreement that our engagement is over, a mutual decision we both hold to. You must move on, otherwise we'll both be trapped by something that can't ever be. You must tell me you agree that our past relationship is over."

She could feel him squirm, try to avoid facing up to the reality, but she persisted, and finally he said, "I agree."

The idea of talking with him about Anne was in her mind, but today had been enough for them. That would be a step too far, a thing that could wait for a future time. Instead, they both tried to make polite conversation, but it was too hard. After about five minutes, she said, "I'd like you to go now. It's just too much right now. There's a part of me that's sad it's come to this. I hope, in weeks or months to come, we can be friends again. Try to remember me as someone bright and happy, not as someone whose life is in broken pieces."

He nodded and they stared intently at each other for a few seconds before she said again, "Please would you go now."

They hugged tightly for a long seconds, then he was gone.

Susan was pleased the talking was done, but with it finished, she felt so alone and empty.

A week passed in which she barely spoke ten words to the warders, and she hadn't said a word to anyone else. It was all so dark and dreary.

Part of her was tempted to put the crocodile stone aside, so as to have something to fill her mind. Even that awful spirit seemed preferable to nothingness, but for now, she resisted.

She wrote a letter to David's parents and another to the Director of Public Prosecutions and asked the warder to send them. When that was done there was just silence again. It was an endless emptiness that went on and on and on.

Susan was halfway through her second week of solitude, the days all muddled in her mind, when someone called her name. She looked up. The warder was seeking her attention.

"You have a visitor."

She had no idea who it could be. Neither Vic nor Charlie had returned. Perhaps it was one of them, perhaps the policeman from the plane or a lawyer from the DPP. She heard a big booming voice come down the corridor. It sounded familiar, but from where?

"Now where is that girl? Surely, she can see me. I've driven for eight hours to visit. Surely, she can find some time."

She opened the door to the visitor's room. A burly stockman greeted her. Genuine delight was on his face when he saw her.

"Buck," she cried in pleasure, almost flinging herself at him.

After hugging her hard, he held her at arm's length, looking at her critically. "What's happened to that lovely English bloom? You're getting thin and pasty in this awful place. Sorry, I couldn't bring Firefly with me on a horse trailer. He would have really sparked you up."

Now she was laughing, and he was laughing too. It was the first real laugh she'd had in longer than she could remember. Tears streamed down both their faces as the laughter eased and she caught her breath again.

"That's better," he said. "Needed a little ray of sunshine. I'm sorry it's taken me so long to come and see you. I only heard about this two days before Christmas, and then Vic was missing, and there was the cyclone and lots of flooding so it's only now I could get away."

Susan looked at him perplexed. "What did you say about Vic being missing? Vic the helicopter pilot?"

Buck looked at her, puzzled and anxious. "Yes, that Vic."

He smacked his hand to his forehead. "Oh Lordy, don't suppose many papers come here, or that you listen to much radio or see much TV?

"Vic told me about Mark just before Christmas. Then, the day before New Year's Eve, Vic and his chopper vanished somewhere en route from Wyndham to Timber Creek. It's been a month now, so nobody holds out much hope anymore, though he's such a tough bugger that if anyone can survive out in the middle of nowhere, it'll be him. I'm not prepared to fully write him off just yet. At least nobody's found a crash site or a body. But I have to admit it's looking real grim."

Susan slumped down into a chair and laid her head on the table. All her jollity had drained away. It felt like someone had put a pin in a balloon.

Since giving Vic the diary, she'd held a thread of hope that he may help her find a way out her situation. Now that bubble had popped. But, even more, she grieved for the loss of that one person who had showed he genuinely cared about what had happened to Mark.

Beyond that, she liked this man, really liked him, his humour, his vitality, his zest for life, his dark, handsome, wiry features. On that day when he'd jested that she pass Mark over in his favour, and she'd riposted that he'd had plenty already in the mile high club, part of her subconscious had known if she wasn't already with Mark, she would have done the mile high thing with him too.

It wasn't that she'd sought anything other than Mark, but she'd recognised this man also had a primal attraction to her. But that was history. Like all that was good in her life, he was gone too. She'd thought her life felt empty before, now she understood what true emptiness was, that place when all her future life hope ran into a dry well.

After a minute, she realised Buck was still standing there looking down at her. His expression was serious. "What an idiot I am," he muttered. "Assumed you'd know if you knew Vic at all. It was a major land and sea search. It was on top of the news every night for a week."

She lifted tear glistened eyes and tried to conjure a smile. "No, it's not your fault. As you say, I barely knew him. I only met him the once, with Mark. Then he came to visit me the day before Christmas. It's just that, of all the people I've met since I came here, he's the only one who really cared about what I'd done and who cared about losing Mark. For everyone else it was just a story of a crime to be solved. Mark could have been anyone for all they knew. Vic did care though. He'd lost his brother. That's what he called Mark. He was so angry with me for killing him."

She saw surprise on Buck's face at her open admission. "That's right," she said. "I did kill him, and I am going to plead guilty. I made an awful mistake. I can't explain it more than that, but it's way past time for any more pretending."

Buck sat on the seat opposite looking stunned too. He shook his head as if it was hard to think of anything useful to say. After a while, he leaned back, folding his arms. "I came here with a plan to help you, imagining you wanted to get out of this place. But the more I look at it, the more it seems you've decided you like it best here in this cage. So much so that you seem determined to stay here, come what may.

"Maybe I'm a bit daft, but there's an elephant in the room, and it seems everyone is trying to pretend it is not there, even as it's trampling on us.

"There's plenty I don't know, but I've just spent an hour talking to Sergeant Alan Richards, and I'm starting to put a few pieces together. It's far from a full story, but I'm about to tell you what I know, what I don't know, and what I think.

"You can nod, or you can shake your head. You can look blank, or act dumb, whatever you choose.

"But this story I am going to tell you needs to be said, and like it or not, I'm determined to make you stand up and fight, even if it is only to fight back at me.

"Mark was my friend too, as was Vic. One's definitely dead, the other may well be. It seems to me I'm the only one left standing in your corner. And the person you have to thank for that, like it or not, is Mark. He appointed me, so I'm here because I know that's what Mark would have wanted.

"He wouldn't have cared a fig what this story said about him, but as sure as I know my name, I know he would have wanted your freedom, not to mention to give freedom and the chance of a better life for his child that I know you carry."

Susan could feel her resolve begin to crumble before this onslaught, the tears only a second away. She put her hands to her ears. "Please, Buck, please, stop now. Don't you see that's what this is about? If it was just about me, it would be simple, but it's about the future of our child. Others can think what they like, but I carry this responsibility, and it's only for me to decide from here.

"I can't bear to have my child know the truth about his father. I knew another Mark, a good Mark, but once the genie is out of the bottle it can never go back in.

"I'm imploring you. Don't go there. It's not a good place. I would rather spend my life in jail and die with the secret. Yes, there is a secret, a terrible secret, and I can't tell anyone, not even to you. For a minute, I entrusted it to Vic despite my fear.

"But it's an omen that he's gone now too with the secret untold. So, it won't come from me, and I'll help no one who tries to go there. I'll kill myself after my baby is born to keep the secret locked away if I must.

"I won't help you. I'll stop you if I can. For my sake, for Mark's sake, for Vic's sake, but most of all for our child's sake, just let it be, and please go now and stop seeking the truth."

Buck looked completely stunned. He turned to walk away but then stopped and looked at her with great sadness. "If that is your wish, I will respect it. Before I go there is something I must tell you though. On the night at the station when you stayed there, Mark came to see me. He asked me to witness his will, and he named me as an executor of his estate. He named you as the sole beneficiary, and in doing so, he placed on me the responsibility to help you in whatever way I can.

"I know he wouldn't have wanted it this way. He named you because he loved you. From here, whatever I do, it will be a betrayal of either him or you. I'm only going to do what you ask because I think he would have had me abide by your wishes, even if they're wrong."

Susan looked at this strong man she had bent to her will and felt ashamed. Why were there no good choices left, and why did it always have to be so hard?

She walked over and put her hand on his arm. "Thank you, Buck. It is hard for me and even harder for you. Mark couldn't have asked for a better friend. I know about his will, and I know about his love. I wish with all my soul I could bring him back, but I can't. Now I must live without him in an empty place."

"Wrong though I know you are, even Mark would have been impressed by your courage. Goddam, you're surely one obstinate woman." He gave her a half smile.

Suddenly she refused to be bowed.

She smiled brightly and looked up. "Thank you so much for coming and visiting me. It was good to laugh and remember happy times. Please stay my friend and come to see me when you can. It would mean much to me."

84

Chapter 9 – Who is Vincent Bassingham

Alan rang Buck just before he logged on to work in the mid-afternoon, having been told he'd have finished his prison visit by then. Buck picked up on the first ring.

"Well, how did the visit go?" Alan asked.

He heard a hesitation, but then it cleared, just a half grunt then nothing for a few seconds. It was as if Buck was reflecting for a second about what to say.

"I was just doing a mental backflip about the visit, but we've been straight this morning, so we might as well stay straight and let the cards fall where they may.

"I can't tell you much. She was her normal charming self, quite gorgeous actually. I told her I was sorry I couldn't bring Firefly, the horse she rode last time. She started laughing. It was the most delightful and unaffected laugh. We both laughed till tears ran down our faces.

"But then I told her about Vic. Like you, she hadn't heard the news, had no idea it had happened. When I told her he was missing, almost certainly dead, it was as if someone put a knife through her soul's brightness. Her light was gone. She sat in the chair, her face on the table, tears streaming down her cheeks. She looked so defeated.

"She'd flown with Vic in the gulf with Mark, and he'd visited her the day before Christmas. She said he was the first person she'd met who really cared about Mark. Now he's gone she's devastated, as if an empty void would swallow her.

"And she said she'd told Vic something really important when he visited, said she'd trusted him with a secret. It was like she had some hope he could help her get out of this mess. With his loss her hope had crumbled. She looked so forlorn.

"I told her Mark had entrusted me to try and help her. Then I tried to push her into telling me what the real story was. I started to spell out what I thought might have happened, but she has a steel core. I've never met such a tough cookie. For a minute, I thought she'd crack and give me something, but it was like you told me about that day you first brought her in for questioning in London. She starts to soften then something happens. This staggering self-control pulls her back. She's determined not to say what happened even though she knows, you and I know something truly awful happened on day, or maybe the day before.

She'd found something out about Mark. He wasn't who she thought he was.

"We're only guessing, but she knows something real. I don't begin to know what it is, but she's determined to never let it out. She more or less told me she had a secret that could never be shared and she'd protect it with her life. She even suggested she'd kill herself rather than let it out. She told me her silence was to protect her baby.

"She knew about the will. She said she'd killed Mark, but in doing so she'd made a terrible mistake. Now she intends to plead guilty and take the punishment for her crime.

"She implored me not to try and seek the truth. She said it was better I didn't know. In the end, I gave her my word I wouldn't try and find out whatever secret of Mark's she's hiding. So, in a way, I'm compromised by her determination for secrecy too. But I didn't promise not to share my knowledge with you.

I've been thinking what to do for the last hour since I saw her. I'll be honouring my deal and digging no further.

"But Mark was my friend too. I shared good times and bad with him over eight years. But he's given me responsibility for her and so I must decide what he would want me to do. If it came to a choice for him between him and her, I know with certainty he would have chosen her. It was obvious every time he looked at her. There was something so tender and protective in his eyes when they were together.

"I can't sit by and watch her spend twenty plus years in jail to protect something she knows about him. I'm completely sure Mark wouldn't have wanted that. Perhaps what I've told you about his real name will open a way up to find out who he really was and uncover his past life.

In a way, it makes strange sense; the man with no history is like the man who can never allow his history to be known.

"Perhaps he killed his parents as a child or murdered a brother or sister in a fit of rage. Perhaps he's wanted for a terrible crime in another country. She knows something.

"If Vic was here, perhaps he would be able to help, but my hope's dying that Vic and I will again sit together by a campfire and share more stories.

"I leave it for you to see if you can get to the truth. Perhaps the name Vincent Bassingham could open up his history and reveal his real story."

Alan felt a weight descend on him as these words were said. It was up to him, yet his bosses had effectively closed the door on him officially working on the case. He had to find a way.

He was glad Sandy was back in three more days. He thought it might help to seek her wise counsel on this matter. He'd struggle to find a way to chase this down without real evidence.

He contemplated making a sworn deposition saying he received this new information about Mark from an anonymous source. That might be enough to give him a basis to investigate. While he was bound by his word to Buck, notwithstanding that he was an officer of the crown. Still a name was a name.

Knowing he could do nothing further this week and his life was about to be consumed by his new job, he jotted down the name Vincent Mark Bassingham but otherwise parked it.

The next three days were frenetic, and he barely had time to think. He was whacked when he logged off late Saturday, having just worked over forty hours in the last three days. He went home, showered, shaved, and fell onto bed, having set the alarm to get up at 11.00pm to meet Sandy off her Sydney plane.

His homecoming with Sandy was lovely, bed was even better, though a bit more sleep would have been nice. In the early morning, after renewing their intimate acquaintance yet again, Alan told Sandy about the name Vincent Mark Bassingham and his need to find if this was the real identity of their man.

After a minute of silence, Sandy looked at him and laughed. "Well, you might have been pulled off the case, but no one has given any such instructions to me. As best I can recall, I'm still the official pathologist on the case.

If I have a man with two names and possibly a third, then clearly I still have an identification to make. That's good grounds for further investigation of his identity so I can try and locate his next of kin and try to correctly inform the court of his true identity, perhaps even to investigate, based on his DNA, whether he's related to any of the identities he claims.

"Leave it to me. Vincent Mark Bassingham is such an uncommon name that I'm sure finding something will be possible, even if it takes a month or two."

"It's funny, but when you came back and I was by myself in Sydney, I sensed my work on this case was far from finished. Perhaps it's a kind of thought transference from Susan and that strange crocodile spirit I've sensed. I want to do whatever I can to try and help her. In the same way that Vic talked about Mark as his brother, I feel Susan is my sister.

"I think I'll arrange to visit her in jail. After all, I've never actually met her, just glimpsed her in court, despite how well I feel I know her.

Maybe if it's just the two of us, talking woman to woman, and she feels the same way about me, I'll get a new lead."

Chapter 10 – Meeting of Spirit Sisters

It was Wednesday before Sandy could arrange a visit. She decided to do it in a fully official manner, to dot all the i's and cross all the t's. She started by explaining to the senior pathologist that the murder victim had been identified by more than one name, so she wanted to determine the victim's real identity. She proposed she start with a visit Susan to seek further information on any known identities. She'd then pursue other leads which might be of value, particularly DNA based.

Her senior officer agreed this was the correct thing to do and sent her an email of confirmation to allow her to proceed. Once this came through, Sandy talked to the prison officers and scheduled her visit for eleven the following day.

On arrival, a warder asked Sandy if she needed her to stay in the visitor's room with them.

Sandy shook her head. "No thanks. I'm sure I'll be fine with her alone."

"Okay. Just push this button here to notify me when you're finished. There's also an alarm button should you needed it." With that she nodded and left to fetch Susan.

Sandy looked around and saw a CCTV behind her. All of this was all on camera and she thought it likely it would be running through to a central console somewhere.

A minute later, Susan was brought in and directed to the seat opposite her. Once they were alone, Sandy got her first up close look at Susan. She was surprised that she was prettier and more diminutive than the image she'd formed of her. From across the courtroom and in her dreams of Susan's face, seen through the mirror of Susan's own mind, she was a bigger and plainer person.

Perhaps this image was influenced by media portrayals of her as some sort of seductive monster. From Alan's description of Susan, she'd imagined Susan would be more fragile and vulnerable. If it was her sitting in Susan's seat, she was sure that would certainly have been the case.

The real Susan had a very self-composed presence about her. The image that now formed in Sandy's mind was closer to sprung steel than a porcelain doll, despite the pretty face.

Before Sandy could make any kind of formal introduction, Susan said, "I'm so glad to meet you at last, Sandy, as I feel I already know you since the night of my dream of you when you were at the billabong, and more since you gave evidence in court. I have this sense of having known you for a long time."

The words were surprising. They were what she'd been thinking but had been reluctant to say. To put the thoughts into words seemed a bit crazy. Yet Susan spoke as if it were perfectly natural to know somebody from a dream shared months ago when they lived on opposite sides of the world. It felt a bit creepy, this thought communication thing.

Yet she'd encountered so much that was strange in this case, starting at the billabong when that hugest ever crocodile seemed to have sought out her and Alan. It had swum up right next to them and stared as if trying to tell them something.

There was how Charlie told her of the bad crocodile spirit of that place needing to be placated, how it had fought him in a tug of war for the man's head he'd caught. There was also Sandy's knowledge of Susan's face before they'd met.

Really this shared connection was no more unusual than everything else that had happened.

"I'm really glad you've come to visit me," Susan continued. "I've felt very much on my own lately, and all visitors are nice, but especially you. I've been wondering if I'd like you as much in person as I'd imagined I would through seeing into your mind. I do like you.

"After that day on the aeroplane with Alan, I feel like the three of us have been friends for a long time, although today's our first meeting." With that Susan held out her hand. "I'm glad to finally meet you in person."

Sandy felt delighted and charmed at this positive response but also a bit flummoxed. She'd come to meet a person she'd sensed was in great need of help, yet this young woman opposite, very much her own age, seemed like a gracious host welcoming her to her house for a garden party, not someone facing a murder charge for killing a lover and feeding him to the crocodiles. It was all so incongruous. She thought it would feel more real if a needy or angry person sat opposite her.

Her puzzlement must have shown on her face because Susan said, "You're probably wondering why I don't appear tormented or crazy because of what's happened. In a way I am. I've had very dark times in my own company feeling endless regret. It's an awful, empty place. But I'm coming to realise I must make the best of what I have, treasure pieces of blue sky and sunshine, like your visit today. I'm trying hard to learn how to live in the moment and act with joy. Sometimes all I see is darkness, and I feel my whole life has burned away, leaving only cold ashes which fill the barren place surrounding me. But then you come along, and the darkness lifts away for another hour.

"Still, you didn't come to hear me tell you about my feelings. You came seeking information about who Mark, the man with different names, really was. Am I right?"

Sandy nodded, even more amazed. Was there anything this woman didn't know about her private thoughts? It was like her mind was an open book allowing direct thought transference.

Sandy sensed the purpose of this visit was being pushed away from what she'd intended. Was this deliberate on Susan's part? She was certainly an adept mind reader. Now she gained a sense she was being manipulated by a superb actress, one who could kill her lover in one minute and then share cake and tea in the next.

She made herself rise to the challenge and felt a sense of satisfaction come back from Susan. She'd been testing her, seeing what substance was present in her character. Now she was pleased she'd pushed back, making her a worthy friend and contestant. So far, it had all happened unsaid within the space of their two minds.

Sandy pushed her body back in her chair, stretched, and said in a measured way, "You're right. I do want to ask questions while here. But that's only a small part of the reason I came.

Mostly, I too wanted to meet you and see if our imagined friendship was real. To talk to you as I would to my other friends, and to see what you were like.

"Will you tell me how you find it being here? Share what's good and what's bad? I can't imagine how I'd cope with being locked up in this place. I'd go crazy alone by myself day after day. Alan's told me you're expecting a baby. How's is your pregnancy going so far?"

"I'd like that, just to talk about ordinary things. Since coming here, I've barely spoken to anyone. I feel consumed by silence.

"Before we talk about other things though, I must tell you I killed Mark, very much the way your report described. I don't want to talk about what happened on that day. That's off limits.

"Anything else I know I'll tell you. I'd love it if you'd be my friend and come to visit me when you can. I can't offer much in return, but I can return friendship."

They sat and talked like sisters who'd known each other all their lives but hadn't met for a decade and now were full to overflowing with endless news to exchange.

Once or twice, Sandy wondered if she was crazy for going out of her way to befriend this person who was already a self-confessed murderer.

Susan again picked up on her thoughts. "It is crazy that we should be friends like this. But try to think of me as a silly young girl who became infatuated, did a thing she regrets, and now must make recompense."

For a while, they talked about their shared interest in and knowledge of pathology. "What struck me when I went to the billabong was the clean up after was done by someone who knew what they were doing and planned it carefully," Sandy said. "It so nearly worked. If the head hadn't been found, or if it had rained first, nobody would have known. Is it luck or destiny it turned out this way?"

Susan answered with perfect clarity. "It's better this way. I thought I could run away and hide from what I did. Now I know I couldn't. I'm glad I don't have to live with that lie. It would have been like a cancer inside me, eating out my insides across all my future. For me, truth is better even if my expected future is a bitter pill to swallow."

When they talked about the baby, Susan told her about David and Sydney, then meeting Mark again in Alice Springs, how excited and infatuated she'd been, how her pregnancy protection had been lax. "As best I can tell, I got pregnant in mid-August. That makes me between five and six months now.

"It's funny, but none of the officials seem to have noticed though it is now really beginning to show. I've told my friends, but it never seemed important to tell others. I've asked my parents to adopt him when he's born. His middle name will be Marco, like his father's was. Mark told me his proper name was Vincent Marco Bassingham.

It's the only thing I know about his life from before, except he told me he had a happy memory of fishing with his uncle in Brisbane. Oh, and he told me his mother died when he was a boy. I don't know her name, but she was Italian, and the name Marco was her brother's name. He died young. He told me he ran away from remand school after getting caught shoplifting when he was about twelve and how he hated his father, who was a bully. He said he'd not seen him since.

"If you can locate Mark's true family, that would be a good thing. While he hated his father, he seemed to like his uncle. Perhaps it may be good for our baby to know any extended family from Mark's side. That's why I am happy that you try to trace his uncle. Having Mark's DNA should assist in confirming any family links you find."

"Would you like me to notify the prison of your pregnancy?"

"Yes, it's a good idea now I'm far along. Thank you."

In the end, their visit was cut short by the warder letting them know that the time was up.

Before she left, she notified the prison office of Susan's pregnancy status and asked whether it would be possible for her to organise a doctor to visit or whether such matters had to be handled by the prison. They said they were uncertain and would call her back.

As she walked away, Sandy felt pleased but perplexed. Her liking of Susan was real and instinctive, and their friendship felt natural and easy to her. It was as if they were very much kindred spirits. The term 'spirit sisters' resonated in her mind. Susan had great charm and was almost impossible not to like. She sensed Susan was telling the truth about the terrible dark times she had lived through since the event of Mark's death. She also had to admit that her own ego felt gratified that what happened on that day had been just the way her pathology report described it, an affirmation of her professional skill.

But there was an undercurrent here she couldn't quite put her finger on that made her uneasy. She chewed over it in her mind, and by the time she reached her car, it came to her.

Obtaining the past information on the identity of Mark was too easy. This consummate actress was steering her. She'd no doubt Susan had told her the truth about the likely true identity of Mark, along with the fragments of childhood memory that he'd conveyed, even down to the remand school. These were given as details to check and help locate a person. It was in stark contrast to the secret of who Mark had been at the time of his death.

When Susan had told her about these things, she'd accepted Susan's facile reason for the disclosures, that it would be good for her baby to know something about his father's family.

She and Alan had previously discussed how Mark's former identity might be the lead that could crack the case open and get to the true Mark.

Their hope was based on the idea that in Mark's distant past, there might lie a clue to who he was, something to explain what had happened between him and Susan.

She realised now that Susan had detected her desire to go down this path and had steered her actively towards it. Susan was deliberately hiding a secret, and yet she had steered Sandy towards what she and Alan thought may be the key.

The name that had been whispered to them, Vincent Mark Bassingham, was now official. It would justify an investigation into birth records, marriage records, next of kin records, DNA checks, thus giving the victim a face and identity.

Susan had readily assisted in providing the information for this search. But why? It seemed much too easy.

Chapter 11 – Susan's Plan

Yesterday afternoon, Susan was told Sandy, a forensic pathologist, wanted to visit her, ask some questions about her knowledge of the prior identity of Mark before she'd met him.

It immediately raised a red flag in her brain. Her overwhelming motive for everything she'd done since his death was to hide the real Mark from public view. When they'd first arrested her, it had seemed officials were happy enough to let Mark fade from view. They had a license ID for a Mark Bennet, and she assumed this would leave a trail for people to confirm the identity of her Mark and having got this information the investigators would let it drop.

But once his second assumed name, Mark Butler, had been discovered, it raised the question of which was his true identity.

Susan thought of the dream she'd had last night. In it, Mark's secret was in great peril, with people investigating what happened on her trip from Alice Springs and tracing her phone calls and text messages to Anne. In the process, they were starting to link Mark to his victims. If Susan's text asking Anne to investigate the missing girls and Anne's reply was found, then everything would unravel. She didn't think Anne would volunteer this information readily, but she knew Anne was conflicted. On balance, she thought her friend's loyalty to her would come first.

Anne didn't know the full story, but she did know the names of the women Susan had asked her to look up, and Susan had effectively admitted they were connected to Mark. Anne could surely see the link between her, Mark, and those cases. And she also knew of the existence of Mark's diary. But with Susan's admission to the murder and her stated intention to plead guilty, she felt she was closing a door on the danger of that revelation becoming common knowledge.

The dream though seemed to be warning otherwise. In it Alan and Sandy were exchanging the name Vincent Mark Bassingham, saying they would trace that person, with Sandy further planning to use DNA to make a link to other family members. They talked about him being the key to finding out who the true Mark was. Through her mind link to Sandy, she knew of Sandy's burning desire to get to the real story, the why of what had happened.

They thought they were doing this to help her. It was like the Biblical line from Presbyterian School she remembered from her childhood, 'Ye shall know the truth and the truth will set you free', but for Susan this truth was not freedom but a whispered secret. Its retelling would be all anyone knew of this case; its memory would follow on for decades.

The interest in the case was already sensational enough. It didn't bear thinking about how a new revelation would play out. While she'd previously considered the option to plead self-defence, reveal the truth about Mark and then vanish under a new name once she was released, she knew it would be easier said than done. In this internet age having no digital footprint was extraordinarily hard, even more so if she wanted to still have her family and friends, the people her baby would need as a growing boy, around her.

She's quickly dismissed the idea because it was fundamentally disloyal to Mark. It would turn him into a monster when the truth was far more complex.

She was glad he was the father of her child. She didn't believe he was evil absolute. She'd glimpsed and tasted goodness at his core, despite all that had happened. But that story would never hold up in the court of public opinion, and she wouldn't allow his memory to be treated that way.

In the dream, Alan was revisiting all the information he had about Susan and Mark to see if any of it would offer more clues as to who Mark was and why Susan had killed him. He was poring over all the records he'd tracked down about Mark, and in the process he'd obtained Susan's Australian mobile number and a SIM card she'd bought in Cairns.

It was funny no one had gone digging into this before, but once they'd identified Susan, it seemed all those other minor details were ignored as extraneous. Her dream told her Alan had been taken off the case, but Sandy would step into the breach. They were still working together and exchanging information.

She sensed Alan's frustration. He was hamstrung by other work and had little available time for this case. His boss had told him to drop it; the case against her was open and shut, and no one cared about the why. All that mattered was her guilt.

Susan wished Alan would just drop it like the rest, but she knew he wouldn't because he thought an injustice was happening, and he wanted to prevent that. In part, it was because he was the person who'd first uncovered the murder, meaning he felt obligated to have the whole truth told. He also thought he was helping her.

When she'd met him on the aeroplane, she'd willed him to help her, just like this. But that was back when her mind was in a big mess. Now she saw clearly that Mark's secret must stay hidden and wished she'd not encouraged Alan in the way she'd done. How could she find a way to prevent his desire for truth from succeeding?

In the dream, Alan linked a number on Mark's phone to her, and following from that, was now tracing all the calls she'd made. The only item of concern was her text to Anne and Anne's reply.

Waking from that dream, she'd realised she must find a new diversion to throw them off the track of tracing this, to make them feel they had another better lead to follow and to put their free time into that.

The name Vincent Mark Bassingham kept coming into her thoughts. They'd follow it like bloodhounds on a scent.

At first this idea filled her with fear. Then it dawned on her. Let them follow it; it was the name of a child of twenty plus years ago, a boy who'd run away when he was abused by his father. That's all they would find from that name. The adult Mark became would not be there.

From what she knew, Mark was around twenty when he went to the Middle East. It was only then the callous, wanton killing began. Discovering that Mark was what most terrified her. By then, he was a man who worked under many other names, taking great care to hide his true identity. The child was not the man nor the man the child.

She needed to throw a false trail, one that seemed to lead somewhere but actually led away, where the sum of a month or two of investigation would be zero.

They would know his real identity, know a few bits about his difficult and abusive childhood, things that could perhaps bring some sympathy, but then it would all vanish, and Mark would just be someone who'd changed his identity because of a violent father and who'd made a new life in the NT under names based on his middle name and initials. Not so remarkable really.

This information would feed the gossip mills for a day or two and then would become yesterday's story, his old and new identity fading into history.

The police would start calling him Vincent. She would admit to Vincent's murder. Adult Mark would be gone, and she would be convicted and sentenced, one of many prisoners serving out their time, soon forgotten, as public attention and police investigations moved on to new, juicier stories.

That is what she would do. She would confirm the name they were seeking, encourage them to follow this trail, while letting the real story, the one she was protecting, slide away.

But she must be careful. Sandy was very clever too. In the same way she could glimpse parts of Sandy's mind, Sandy could do the same to her. It was a cat and mouse game, throw a bait one way for the cat to pounce on while you quietly crept off in a different direction.

She wished it was a guilt free and painless process. She liked Sandy and would gladly accept any friendship offered. She felt the same way about Alan and Buck, yet here she was acting out a role for their apparent benefit, which had the real purpose of deceiving them. She didn't feel good about herself. The old, decent Susan was fast sliding away, being replaced by a manipulating and conniving actress.

In trying to hide the true Mark, she'd become a shadow figure of her former self. Now she was the great dissembler, one who showed people a face they wanted to believe in and used all her tricks to make it seem true. She'd become a second Mark, a person trapped by bad decisions and poor choices and so forced into perpetual dishonesty.

The only person who'd seen through this was Vic. On the day he'd visited, he'd refused to accept meaningless answers. Now he was gone too, and she was left alone, ever and always alone, in this endless void.

Chapter 12 – The Children and the Crocodile Stone

Two days after Sandy met Susan, she was notified of a doctor coming to visit her to examine her baby. She was told Sandy had arranged this visit. The doctor was someone she'd met through medical circles.

Susan was unsure but agreed. She wanted her baby to get the best treatment. Once she'd met the doctor, she'd decide on what else to do and how to pay.

At ten o'clock, she was escorted to the visitor's room to meet the doctor, Christine something, a gynaecologist who'd qualified as a specialist last year, joining a busy practice at Darwin Private Hospital. She'd understood this doctor usually saw private patients, not prisoners, but had made these arrangements as a favour to Sandy.

As Susan came into the visitor's room, a pleasant lady in her early thirties rose to greet her. Susan liked her instantly, the no nonsense professional competence and ready smile.

She asked Susan to lie on a towel on the table, and she checked her carefully by palpation and with a portable ultrasound machine. She soon had a picture of her baby on a laptop screen attached to the ultrasound. "Would you like to know the sex of your baby?"

Susan nodded.

"As best I can tell it's a girl. You're having a daughter."

Susan was thrown. "Are you sure? I was certain it's a boy."

Christine reworked the image, zooming in again and going to the lower body. "Well, it's hard to be 100% at this stage, between five and six months, but it's pretty clear. You can see there's nothing there where the penis and testicles should be. The baby seems a bit small for your due date in relation to how big your tummy is. We should run a few tests just to confirm everything's okay, bring you in to hospital for a day next week to check it out more thoroughly."

Susan nodded, not wanting to take a chance with the health of her baby. While they discussed the tests for next week, Christine left the ultrasound head resting on Susan's belly, the laptop screen facing her.

There was a movement. Something that looked like a leg zoomed into view, showing a tiny foot with five toes. It seemed to come from a different place than where the baby they'd been looking at was. Susan pointed, open mouthed, and Christine's eyes followed her finger.

"Oh my God, that leg does not belong to the child we've been looking at. There's a second baby."

After five minutes of further checking, it was clear there were twins, a boy and girl. Now the sizes were right.

Christine finished a few minutes later. When Susan started talking about working out a payment plan for future treatments, Christine waved her aside. "Plenty of time to sort that out later, and Sandy told me she would pay if needed.

"First things first! With two babies there are extra risks. I need you to come into hospital next week for more tests. I'll arrange everything with the prison authorities."

By the time Christine left, it was organised. The hospital visit was booked for the next Monday. A prison van would take her, and she'd be escorted by a warder for the day. Not that she was considered a significant risk, having returned to Australia voluntarily, but even so it was the required protocol.

Susan woke early on the Monday, feeling an eager anticipation to leave her cell and walk in the open air. It was the first time she'd left since her court appearance over six weeks ago. That seemed like an eternity in the past. She walked outside in handcuffs, acutely aware of the shame of being treated like a wild animal.

Someone must have tipped off the press. Several journalists and camera operators were gathered in the car park, long telephoto lenses pointing her way. Her protruding stomach was there for all to see as she walked the few steps from the prison door to the waiting van. She was whisked away, glad to be inside the van's windowless sides.

Her day was spent waiting between different tests and procedures, enclosed in a locked room, up on a high floor. At least there was a TV she could watch, her first real taste of the happenings in the outside world since her arrest in England.

In between procedures she sat with her eyes glued to the screen. The morning broadcasts were a rolling rotation of chat shows and soap operas. When the midday news came on, she felt disconnected from it and decided she'd flick back to a soap opera. There was too much pain as she watched normal people go about their real everyday lives.

But before she could change the channel, a headline flashed up. 'Remnants of missing helicopter found'.

Now the TV had her full attention. The report was to the point. A fishing trawler had picked up refuse floating in the water about one hundred kilometres west of Darwin yesterday and brought it to port last night. This morning, experts from the

Department of Aviation examined it and confirmed it appeared to be an extensively damaged fuel tank of a Bell 47 helicopter.

The reporter stated, "The helicopter is likely to be that of Vikram Campbell, missing and whereabouts unknown since 30th December. It's probable the wreckage washed out to sea from the rivers of the Joseph Bonaparte Gulf following the cyclone in that area in the days after Mr Campbell's disappearance.

"A new search of this area for any additional wreckage will commence tomorrow."

The news left Susan profoundly depressed. She'd had a little hope before, despite Buck's optimistic unwillingness to concede the likely, but now all her hope was extinguished. Vic's helicopter really had crashed, and looking at the damage, the outcome of Vic's fate was obvious. She knew they must go through the formalities of the search, but there would be no happy ending, even if further wreckage was found. Vic's death only reinforced her determination to keep on the path she was following. She sat musing on the way her life was going, drifting further and further downwards into darkness.

Suddenly, her own image on the TV pulled her attention back. It was a telephoto image of her taken this morning, a woman with a bloated belly walking the few steps to the prison van. She listened to the reporter.

'Breaking News: Crocodile Man's lover and alleged murderer has been taken to Darwin Hospital this morning for medical tests to confirm her pregnancy. Could Crocodile Man be the father of her child?'

She remembered grainy images she'd seen of Lindy Chamberlain's pregnancy, taken at a time when she was in prison, and the awful speculation about her baby being a Devil's child was swirling in the press. Was that to be her fate – the mother of another Devil child? Susan wished she'd stayed in prison and let their doctor deal with her.

She just wanted to return from this hostile place to her cage again. It kept the outside away. It was better to be alone than to have to watch this feeding frenzy as a voracious public took delight in news of one tragedy after another.

She realised her mind was slowly being refilled with the missing crocodile spirit. She had left the crocodile stone in her cell, and with it her defence was gone.

As the day wore on, she could feel it pushing and insinuating its way back into her mind, but she didn't care anymore. It was easier this way, lost in a mindless oblivion.

As she let the crocodile spirit retake her mind, she again felt Mark's presence. He seemed real again inside her head.

She'd had missed him so much, and here he still was. In her pointless search for freedom, all she had found was an empty place where nothing and no one lived. At least here, in her mind, she had a companion again and one with far less power to hurt her than what lay outside.

Happiness that she was carrying his two children bloomed inside her. They could continue her and Mark's lives in the outside world. They would be company for each other, grow up strong and healthy, with no taint from this past. She knew her parents would take good care of them.

When they were taken from her, she would say a final goodbye to them and her parents and to all this awful life had dealt her. It was simple. She would leave this world.

Before she departed she would write a simple will and ask they put her body into the ground next to what was left of Mark's.

She would return to him, and as two crocodile spirits together, they would watch from afar.

That was as close to heaven as either of them would ever get, but if she was with Mark, it would have to be enough.

Chapter 13 – Return to London

Anne found the return flight to London to be a poignant time warp. She was leaving a place of heat, humidity, and relentless anxiety at watching her best friend's life as it disintegrated, trying not to get drawn into another relationship and worrying about keeping her job and how to deal with her increasing pile of undone work in London. All of that was being left behind as she returned to her home, her flat, her network of friends, her family, and the ability to rescue her job and create order in all that undone work.

She should be feeling relief and excitement at her return. Instead, she felt strangely let down and empty, as if she had now moved her centre of existence to the other side of the world, and London had become the unreal artefact, while a hotel room in Darwin had become her new permanency.

It was not that she wasn't looking forward to seeing her family and friends again, or having her own things in her own place, or even creating order from the chaos she knew would await her at work. She was, and yet it was as if the centre of gravity in her world had shifted to a previously unknown and unimagined place.

It wasn't just David, Susan and their lives there, though it was a partly that. It felt as if a part of her, one she hadn't known existed, was captured by the spirit of Australia. It was about identification. She, a quintessentially English girl, now felt part of her soul lived across the sea in another strange, harsh land. It was a far less pleasant place to live than her home in London, but an attachment to it was within her now. She'd been ambushed and captured.

Still, she must park this nostalgia for now and knuckle down to do all the things her life in London demanded of her. She'd made a promise to ring David at least once each week, but she suspected she'd call more often.

It was midday Sunday before she cleared the airport. She then spent two hours at her flat, recreating order, before heading out to dinner with her family in Reading. They weren't quite neighbours to Susan's family, but near enough, and that's where her friendship with Susan had begun at school.

She didn't stay late after dinner but headed back to town, knowing she needed to be up early for work in the morning. Her jet lag wasn't too bad, thanks to the business class seat David had bought for her.

The first week back flew by so quickly she barely knew where time went. During the second week, she started to catch up with friends, all of them anxious for news of her and Susan.

It was hard to tell them much, but she realised the interest and understanding were only superficial. They were busy with their own lives.

She and David had taken to calling each other in alternate turns, mostly every second or third day. It was wonderful to hear his voice, and she always felt like she was walking on air afterwards. They both had plenty and yet nothing in particular to talk about, but what both said they most wanted was to hear the other's voice.

While neither quite said it, since Sydney, they'd transitioned into something more than friends. One day in the second week, she expected him to call, but he didn't. She slept fitfully that night and early the next morning she rang, knowing it was now evening in Australia. David picked up immediately, and she asked if he was okay. Something in his voice said otherwise.

"I visited Susan yesterday, and she broke off our engagement and forced me to agree it was a joint decision.

It's funny because I've known since before Christmas it was inevitable and my mum agreed too, yet when she said it and made me agree I felt so gutted.

"She made me finally confront what I should have always known that despite my dream of perfection with her, it would never be. Maybe it never could have been. At one level we were pulled together, but at another we were never quite fashioned to fit together. I did love her though. Part of me will always be a bit captured by something in her, but I've had to force myself to face up to the fact it's over.

"I'm sorry I didn't call yesterday. I was just too raw to talk about it. I needed some time to process and grieve. I'm sorry if I worried you."

"When I saw her that week in Darwin, Susan told me something similar," Anne replied. "She said that deep inside, she knew from the outset it was not meant to work, yet there was a pull of attraction that drew you together, at least for a time.

She told me that being with you seemed like an idea of perfection, but it was a dream of perfection that wasn't real. It did hurt her to have to make the choice to leave you.

"I'm glad you've both reached a similar place. She's still my best friend, and I hope you can stay friends too."

"Of course. We'll always be friends. Far too much has passed between us. It hurts, but I know it's a good thing for us to move on with our separate lives now.

"Speaking of which. How soon can you come back out to Australia? I can't wait to see you again."

"I've almost caught up on my work, and I've asked about taking some more time off so I can be there for Susan's trail in just over a month. They've reluctantly agreed to give me a fortnight off for that. That's the best I can do. I'm sure that fortnight is unlikely to be a bundle of joy, but I'm looking forward to seeing you again too."

"Okay, perfect. Tell me your dates as soon as you know them. Once I hear from you, I'll book your flights and be there to meet you at the airport."

Chapter 14 – Finding Vincent Marco Bassingham

Sandy pushed on with her work of locating the real Mark.

First, she double-checked the names Butler and Bennet. Neither was obviously false. They had a trail of sorts, but after following both back a few years, they rapidly descended into mush. In both cases, they were common names with far too many people to easily trace. Without a known birth location, it was hard to follow them up quickly.

Next, she began tracing Vincent Bassingham. Unfortunately, the details of past births, deaths and marriages were held separately in each state and were not fully computerised. This meant some manual leg work dealing with up to seven state administrations and systems, as well as checking the records held here. In her experience, requests coming from the Northern Territory didn't get top billing.

That would mean phone calls to clerks to seek their cooperation and stress the priority. It would have helped if she'd had a real age for Mark, but the two licenses gave ages almost three years apart. She'd need to cover a fair range of possible birth years to ensure she didn't miss him. Neither Susan nor Buck were one hundred percent sure of his name's spelling. The best help was the last name, which had a range of spelling variants, was reasonably uncommon.

Based on Susan's story of an uncle in Queensland, she started in Brisbane but drew a blank in both the regular name version and the likely variants. NSW and Victoria were the same. It was perplexing. She'd been fairly sure she'd find a record in one of these most populous states providing a clue to Mark's identity and background.

Apart from the NT, she worked her way fully around the country. Somehow, the idea of Mark being born in The Territory never occurred to her. Two of her precious weeks passed, with nothing and she was left feeling frustrated.

She went to visit Susan each week to keep her up to date with her progress, or lack thereof. She was worried about Susan. She'd read about her visit to the hospital in the NT papers and seen it on the news. Somehow, the press had found out she was expecting twins. Its coverage spawned vile forms of speculation by internet trolls who posted endless awful things like kill the bitch, feed her to the crocodiles, cut out her babies, watch the crocodiles jump and feast.

It was shameful what people did with all this stuff, and she was glad most of it seemed to have passed Susan by. She wished she didn't know about it herself, but it was surprising how much of this rubbish came up in her searches.

The warders had taken to bringing Sandy directly to Susan's cell for their visits. This gave her an insight into just how desolate Susan's life was. Her sense of Susan as an actress who turned on and off her performances had grown ever stronger, although the Susan she now visited was a much-diminished person, a much better fit to her former mental image of her. A worrying lethargy and fatalism sat about her, as if she'd resigned herself to what was coming and had given up hope.

Each time Sandy came in, she would see Susan pick up the flattened oval crocodile stone, the one Charlie told her about, to keep the evil crocodile spirit out of her mind. If it worked, she wondered why Susan didn't keep it with her all the time, put it in her pocket. That seemed to be the way she used it when Sandy first met her, and Susan had been a lot sharper then.

Now when she first arrived, Susan seemed to be completely spaced out, unaware of her surroundings, with her mind lost in another place. It would take a few minutes of her holding the stone before any glimpse of the original Susan was visible. Her answers were often vague and woolly. "Yes, if you think so," or "Whatever you think; I don't know."

She was so different from the person with the razor-sharp mind who Sandy had first met. Sometimes, flashes of that old Susan returned. Sometimes they would still laugh together till their sides hurt at the silliest things, and Susan was always much better after this.

She tried to get Susan to tell her about her feelings and got occasional insights. On the last visit, Susan had told her about her hospital visit, at first feeling excited to discover more about her twins and to leave the prison. Then how that feeling collapsed on seeing the lunch time TV news, the first TV she'd seen in months.

The first news item was about the wreckage of the helicopter crash, which meant Vic really was dead. Susan said this with such a flat, despairing finality that it broke Sandy's heart. Such a palpable feeling of emptiness and desolation flowed from her. Why was Susan so upset about a man she barely knew? Perhaps because he was a close friend of Mark's.

Susan's mood seemed even lower as she told Sandy about seeing herself with a fat, bloated belly on TV. She said it reminded her of photos of pregnant Lindy Chamberlain in prison, with people saying she was expecting the Devil's child, only now it was her who was the focus and people were calling her babies the

'She Devil's Children' and making sick jokes they weren't human but crocodilian.

It was such an excruciating description of a visit that Sandy had hoped would be an escape from the dreariness of this place. But even more upsetting was hearing Susan say that at least it would be over soon. Her babies would be born and have each other and her parents. They wouldn't need her anymore, so she could escape all this. There was a chilling finality to this statement. It felt like a suicide note.

Today was Sandy's fourth visit, meaning three weeks had passed since she first came. It was only a fortnight until the trial. There was a pre-trial conference next week where lawyers would meet with Sandy to discuss preparations for the case.

They would then meet with Susan on the next day to discuss the evidence they would lead and how it would all run.

As she walked towards the prison, Sandy ran through how the case was unfolding in her mind. Susan had refused all offers to employ a defence counsel, saying she was pleading guilty and could speak for herself. Everyone was deeply uncomfortable about the way events were shaping. Even the prosecution didn't like it, despite it making their work easy. Public opinion was starting to swing behind Susan, suggesting the investigation must have been incompetent, as the prosecution hadn't come up with a better explanation other than a lover's tiff gone wrong. It just didn't seem to make sense as the murder was being portrayed as highly planned and calculated, suggesting a deeper motive. It was also reported as out of character for Susan based on her past life.

This, with Susan's unwillingness to make a defence as to why she killed Mark, seemed incomprehensible to the media.

Sandy knew Susan really wanted the trial to be over. The prosecution wanted it wrapped up too. Their case was solid, and officials believed that any adverse public opinion would fade once the trial was out of daily news cycles, so it was agreed the trial would proceed as scheduled.

While Sandy found it problematic that the reason for Mark's dual identity hadn't been solved, neither the prosecution nor Susan was overly concerned. He was a person, and they had his body, so it was murder. Investigations about his identity could take their own course.

One fly in the ointment was an independent barrister who was now advocating for a parliamentary or judicial inquiry, lobbying key people for a full and proper investigation into the identity of the victim before the trial went ahead.

Sandy half wondered if this was being done as a delaying tactic by Susan's friends or family to try and buy some space. She wished it would succeed as she wanted to gain more time for her own search. She knew Susan's former fiancée, along with her best friend, Anne, were flying into Darwin again this weekend. She wondered if either of them had had a hand in this lobbying and advocacy.

Today when Sandy visited, Susan was different. She'd washed her face, done her hair, and put on a pretty dress, one loose fitting enough to diminish her pregnant look. She smiled brightly and gave Sandy a hug and kiss as she came in.

Sandy should have been delighted. Instead, her radar went into red alert zone though she tried to hide her concern.

Once Sandy sat down, they talked about who the real Mark could be and about lines of investigation they could follow to get to the real person. "I've been racking my brain for any other clues from the time I spent with Mark. I wondered if he could have been born and lived as a small child in the NT or perhaps been born or lived for a time in either London or Italy."

Sandy nodded. "Definitely lines of inquiry worth pursuing."

"I'm sure Mark told me that his father's name was Vincent Bassingham. That was part of his unwillingness to take his father's name at school. Perhaps you could try to trace his father, maybe find a birth or marriage certificate for a man by that name?"

The suggestion was eminently sensible, so she agreed to try. But suddenly, Sandy saw with a shocking clarity the difference in Susan was all a ruse. She'd always had a vague, unformed suspicion Susan was steering her. Now she knew it with certainty. She glimpsed a gloating place open in Susan's mind as Sandy took up her ideas. Susan was directing her to these places, and she was secretly gleeful Sandy had taken the bait.

She tried to pull back from her desire to look into Susan's thoughts. This was danger. If she saw what Susan was thinking, it was likely Susan saw what she was thinking too. In a split second, she saw fear in Susan's eyes that she'd let Sandy see too much.

Now Susan was backpedalling. "Perhaps that is a silly idea after all. It is not really so important to know who Mark was."

It was such a subtle and skilful seduction, a piece of consummate acting. Anyone who didn't have Sandy's insights into the way Susan's mind worked would have missed it. But she knew and Susan knew she knew. She'd have to think about this, talk to Alan that night.

She started to pack up to leave, but now Susan wanted to slow her departure, to keep her talking while shifting the topic, and that way to break the link of the insight from its importance.

Sandy sensed desperation she'd not seen before. Susan was really trying to hide something about Mark. She let these thoughts wash through her mind like an unconscious flow, making no attempt to trap and catch them, hoping that, without formed intent, Susan could see no more of her own thoughts and plans.

She forced her full attention back to Susan and felt affection for her flooding back. Despite the deception, there was real goodness in Susan, a simple and decent person who needed all the help she could get. Spontaneously she hugged her. "I'm so glad you seem to be a bit better today."

Susan hugged her back, feeding on her warmth, opening her mind to Sandy unconsciously.

For a split second, Sandy saw an outline of a dark, terrible secret. She knew with certainty this was the real reason behind Susan's act. It confirmed her fear that Susan had a future plan which ended once her children were born. She'd give her children to her parents to care for, safe in the knowledge they would have each other and be well cared for. Once they were safely home in England, Susan would end her life and join her crocodile spirit partner. There was a bursting joy inside Susan at this idea, making her incapable of hiding it. It chilled Sandy to the bone, though she knew she mustn't let Susan know what she'd seen.

That night she and Alan talked it through. Alan was finished with his surveillance operation and now had two days in the office to clean up paperwork before starting on a significant new case. "Finding Mark's real identity is important, but I'm nearly certain

Susan will enter a guilty plea at the trial, so you may be wasting your time trying to help her that way. I think you'll be safe to park your concerns for a week or so anyway. I'm pretty busy next week with the trial approaching. I have evidence to go through, meetings with lawyers, some statements to go over and polish that we'll put before the court to help secure a conviction. Finding Mark's identity is secondary right now. I have to prioritise."

"But you know plenty of people change their pleas, even as little as five minutes before they stand in the court. That right is available to Susan. We don't know for certain she won't take it. We have to expect this could end up being a full jury trial, prepare accordingly and have as much evidence as possible because everything will be contested."

"Look, I do have a little free time, but not a lot, to try help you pursue Mark's identity. But like you say, it seems she's trying hard to manipulate you to only pursue that one path.

"You may succeed, but it'll be at the eleventh hour by this point and then we'll all be in court with no time left to pursue any other lines of enquiry.

"I'll help you where I can, but I think I should also try to find time to pursue leads relating to Mark's life since he came to the NT. That's possibly what Susan is trying to steer you away from.

"I'll focus on the details of their trip between Barkly Homestead and Timber Creek, particularly the day after they flew in the helicopter with Vic. That seemed to be the part of the trip where something in their relationship changed, or maybe Susan found something out that could have led to Mark's murder. There must be something in those final few days.

"From my meeting with Vic I know the date of their flight in the Gulf and that they were heading on to Seven Emus and Borroloola the next day, then to VRD the day after. Buck said they'd stayed at Heartbreak Hotel and made brief stopovers in Daly Waters and Top Springs.

"I must find time to revisit all these places in case there's something important we missed at one of them. If that trawls up nothing then, after the trial and before sentencing, which will likely be deferred, I'll try close out all the other loose ends, particularly any Katherine connections. His Mark Butler identity seems to be centred there."

"Okay, it sounds like a plan," Sandy agreed. "And next week I'll put maximum effort into working out who Vincent Mark Bassingham really was."

Alan used his next two days to get all his other affairs in order and to start making discreet inquiries about whatever contacts Mark had in the Gulf or VRD. He started with a call to Buck to update him and seek insights into people worth talking to who lived out that way.

"People who knew Mark are spread all over the Northern Territory and the Kimberley region if I'm being honest with you. I remember him talking about working in the north of Western Australia, some of that time spent at the Argyle Diamond Mine and some time on stations. He also worked on some dude lodge up around the Mitchell Plateau and said he'd done work on aboriginal communities out towards the Tanami, Hooker Creek was one. I know he was good mates with Michael Riley, the publican at Top Springs Hotel, a mad Irishman if ever there was one and a bit fey. My sixth sense tells me Michael Riley's guesses could be well worth listening to."

In the end, Alan and Buck concluded the rest of Mark's contacts were too scattered, and the places those people lived hadn't been on Mark and Susan's trip. It sounded like Michael Riley from Top Springs was worth talking to though.

When Alan mentioned the name to Sandy she said, "That's funny. I'm sure I saw that name in the log of visitors Susan's had. She hasn't had many other visitors, so I remember that name as it sort of stuck out as a person I didn't know when I read it."

Alan had already talked to the publicans at Daly Waters and Heartbreak Hotel. He doubted he'd get more there, though now his focus was different, so who knew. But he'd never covered the part of the trip from Redbank Mine to Heartbreak Hotel in the Gulf, with likely stopovers at Borroloola and Seven Emus. He'd needed to follow up these leads, and a visit in person would be best.

If he cracked a whip, he reckoned he'd cover the ground in three days. He tried to think how he could slot it in. Trouble was the pre-trial conference was next Wednesday. He had a lot of work to do getting ready for it, as well as running down the identity angle before then. The trial proper started the following Tuesday, meaning he'd need to be back in town on the Monday for final barrister meetings and also any last-minute pre-trial work. That left a four-day window, but he ruled out Thursday knowing he'd have follow up work to do after his first pre-trial meeting. That left Friday and the weekend. He hated giving up his weekends with Sandy, and they'd both been really busy lately, leaving very little time for play, and he really wanted to play some more – with her!

It came to him like a flash of light. They were both working on this case, so there was no reason she couldn't come with him. Often their shared insights were way better than what they perceived individually.

He picked up the phone and called Sandy. "Fancy a trip to the VRD and Gulf next weekend? Leave Friday early and back Sunday, probably late. I'm trying to backtrack and trace the trip Susan and Mark made. There must be a clue somewhere. I've yet to clear it with my boss, but I think I can swing it.

"He's starting to feel the political heat about Susan. He called her 'Saint Susan' this morning, said he was scared they'd canonise her next week before they burnt her at the stake for murder the week after. A sort of Joan of Arc trick was the way he described it. I know he's getting desperate for something better than the explanation we have now that a nice girl suddenly went crazy."

"Shut up and stop talking. If a real dirty weekend away with you in the bush beckons, then you can count me in."

When she hung up, she had a lascivious smile on her face. Her colleague across the bench looked at her with surprise, and she felt her face flush bright red.

Sandy set to work following up the suggestions Susan had given her about trying to locate the real Mark.

She could have kicked herself for having ignored the NT as his possible birthplace, and the English and Italian connections were definitely worth following.

Half an hour later, she rang Alan back, and her hands were shaking. "I can't believe I missed it. I have a birth certificate for a

Vincent Marco Bassingham right here. He was born in Darwin on November 3rd, and he would have been thirty-five years old this November gone if he was still alive. His parents are listed as English migrants, though his mother's nationality is listed as Italian. His mother was Rosalie Adriana Moretti, and his father is Vincent Bassingham, no middle name.

"It suggests we have our man, although I do suspect they didn't live in Darwin for very long. Now I need to try to work out where they lived after that.

"I'll visit Susan to see if she can share anything Mark might have told her about his mother. I'm almost sure he told Susan she committed suicide. There was also a suggestion the police wanted to lay charges against her husband for beating her up, and there may have been other violent incidents where he was charged. Perhaps there may be some old police records in this name. How about you try and locate any police records for his father, and I'll try and find out where his mother died. It shouldn't be too hard if I can get an approximate date of death, even if we don't know the location. Death certificates are pretty reliable, and ones from that era are computerised across Australia now. Once I can pin the date down to a year or two, it should only take half an hour.

"Anyway, bye for now, but don't forget about our weekend away. I can't wait to get you down and dirty in the real bush and see whether there's a real bushie lurking in there, or just an Akubra wearing city slicker." Sandy felt herself flush red again as she ended her call and looked up to see her workmate was looking curiously at her again.

By the Friday afternoon, Sandy had all the pieces together. She'd found a real Vincent Marco Bassingham, who had vanished from remand school at thirteen only to turn up a couple times over the next five years in slightly suspicious circumstances, being linked to deaths of other unsavoury people he'd worked with, but with no real evidence of his involvement, just a couple notes on files of a suspicion. Then he'd faded from view over fifteen years ago.

She'd tracked down his family and had a death certificate for his mother, Rosalie, in Melbourne when he was seven. There was a charge of assault for his father from ten years ago in Melbourne, which was dropped when the victim refused to testify. They'd even located Rosalie's now elderly parents in Naples, Italy. They'd confirmed Rosalie had a dead brother called Marco, who'd died in a tragic accident a year before Mark was born. A brother called Antonio lived in Brisbane. He'd agreed to provide a DNA sample, with results to come through next Monday in time for the pre-trial conference. With Antonio's DNA, they'd know for certain if their victim was Mark, although Sandy was already ninety-nine percent certain he was.

She felt almost pumped as she walked out of the office on Friday, at least until she thought of Susan. She was scheduled to meet her on Monday. Usually, they met on a Wednesday, but it would have to be earlier with the legal proceedings scheduled.

When she thought of Susan sitting alone in her cell, lost, defeated, resigned to a life in jail, probably already planning for her suicide in just a couple months, it all seemed suddenly so futile and pointless. Yes, they now knew Mark was really Vincent Marco Bassingham, and they had traced his family, but so what? Wasting a month of their time and diverting attention was what Susan had wanted.

But it was not what Sandy wanted. She must keep fighting to save this silly girl, even if Susan didn't want to be saved.

Sandy was flooded with a terrible feeling of guilt. She pictured herself listening to the radio in two or three months' time, hearing an announcement that Susan was dead and there were no suspicious circumstances, in other words suicide.

That was one post-mortem she could never bring herself to do. No, she would never cut up this beautiful girl's body. Instead, she would sit alone as someone else did it, feeling an irreconcilable guilt that if she, in her cleverness, had not spotted the clues by the waterhole, then the case would have died right there and then. If this case had died back then, a good person would still be alive, and only a bad person would have died.

She took a deep breath. She could not go there. She understood now, suddenly and very clearly, Susan's dilemma. Bad choices could never be undone. In the trying lay madness.

Well, she must work even harder to ensure another choice was available for Susan, one that wasn't bad, unlike all the ones she could see now.

Chapter 15 – Just a Guilty Plea

Susan sat in a conference room with a prison officer by her side. Sitting opposite was a barrister and solicitor for the prosecution. On one end of the table was Alan, there as principal witness for the prosecution, though he was only there to clarify any evidence that was unclear and not to otherwise speak, or so it had been explained to her.

She wished she could have a few minutes to talk to him alone. She hadn't seen him at close quarters since they'd spent a day sitting next to each other on the aeroplane that returned her to Australia. Not that she had anything specific to say, but she felt affection for him and knew he was trying his best for her, despite her best endeavours to lead him and Sandy in the wrong direction. That was a necessity, not personal. She would have liked to exchange a few friendly words. Friends she could talk to were so few. But instead, she turned her attention to the business at hand.

Everyone had tried to get her to retain counsel to represent her in the trial. She declined all their offers, and in the end, the judge made a ruling that while he would not appoint a counsel against her wishes, he would appoint a legal representative to act in the court's behalf and to seek to protect her interests where feasible.

She didn't care. She was glad she'd got to this far without further delay. It was nearly over, and she wanted that more than anything. Today was only about confirming basic facts to save an argument over them in court. "To narrow the scope of what has to be determined during the trial," was how the prosecution barrister had put it.

She nodded when someone laboriously explained it all again for the umpteenth time. "Yes, I get that," she said. "I don't need you to keep repeating it. I'm not clear why you're bothering with all this when I've told you I plan to stand up and plead guilty. The way I see it, at that stage it should all be over. Hence, I struggle to see what this whole drawn out process is about."

The prosecuting lawyer, the man who would stand up and try to bury her on behalf of the state in six days' time, rolled his eyes in a show of weary exasperation. "Nevertheless, Miss McDonald, we're obliged to go through this process to outline evidence we will lead, so there are no surprises, no suggestions that we have relied on information not provided to the defence in establishing your guilt."

Susan rolled her eyes in return and replied, unconsciously mimicking his weary exasperation. "But you don't need to prove anything. In my plea, I'll admit to the truth of the key facts which you state. These are that I killed Mark Bennet, or rather I should now say, Vincent Marco Bassingham, by striking him on the head with a piece of wood, and as he lay on the ground, either dead or unconscious, I don't know which, I dragged his body to the edge of the billabong where it was taken and consumed by three large crocodiles which tore his body apart between them."

Alan's eyebrows raised in surprise. Her description of multiple crocodiles and what she'd done as Mark lay on the ground were new admissions. She'd stated these facts deliberately, done it to forestall any discussion that might ensue about how the separated body parts arose. Strangely, no one else but him had seemed to notice.

"Yes, Miss McDonald, we know all that," the prosecutor replied. "Like us, you've made your points before, but I do need to go through the rest of the evidence we will lead.

"We will establish you met Mr Bassingham in Cairns, when diving with him. We will establish you met him again in Alice Springs, that you travelled with him to Yulara, and then over the next week and a half, you went on to Timber Creek through a range of Northern Territory locations including the Barkly Roadhouse and Heartbreak Hotel. Do you agree to those facts?"

"Yes," Susan said. "As you're aware, I've already provided that in an amended statement to the police."

"Then we will establish you continued to travel on with him to the billabong on the Mary River where his body was found."

Susan sat up and looked at him intently. This was something new she'd not thought about. "How will you establish that? I've admitted to being with him at the Mary River on the morning of that Saturday in August when I killed him. I've made no admissions about how I got from Timber Creek to the billabong, so how do you propose to establish that?"

He looked caught out.

She continued, "I don't propose to admit that fact, as nothing turns on it. It's only relevant I was at the location where he was killed, at the time he was killed, in order to establish I could have killed him, and I've already admitted to that. So won't be making any admissions of how I got from Timber Creek to the billabong because it's not relevant. As far as I can see, you've no evidence of how I got there. So, I'm sorry, but I won't agree to that as evidence. You can contest it in court if you choose."

She glanced to the end of the table where Alan sat. He was trying to maintain a poker face, but the edge of a smile was creeping into his eyes. He was enjoying this. She had to admit she was too. It was a long time since she'd used her brain in an intellectually challenging way. Perhaps her day in court would be more fun than she'd thought. Unfortunately, the prosecution seemed to lack any sense of humour and kept grinding away. She made herself play the game. Yes, she agreed to all the facts relating to the murder that she'd already admitted to. Duh!

Now they moved on to what happened after the murder.

"We will establish you systematically set out to hide the evidence of the murder," the prosecution droned on. "That you scraped blood stains away from the place where his body first lay and from where you dragged him to the water."

"I don't consider it is relevant as to whether or not I murdered him. While I don't admit it, you can seek to prove it if you wish."

The prosecution nodded and continued, "We will further establish you burnt all the items belonging to the victim in order to conceal his identity."

"I don't consider that's relevant to whether or not I murdered him, so I don't admit it, but you can seek to prove it if you wish."

"We will establish that you removed and destroyed all the victim's identity papers and other items which belonged to him, yourself, or to other persons unknown, which may have provided a link between him, yourself, and the murder site."

As the words 'persons unknown' were said, the four passports she'd tried to forget since that day came bursting into her head, along with Mark's diary.

Instinctively, she shook her head. "No, that's not true."

While the prosecution had barely seemed to notice her response, Alan looked at her sharply. He'd picked up her slip but he said nothing.

"I don't consider it's relevant to whether or not I murdered him," she clarified. "So, I don't admit it. You can seek to prove it if you wish."

After another half hour, it was all done. It was really a waste of time, but so be it. She'd fight all those items she wasn't admitting to, line by line, on the day. A few they could prove, most they could not. The contest would help her get through what she knew would be a gruelling time at the trial, while her parents and friends watched on.

It was okay to play at it here. It was just pretend blood sport, but in there, it would be for real. She was glad she'd come here today rather than refusing to attend. It had toughened her up for the real thing when there would be a crowd baying for her blood and her parents and friends watching it all in horror.

But she also knew she'd made a mistake, an admission which might provide a wormhole for Alan to burrow into. She thought he'd be hard pushed to find anything on the basis of that little admission, but she wasn't completely sure.

She'd as good as said there was still stuff she'd not destroyed, and the inference was it was still out there to be found. Of course, finding this material would be much harder, but she knew it wasn't impossible.

She was glad nobody had thought to use sniffer dogs when they'd first searched the site. Even after a month or two, they could have found the passports where she'd buried them. Now, with the wet season's rain, she knew that chance had passed.

Still, she felt a grudging admiration for Alan. He was nothing if not sharp.

Doubt nagged. She was no longer so sure all her secrets would stay hidden. If they ever found the metal box with those things of Mark's she'd buried in it, it would all be over.

Chapter 16 – David and Anne

David and Anne both flew into Darwin on the Sunday before the trial, though David arrived on the lunchtime flight, and Anne didn't get in until later in the afternoon. Susan's parents had arrived two days earlier, minus Tim, who'd stayed on at university knowing there was little he could do for his sister.

Anne felt like a giddy schoolgirl as the plane touched down. She couldn't believe her excitement at the prospect of seeing David again. She felt almost disloyal to Susan for allowing David to dominate her mind, but alongside this, she knew Susan would be happy for her.

She and Susan had exchanged two letters since she'd left Darwin, and their friendship was again as strong as ever.

Susan had specifically mentioned David in her last letter and wished Anne well when she met him again on this trip. At the side of her writing, she'd placed little cryptic symbols and drawings of families and babies, as if to hint she should go for it. Even before receiving this letter, Anne had well and truly decided to throw caution to the wind and let whatever would happen, happen, with no restraint on her part.

She just hoped David wouldn't find it too painful watching Susan's trial. Anne had very low expectations that anything good would come out of it. She understood the sentencing would be delayed for a couple further weeks to allow submissions to be made, specifically on the punishment and particularly the length of the custodial sentence.

She decided she'd put all her effort into this space, as she knew nothing would change Susan's mind on her guilty plea. She did hope though that once a guilty conviction was made, she could convince Susan to explain her fear, and this, along with many glowing character references, could be used to get a large reduction in her sentence.

Anne waited, suppressed impatience mingling with nervousness fluttering in her chest as she waited for everyone to file down the aisle of the plane and queue their way through customs. Then, at last, she was outside, and there was David in a blue short sleeved shirt, his muscular arms and tousled blond hair looking as gorgeous as ever. He was a bit slow spotting her as she was behind a bigger group.

She ran around them and flung herself into his arms. He let out a whoop of delight, picked her up, and swung her around, planting a big kiss on her lips. It was more than a friend's kiss.

They talked frenetically on the way to the hotel where he'd again booked them adjoining rooms. They checked in and she freshened up, then they went down for a drink and dinner. Over dinner, she felt obliged to turn the conversation to the serious business they were here for. They spent the next hour discussing all the ways they could approach the court case to try and improve what happened, whatever the outcome might be. Anne was tempted to tell him about the text from Susan all those months ago, but something held her back.

The wine was beginning to make her feel sleepy, and she realised with the frantic rush to pack and leave and the two short days on the flight, her time was out of sync. It'd been lovely in business class, but she'd not slept as well as she did on her last trip. This time a mix of anticipation and anxiety that everything hung in the balance for Susan from here was in play.

She felt a huge yawn come over her. David signed for the bill and escorted her upstairs telling her she needed to get to bed and have a good night's sleep.

It was disappointing their night had ended so soon, but almost as soon as Anne lay down, she fell into a deep sleep. She woke at four in the morning feeling cold, wishing there was another warm body alongside her. It popped into her mind that there was a warm body through the connecting door between their rooms. What was she waiting for? When she tried to open the door she found it was unlocked.

She made out David's shadowy outline in the bed. He was sleeping soundly. Part of her felt disappointed, but another part was pleased she'd be able to surprise him when he woke. She cuddled in next to him, laid her head on his chest, and fell into a dreamless sleep.

In the early morning light, she woke and saw David lying there, not moving but looking at her intently.

"You're so beautiful," he said, and gently stroked her hair as she turned to face him.

They didn't make love then, but there was something nicer in their casual friendship and intimacy. As they got up to face the day, she went into her room and carried her things into his.

"I hope you don't mind," she said as she saw him watching her closely. "When I woke by myself last night, I wanted much more to be with you and was tired of stopping myself on account of anyone or anything else. I figure we can both share this room if you'd like us to too? We can keep the other room as well, just for appearances, if you like."

"I'm glad that's how you feel," David said. "I've felt unsure how to be around you. I've been wanting us to be more than friends yet feeling constrained by what Susan and I had before, even though by the time I met you in Darwin last year, it was already over. Like you, I don't feel inclined to waste time wishing for something when the alternative is to enjoy it now."

Anne kissed him on the lips lightly before turning her back to him and slipping out of her dressing gown.

She walked naked into the bathroom, giving her bottom a saucy wiggle as she closed the door part way, leaving enough open so he could see her as she showered.

She caught his eye as he watched her, and she could sense his desire as she turned on the shower. "Why don't you come and join me? We can wash each other's backs," she called out.

He undressed and got into the shower alongside her, his erection throbbing.

She bent forward and kissed it, then took it into her mouth. She looked back up at him and said, "There's another part of me that needs to feel it even more."

Without speaking, he nodded then put his hands behind her thighs and lifted her up and onto him.

"That feels wonderful," she said as he pushed himself all the way into her.

After a moment, she said, "Let's stop messing around and go and fuck properly. I want you to fuck me as hard and long as you can, and then I want to do it all over again. I'm so horny to feel you moving deep inside me, and I want it to happen right now."

The sex was better than she could have imagined, and the emotional connection made is doubly intense. Even on that first time, they both came together. Soon they were doing it again, and then they slept for another hour and then made love again. About nine o'clock, they decided they must eat breakfast and face the day. While they ate, Anne told David what Susan had said about them getting together.

"I think I am the luckiest man alive having had relationships with the two most gorgeous women in England. But, after tasting second course, I don't want to go back to the first."

Anne replied, with a playful smile, "I don't mind her being before me. But she'd better not ever come after me, or I'll cut that thing off."

She said it with such ferocity that he believed she would.

They visited Susan after lunch and when she noticed and commented on the closeness between them, they told her about their new relationship.

She seemed genuinely pleased. "It's funny, but I knew from the first day you met Anne that she was my main danger with you, not a crocodile. Right back then, I felt a little jealous of your instinctive reaction to Anne. It was like she and you had a deeper level of attraction than we ever did. I see now it's how it was meant to be. So, truth be told, I'm glad for you both and not jealous, well, not more than a tiny bit."

She turned to Anne and giggled. "Not the little brother for you Anne, imagine that."

Anne giggled too, and soon the three of them were laughing and hugging together. It felt good to all of them that that part of their lives had moved on.

Now Anne turned to Susan and in a serious tone said, "We're here at your disposal and want to do whatever we can to help.

Can I find a lawyer to represent you in court? I know you said you don't one and that you can speak for yourself, and that's your right. But having someone in your corner watching to make sure the other side acts fairly from a legal viewpoint could be useful."

Susan laughed. "Ever the legal secretary, eh! Actually, I sort of have one. The judge has taken it into his own hands to appoint someone in that role. He sat in at the pre-trial conference last week, and I could see his mind was sharp. Truth be told, I kinda liked him. He didn't try to barge in when I was speaking. As long as he doesn't try and take over and does not change what I have to say, you can retain him on my behalf. His name's James Williamson. Feel free to retain him but Just make it clear I don't intend to change what I've already said. I'm merely asking the court to make its judgement on the facts. I'm not asking for any deals or any other special consideration."

She looked between Anne and David. "Did you know I'm going to have twins, a boy and girl? My parents have agreed to adopt them when they're born and take them back to England to give them a good life. I know I can't offer them anything from here, so I'm glad that's sorted.

"There is just one thing I'd like to ask you both, whether you stay together or not. I'd like to name them Anne and David, with Marco as the middle name for the boy and Rosalie for the girl. It was Mark's mother's name.

"It would make me happy if you'd agree to those names. And I'd also love you to be their godparents. I daresay my parents will have them baptised in the Presbyterian Church in Reading, so perhaps you could go along and make your promises on my behalf, seeing as I won't be able to come.

"After, I'd like you to be like an aunt and uncle to them. Should anything happen to my parents, I'd like you to take responsibility for their upbringing. You don't have to adopt them, but it will set my mind to rest knowing they can stay together in a good happy family, being well provided for.

"Can you agree to all that?"

Though Susan could see it was heart wrenching for them both, they agreed. She was forcing them to confront the future that lay before her and that would affect them both as well.

Susan turned to David. "You've been unbelievably good, kind and forgiving to me through all this. I'm sorry for all the hurt I've caused and for not being more honest with you at the outset. It would have spared you this. I also want to thank your parents again for their kindness. I wrote to them in January, but could you pass on my thanks and say how sorry I am they've also have had to endure this."

David had tears glistening in his eyes as he replied, "I've never regretted a minute I spent with you. You have nothing to feel bad about in anything you've done towards me. And, of course, I wouldn't have met Anne but for you."

Susan took their hands in hers. "Thank you for visiting. You should now go and do what you have to. I can't wait for it all this to be over and to get out of this place forever. I'm glad it won't be long now."

She said it with a bright and happy smile, as if in a month or two, she'd walk out again into the bright sunshine and be free.

Inside Anne something quailed. Those were almost exactly the same words that one of her other dear friends used last year the day before she took her own life.

She walled off that thought. Surely that wasn't what Susan meant. There must be another way out. Now she felt really trapped. Should she break her promise to Susan and tell all? But as she walked out, she looked back at Susan's desperate pleading eyes. It was a look right into her soul.

Anne knew she was still bound to Susan, and there could be no good way to reveal Susan's secret, at least not without a betrayal of her friend.

Chapter 17 – The Bush Trip

It was Friday morning, and Sandy felt excited. A bush trip with only the two of them! They were heading down to Timber Creek via Katherine. Buck was putting them up at VRD tonight. Tomorrow, they'd head east, stopping at Top Springs for morning tea, then on to Daly Waters and Heartbreak Hotel before Borroloola was their overnight stop. The drive would be a long, seven hundred kilometres. Next day they'd go even further east to Seven Emus and meet the people there before the long, thousand plus kilometre return drive home to Darwin that night.

Despite the long, boring hours of driving ahead, she couldn't wait to be on the road, both to get a taste of the vast expanses of this land and to be with Alan, uninterrupted for all that time.

These days, they mostly slept at her flat and used Alan's place as a store, although his place was bigger and more comfortable. Alan said he liked her girly things and her smells. Her scent in the bed was a real turn on for him, and she liked him being turned on.

As a teenager, no one had ever told her sex could be so much fun. She'd been a slow starter, but with him, it was just so, so delicious. She felt herself blush inside at the thought of them together. Her mind drifted into thoughts of three days away together and plenty of time for in-bed play.

Last night they'd slept in Alan's flat. It was big and comfortable but a bit impersonal for her taste. Soon, they'd sell it, only keep one place until they married. It would help save money. But they'd slept there because he kept his bush gear there, his swag and the other camping gear he wanted to bring.

Now, it was six thirty in the morning, and she was fixing a quick breakfast while he shaved in the shower. He came out in his towel and swept her into a huge hug that made the towel fall away. She saw his aroused body, and before she knew it, they were back in bed. It was even better than her randy thoughts over her toast.

Afterwards, they packed quickly and headed out. They made the six hundred kilometres trip to Timber Creek in time for a late lunch. They questioned everyone they met who'd known Mark, particularly anyone who'd seen him and Susan together. The pickings were slim.

Tanya, the main witness, was gone. Alan had met her briefly in Darwin before she left to return home, and he'd reread her statement two days ago. Still, it was good to see the place in person. He'd previously sent an officer here to investigate, and even though he'd seen photos, it was different being here in person and seeing things with his own eyes.

Now, he read Tanya's statement again as he looked at the photos. Using the information in her statement, he was able to work out where Mark's vehicle had been parked when Susan got into it. He looked back to the pub from there. The space was in clear view from the kitchen window where Tanya was working, so that part added up. There was no reason not to believe everything was as she described.

The way the vehicle had been parked, facing Katherine, meant the passenger door would have been facing the kitchen window. Tanya described Mark retrieving a pillow from the back of the car and propping it under Susan's head before he got into the driver's side and drove away towards Katherine. The statement fitted with what he could see now. And that sighting had been it. It was the last time anyone, other than Susan, saw Mark alive.

Alan read back over the full statement again. Susan had come out just after eight in the morning, yawning and looking very sleepy. She'd checked her phone for messages before climbing into the car, then laying down on the seat and apparently falling asleep. The car window was open, so Tanya had seen all this clearly. While she didn't watch Susan the entire time, she hadn't seen the passenger door open again or seen Susan sit up.

The morning news on the radio had just come on when Susan got into the car, which meant it was eight o'clock. She was less sure about the time when Mark got into the car, but she'd finished serving breakfasts and was washing up, so it must have been around nine.

It all fitted. It seemed idyllically normal, exactly how he imagined he'd be with Sandy if she'd fallen asleep. The question was what happened to change this idyll?

The description of Susan checking her phone jangled in his brain. He'd never noticed this part of the statement in particular prior to now. Not that it was unusual for someone to check their phone, and the reception out here was limited. But it seemed a bit odd to be checking messages first thing in the morning when half asleep, unless, of course, she was expecting a message. But from who, and what would that message be? Perhaps she was seeking a confirmation of flight details home or something similarly mundane. He'd park that question for now, though when Tanya came to Darwin next week to give evidence, he must ask her more, dig for any little thing.

Speaking of which, he needed to ring his boss in Darwin and give him a quick verbal update. He pulled out his phone. Damn! Just a flickering half bar of signal, certainly not enough reception to ring from here. He walked along the road for a hundred yards. Now he had two bars and the phone rang through.

After he finished his call, they drove on to Victoria River Downs Station, arriving in the late afternoon. Apart from Buck and his wife, there were only a couple of people still working there who'd met Mark and Susan on that night, and they'd already heard Buck and Julie's statements. Again, slim pickings, though one person remembered Mark and Susan had both gone to bed early pleading tiredness, but that Mark had given Susan a very lascivious look as she was yawning, and she had flushed bright red in response. But they'd slept in separate rooms because only dormitory bunks were free that night, and they'd been up at dawn the next day for a quick breakfast before a helicopter flight. That was it really.

Alan and Sandy also retired early after one of those friendly dinners in the kitchen with all the other station workers, presided over by Buck and Julie. The food was plain but satisfying. Alan and Buck were now fast friends, and Sandy could feel herself really getting to like Julie, even though she and Alan had only met her today for the first time. An almost full crew was on hand as the mustering season was about to start. After they'd said goodnight, they got their own room, with a full-sized double bed, and they made good use of it.

They were away early next day. First stop would be Top Springs, and they hoped things would start to get more interesting from there.

The barman, Mike, was sweeping and mopping outside as they arrived. He finished up and wiped the sweat off his forehead with a dirty rag. It was already getting hot. He waved them inside to the bar, cool and inviting in the dim light.

Alan introduced himself by saying, "I'm the policeman who talked to you on the phone a couple days ago. Sergeant Alan Richards. This is my partner, Sandy."

They all shook hands.

"Yeah, I remember," Mike replied. "Was about my old mate, the recently deceased Mr Mark B."

They got to talking. Mike's take was rambling, interspersed with anecdotes, of which there were many. Eventually, he got to the point.

"Known Mark mebbe ten years. Proper good bloke, but wild, with a mean and dangerous streak."

"What do you mean dangerous?" Alan asked.

"Well, they tell me I am a bit fey. Must be de Irish in me. Came out as a young fella from de green land, and back dere tis always talk of spirits and divils, faeries and the like, ye know what I mean. So sometimes I sees what ordnary folks doesn't.

"Ever since I fust met Mark, I could see a sort of divil sitting on his shoulder. Not a proper divil, more like a bad spirit which filled an empty place inside him. Used to call it crocodile spirit cos he always carried dat crocodile totem, sometimes touchin it, like. But I could see it there, sort of in the shadow right behind him. Some blackfellas from round dis way, dey could see it too. So, even before I see him do anything, I knew back then he was the real deal, proper dangerous.

"Den there was the odd story to be told, ye know, bar talk, nuthin nobody'd seen direct like, but somebody knew somebody he'd hurt bad on account of a man had tried to bully him and stuff like dat.

"He'd pass through here a lot, more often than not with a pretty girl alongside. It used to be a joke. Never the same one twice. Once or twice, someone would ask him why all different girls. He would say, 'Easy come, easy go.' You sorta got used to it after a while.

"He was a popular guy, would always buy a drink for a mate, no job too hard for him, and he worked like a Trojan. And he was good to the local blacks. He would fix up der houses, give dem meat, lend dem money, only if he thought it legit though. He was no soft touch.

"So, we all sort of liked him and stuck by him. He was one of us, though nobody ever knew more about him than his first name. He introduced hisself as Mark, sometimes Mark B. I niver knew his proper name, though once I heard tell from a VRD ringer it was Mark Butler. He said he sees it on a bit of paper.

"Anyhows, one night Mark was drinking here, beers and rum chasers. We'd all had a bit, three other blokes in the bar, along with Mark. One fella was a fair tosser, big burly bloke, up from the south for a year or two, good bit bigger than Mark or the rest of us. He was always shootin' off his mouth, kept tellin' how it was all done so much better down there. Sometimes, we'd say if he loved it so much, he should piss off back there.

"Well, after we'd been drinking steadily for an hour or two, all good company like, this bloke turned to Mark and said, 'What no girl tonight? Why do you keep changing them girls anyway? What do you do? Root them, shoot them, chuck them in a hole?'

Then he laughed at his own joke, a sort of nasty laugh.

"There was a split second of dead quiet. I was watching Mark's eyes. Twas dead scary it was, like a cobra about to strike. The most evil look I've ever seen.

"He picked up this guy's beer. He always drunk from a glass like a true city slicker. Mark flings the beer in his face then tips the rum over his head. Then he says, 'Now shut yer fuckin' mouth and don't you ever talk like that again. If you ever do, *I will kill you.*'

"The guy fires right up, 'What'd you do that for? Can't you take a joke?'

"Mark points a finger at him and says, 'Shut the fuck up. If you don't like it, why don't you just follow me outside?'

"Then Mark walks out and closes the door.

"This guy is bridling up, full of piss and bad manners, reckons he doesn't need to cop shit like that; he was just makin' a joke. He thinks it will be easy enough to sort Mark out. He's got the size and fancies himself as a bit of a pub room fighter.

"We all tells him to calm down, not to fuck with Mark, to just be glad he didn't get his teeth broken for the trouble. But he keeps firing himself up, muttering that he won't cop that shit. He'll show him.

"After a minute, he goes charging outside yelling, 'I'm comin' to git you, motherfucker.'

"We sort of ignored him, hoping Mark was gone and he would fall over in the darkness and sober up after a minute. We heard a couple grunts but nothing much.

"After a while, maybe ten minutes, one of the other blokes, Fred, says, 'Think I'd better check outside jus make sure all's fine.' He goes out and a minute later he calls out 'Jasus Fuckin' Christ, boys, I need help. Bring some light.'

"We goes out and finds the big fucker lying in the dirt. It looks like he's been hit by an express train. Face is smashed pretty much to pulp, and he looks like shit, big, ragged breaths like he could croak anytime. Of Mark there's no sign.

"We call the flying doctor. They air lift him out.

"Later, the paramedic tells me it was touch and go. The face looked the worst, but he had several broken ribs, a punctured lung, and a busted liver. Don't know what Mark did but was like he hit him with a sledgehammer a few times.

"Anyway, de bloke gets better, goes back south with a slightly patched up face, not too much worse for wear. Rest of us decide that he got what's comin' his way and say nuthin. And the guy is obviously not goin' to complain to anyone, lest Mark come back and finish the job.

"Well, like I say, Mark's a dangerous man. We knew it before, but after that, word got around, and ye can be sure no one's since tried to pick a fight with him on a dark night."

Now that Mike had finished his tale, he leaned back on the bar, pulled out a can of coke for them each, and cracked his knuckles. "Guess you gets what I mean about dangerous, so."

Alan nodded, while Sandy said, "Do you remember that day he came through with the girl. The one you visited in jail?"

Mike turned to her with a grin. "Well, you're the sharp one, aren't you. Now how did you be knowin' dat?"

Sandy grinned back. "Even a city slicker like me can read the name Michael Riley in the prison visitor book."

"Yeah, sure. Remember her well enough. She was somehow different. She really liked him; could tell that from the start. Not that it was so unusual. Plenty really liked him, though for her maybe, it was a bit deeper, serious like. But what was different was that he really liked her too. It was writ all over him.

"We talked away for a good while, and they had a feed, ye know. Mark and me tellin' bush stories, all fine and dandy. Then as they gets up to go, I had this real powerful vision of her being in great danger. That crocodile spirit. I sees it now coming round to the front of him like it was protecting him. I sensed it wanted to attack her, even kill her. It was not Mark, but the bad spirit. He could not have harmed her; she was like the light in his life, but the spirit held the power.

"I knew then there was danger for her and tried to warn her. Not that I could say it clearly. With that warning Mark got sort of protective of her, and the spirit pulled back to behind him. Then I saw that, while the danger was for her, there was something protecting her, and it would turn the danger back on him.

"In that minute, I knew he was not long for this world. I saw then, in the next few days, a choice would come for him and her. One of them would have to go. The evil spirit would take its own. But Mark had proper understood this bad thing was coming. I knew he'd choose for her to live and him to die.

"There's one more thing I can tell you. Since that silly fucker said that thing about the girls and Mark, it got me thinking. Even though he was mouthing off, it told me something. I think, how Mark acted, it was saying twas at least part true, what was said. Maybe it was that bad spirit acting to protect its own that night by almost beating the life out of that man. Marks hands did it, no doubt, but what I saw in his eyes was not my friend Mark. It was this pure evil beast, one that would keep its secret tight.

"It did not come to me straight out, but over months and years, little pieces joining together in my head since that time when it happened, maybe three years ago. And then, on that day with Susan, it was like a war was happening inside him, a war between that beast and his better part. In the end, I knew his better part would win, but only through letting the beast take him instead of her.

"So, I went and tried to talk to her in jail, to tell her I knew what the good part of him wanted for her, and it was not to end her life in jail to protect his name. Her love for him was too strong. She'd not listen. In the end, I knew I could help her no more. Now you must try.

"She wants to be with him. She thinks the only way is to give her soul to the evil, let the crocodile spirit take her to join him. The only thing keeping her in this place is the babies she's yet to have. Once they be born, she's in great danger from herself."

For the last five minutes, Mike had spoken to them as if from a trance, looking out from somewhere deep inside himself. It seemed he was glimpsing a truth the world couldn't see, something hidden in a place where shadows lived and danced.

Sandy felt goose bumps run up her arms and neck. His words fitted far too well with what she'd glimpsed inside Susan's mind to treat them as an old man's mad ravings.

Suddenly, Mike returned to his normal banter. The shadow was gone. He looked at the clock, went to the bar, and pulled out three beers. "One for the road; one for each of ye. Tis on the house. And another for me, one to give me the strength to finish me day's cleaning."

They thanked Mike for his time and the beers. As they left, Sandy gave Mike a spontaneous hug, a sign of affection that felt like it came from both her and Susan for his attempt to help.

Mike winked at Alan and said, "Watch out. This one's like that Susan girl. She's smart and her mind can see shadows too. Maybe ye both can so take care."

Alan and Sandy exchanged a puzzled look as they left.

Late in the day, they arrived at Heartbreak Hotel with nothing useful found out in Daly Waters. They booked a demountable room for the night.

They were both struggling to come to terms with what they'd heard at Top Springs. To any normal person, it would sound like Mike was mad, and yet...

They'd tried to talk about it, the idea that a part of Mark wanted to kill Susan and that, instead, he had deliberately chosen to sacrifice himself for her. It didn't quite fit with the facts, but there was a truth somehow hidden within this story. It couldn't be dismissed, but it couldn't be understood. They knew there was something vital locked within the puzzle he'd given them, if they could only see it.

The spent an hour in the bar canvassing any information from when Susan had passed through, but the staff here were different now, with nobody who'd worked here from back then.

They were tired from hours of talking and thinking and driving. They wanted to hold close to each other's bodies in the night and push the shadows they had glimpsed far away.

Next morning, they woke to a bright, clear sunny day. The muggy heat and humidity were gone. Instead, a light, cool breeze was blowing from the south-east.

"The start of the dry season," Alan said.

Borroloola was their next stopping place. They knew it was an intended destination for a visit by Mark and Susan, as told by Vic last year, and they may have spent a few hours here. What they didn't know was if anyone would know or recognise either of them from a photo after all these months. They split up and took a part of the town each to work their way round, showing people photos of Mark and Susan and asking if they remembered them.

Alan started at the police station; the local copper might have some clues, if not through recognising one of them by suggesting where to ask others.

Sandy planned to hit the hotel, petrol station and local shop first. She walked into the hotel bar which had only just opened. It was dark and felt cool. She let her eyes adjust and walked over to the counter where a solid, middle-aged man looked up.

She explained her mission and passed over a photo of Susan.

He held it to a light, looked at it for a bare half second and nodded. "Yes, I remember her quite clearly from sometime around last August. A pretty girl with an English accent. The reason I remember her was her nice manners were mixed with something, a sort of anxiety, like she needed to do something unpleasant but didn't want to.

"She ordered a lemon lime and bitters and went and sat in that corner just next to the door you came in through, and she kept glancing towards it as if to check whether someone else was coming. When she was first at the bar, she asked me what time it was. When I told her, just about ten, she said that meant it was around one o'clock in the morning in England.

"Then she asked if she could charge her phone, said the battery was getting pretty low, and she needed to send a text. She didn't want to call her friend in England at that time of night and wake them.

"I pointed to the power point next to that seat. She plugged her phone in and sat there to have her drink. I didn't take a big lot of notice, but I saw her pull out a tiny notebook from her purse and look carefully at it while she was sending the text.

"I thought maybe flight details home or something like that. It took her a few minutes. It was like she was trying to work out what words to say as she did it. She was clearly nervous, the way she kept looking up. Then when it was done, she relaxed. After a bit, she finished her drink, unplugged the phone, and walked outside. Actually, a bloke came inside the front door, and she soon went out with him. Once he came in, she didn't look nervous anymore, more like relieved."

Susan showed him Mark's photo. "Is that him?"

"Could be, not sure. I barely looked at him. Only she obviously knew him and was pleased to see him. But she'd already put her phone away soon as she was finished texting, and the moment he came inside, she left.

"The strangest thing is I'm sure I've seen her picture since, like on TV or in a paper or something, but I'm dammed if I can remember where. It just seems too familiar."

Sandy sat at the bar for a few minutes and wrote out a statement, then read it back to the barman. He confirmed its accuracy, and she asked him for his name for the statement, thanked him and left. She knew she'd discovered something significant, so she rang Alan to find out where he was.

He'd also met someone with new information, a man who'd known Mark. Alan gave her directions to find him.

Five minutes later she entered a corrugated iron building where a middle-aged, non-descript man was showing Alan a photo of two beautiful blue opal stones, one set in a pendant the other in a ring.

"Those are what he collected," the man said. "Told me they were for his sweetheart, nearest he could get to an engagement ring for one who lived on the other side of the world.

"I've had dealings with him from time to time over five or six years, ordering things, selling gemstones and the like. I'm a bit of a wheeler dealer. I have contacts all over the place, and that's a bit the way he struck me, another dealer like me.

"He was mostly pretty guarded. Never said much about his work, but always had plenty of cash. Early on once, he gave me his driver's license details for ID. Mark Butler was his name, though most people just called him Mark or Mark B. He seemed to know quite a few of the people round here, particularly the aboriginals. They would often shout his name when they saw him in the street, and he seemed often to have meat and fish to give away to them.

"I'd not seen him for a few months, but he'd rung a couple weeks before and asked if he could have a delivery made to my place, which he'd collect on his way through.

"It was in a small box, and I would never have known what was inside, except I had to sign for the delivery and say it was received in good order. So, I opened the box, checked its contents, and that's what I saw. I took a picture of them for insurance purposes, just in case they were stolen.

"The thing I best remember was he was different that day. Normally he was serious and deadpan. That day he was excited when he collected it. He had a lovesick puppy look. He opened it in front of me to check, and then he told me what it was for. He also gave me an extra fifty for my troubles."

"Would I be able to get a copy of that photo?" Alan asked.

"Yes, happy to oblige."

They brought it outside, and Alan copied it on his digital camera, thanked the man, and they were on their way.

"I think we've got as much new useful information as we'll get from this town," Alan said. "It seems Mark's main purpose in coming here was to collect this gift, and it sounded like it was intended as a present for Susan. We'll have to check whether anyone saw her wearing the jewellery. It was obviously valuable judging by the photo."

Sandy said, "The most significant thing I found was that Susan sent a text to a friend in England when it was the middle of the night there. Her demeanour suggested she was anxious when she did it, and she made sure to send it when Mark wasn't with her. Her phone was out of sight before he came to collect her. It may be nothing, but my intuition tells me it's important."

"I'm kicking myself for never following up as to whether Susan had a phone in Australia," Alan said. "And if she did, what was the number and where is it now? My first job once I get back to Darwin will be to trace it."

They drove out to Seven Emus for lunch. The people were very hospitable. They knew Mark quite well and remembered him being with Susan who'd enjoyed a morning tea of Chinese dumplings and spiced pork, as did Mark. They described how they were affectionate to each another, but they could tell them nothing else that was useful.

Then it was a long afternoon of driving first west, then north, before, at last, they arrived in Darwin in the early hours of the next morning, both feeling completely whacked. Alan had a new burning priority. He must find the phone Susan had used.

Chapter 18 – The Trial

Susan was awake early in the morning. She should be calm, but anxiety swirled around inside her. This was a critical day, and she needed to get through it without making any major mistakes. She'd felt uneasy almost continuously since that pre-trial meeting blunder, mostly worried about them tracing her phone calls before the trial.

Now, on top of that, was a whole new line of inquiry. Could they find the box she'd buried with the four missing girls' passports and Mark's multiple fake IDs? Why had she left them together? The passports on their own didn't link to Mark but found alongside his own documents, well, that was game set and match for association. Through Sandy's mind, she could read that Alan was closing in on her. Why had she willed him to do this on the aeroplane? An average, lazy copper would have been gloating he'd nailed her and would have looked no further. But this was a man on a mission.

She had a premonition he would succeed. What would she do then? Perhaps she'd find a way to kill herself and her unborn children so that they would all be gone and never have to live with this. But no, she couldn't ever do that. These children didn't deserve to die. Once she was gone, the whole story would fade away, and by the time her children were old enough to know, it would be long buried under yesterday's news.

She realised she was being silly. Nothing had happened. No new, startling revelations had been revealed. After today, it would pretty much be too late. Conviction. Guilty. Move On.

She needed to focus on getting her mind into the right state for her murder trial. She must be a credible witness to her own guilt, not too abject. Let them think she was a conniving bitch who liked playing games with the truth.

She would plead guilty as planned.

But she would now contest the evidence of her attempt at concealment, about what happened before and after Mark's death, and any speculation as to motive. She'd visibly gloat a little at any wins, which would happen if they overplayed their hand.

Most of her challenges would probably fail, but she thought her performance would entertain the assembled cast and audience and give the ever present press another whole new set of dead end leads to follow.

Her performance wouldn't endear her in the public mind. She knew they wanted to think of her as an evil witch, and to judge her accordingly. Well, let them. It would be her lead starring role for today.

***

The trial went pretty much as planned. She was glad she'd her own barrister in the end. He stuck strictly to her instructions, though she could tell that bothered him. But it was her show. She was its star, playing her cast character just how she wanted.

As the day unfolded, she realised this day was little different to other theatrical productions. She had a flair for this acting stuff. She could choose to be Saint Susan today and become a different Slut Susan tomorrow.

Now the stakes now were much higher. They were all playing for her life. But what the hell. She had already conceded that, so there was really nothing more to lose.

It was simple really, like a game of chess. When the game was lost, you knocked your king over. As he lay there, dead on the ground, everyone else saw it and knew it too. It was the sign the game had really ended.

The day ground its slow way forward, and she ground out her best acting, worth at least an Oscar, she thought.

When the prosecution finished its tortuous and contested trail of evidence, she took the stand, swearing to tell the truth. She blocked the word 'whole' out of her hearing and mind. She would tell no lies.

Her evidence took barely a minute. Her guilty plea was entered. She could see everyone squirming, knowing there must be more and wondering about the why.

The judge summed it up and asked if she had anything further to say before he made a finding.

Instead, she looked the devil in the eye and laughed, gave a big grin to the audience. She heard gasps coming from the back stalls at her obvious lack of remorse and noticed a reporter furiously scribbling a line to crucify her.

From a far-off place, she heard the judge asking her, most earnestly, to provide a better explanation, one to help him understand and reach a verdict. He wanted a tale that balanced the need for justice with a story that made sense of the situation for the whole community who watched on, not least her family, friends, and her many other supporters.

She looked him in the eye, smiled brightly again and said, "Your honour, I've told you I killed him. I've told you when and where I killed him and how I killed him. What more is there that you need to know before you reach your verdict?"

She could have sworn he muttered a curse under his breath, and she allowed herself a further tiny smile of victory. He called a short recess and asked to speak to her with her legal representative present.

Susan followed a court official into a small private room where the judge sat waiting, opposite her own barrister. He indicated to her to take a seat, and she did.

The judge explained he saw no choice but to find her guilty by her own admission, but he found it distasteful, unsatisfactory, and disturbing that she would willingly submit herself to spending years in jail without offering any resistance. He implored her to offer him some better explanation of why or what she was hiding or protecting.

"I'll be delaying sentencing for two weeks, and I'll require you to undergo psychiatric assessment as I have some grave concerns about your mental state. Do you agree to this?"

There was a pause while she looked to her barrister and then nodded to give her assent.

In conclusion the judge said, "Please give another consideration to providing an explanation before I return to the court and make a ruling.

Susan could feel a thing like a great weight pulling at her to give him something, at least to admit her fear or say that, in the end, she knew it was a mistake. But every step forward from where she was now opened a Pandora's box: if fear then of what? If a mistake, then why?

She took a breath, hardened her resolve again, and answered, "Your honour, I'm not being deliberately contrary. I would dearly like to help you. I know the court and my friends want to understand why I did this, but I'm not able to say why. I refuse to say why. I'm informed that's my right under law. So, you'll have to rule only on the facts before you. I, like you, wish it was otherwise. But it can't be so."

They returned to the courtroom. The judge ruled that she, Susan Emily McDonald, was guilty of the murder of Vincent Marco Bassingham as charged. He made no findings as to premeditation. He announced sentencing would occur two weeks from tomorrow when he would receive and consider any submissions the parties wished to make. In the meantime, he ordered she go for a psychiatric assessment.

Susan thought she should savour her success, but it now left a bitter taste in her mouth and an empty place in her soul — betrayal on betrayal. She didn't care about the sentencing. It held no fears; it couldn't undo the verdict. Only one last real step remained before she would be free. Well, perhaps two when she counted her babies.

Chapter 19 – Anne's Dilemma

Anne felt appalled as she watched the trial unfold.

This beautiful woman, her friend, was play acting the performance of her life as, with deliberate purpose, she condemned herself to death. She saw it so clearly now. This was not death in some metaphorical sense. This was the real thing. The babies would be born, Susan's parents would adopt them and take them back to England, and she and David would fly there to attend the baptism.

While they were all gathered there, the phone call would come saying that Susan, lovely, beautiful Susan, was dead. Anne could try and protect her, ask for extra watches, removal of anything dangerous, but it would be futile. Susan was way too clever. She would find a way.

After the sentence was pronounced and Anne walked away from the court, she knew she had a choice to make — to let her friend die, or to betray her promise. Suddenly, there was no choice anymore. The answer was clear and simple.

But she must wait until everything was almost finished. She would provide her evidence to Susan's barrister at the moment he stood to sum up on sentencing day, the last possible moment before the judge pronounced sentence, and she'd build in a safety catch in case anything happened to her.

She'd tell David but hold him to the same promise which bound her. She'd transcribe the two text messages. They'd only take one sheet of paper. She'd make a copy for David and a copy for herself. She'd lock her phone in the hotel safe where it could be produced later when required to verify the transcript.

The prosecution lawyers would hate new evidence being produced at this very late stage. They'd talk of being ambushed, using all sorts of fancy sounding legal names to condemn what she'd done.

But the evidence would be accepted, and it would show Susan was in real fear for her life just before the murder. Even if she was guilty, her actions were justified, and they would be deemed as self-defence. There would be plenty of time for the lawyers to argue the finer legal points of that later.

Once back at their hotel room, she sat and wrote the texts out then woke David who was napping in the bed and read them out to him after she'd extracted his promise.

He was fuzzy from sleep at first, but suddenly a light went on in his brain. "Suddenly it all makes sense."

Now he was bursting for action. "We need to trace these girls, follow their last movements, show that Mark could have been responsible for them being missing. I can get ten people on to it in the morning."

Anne shook her head. "No, my impulsive one! I've promised her I won't reveal this. I only choose to do so because I know she'll commit suicide after the babies are born. I'm only breaking my promise to her if there really is no other choice.

"That means as her barrister stands up to speak, he'll be passed the note and asked to read it immediately. He might not like it, but he'll do it, and in the interests of justice, he'll demand it be admitted into evidence.

"It'll almost certainly mean that the judge will suspend his sentencing decision. It's also highly likely Susan will be released on bail. Even doing it this way is very high risk. I'll make sure a twenty-four-hour watch is placed on her cell if she's not granted bail. And if she is, I'll stay with her all day and every day until she gives birth, and I'll make sure she holds and loves her babies and knows she can't abandon them. It gives us a fighting chance. But the element of surprise is everything. That means it can only happen then because if the texts are revealed in advance, she may not wait for her babies to be born before she ends it.

"I don't want to betray her trust, but I will as an absolute last resort. I know Alan is following similar lines. Sandy was asking me about Susan's phone when I saw her yesterday, but I just played dumb. So, they may discover something about these missing women too, and I would rather it comes from them, though once again, later is better.

"Don't get any crazy ideas about becoming a super sleuth. That will be the job of the police. Our job will simply be to give them this clue to point them in the right direction."

She shook her head. "I hope one day Susan will thank me though I very much doubt it. I'm sure this is the right thing to do but I'm still very afraid for her. It's the way she talks about her life in the past tense now. In her head she's already decided it's over. It's the way she smiles brightly as she looks towards an impossible future, and it's the way she acted in court today as if she was playing a chess game for her own life. She acts as if there'll be no tomorrow. That's because she's already decided there won't be."

Chapter 20 – New Search and Phone Links

Alan had only seen the second half of Susan's performance in court but was equally appalled. After today, he had just two weeks to crack this one with but two leads remaining. One was the phone, and one was Susan's admission in the pre-trial meeting, he was certain what she meant was she had not destroyed everything.

He would work to trace her phone, the calls, and particularly the text she sent from Borroloola. Could she have found something out by text which prompted her change in behaviour? But what? A text could only have been a few sentences at most. It could give a date, an ETA, a place, or name. But to try and find information from other parts of the world one needed the internet. She could have used the internet at Borroloola. The corner store had it. But she'd only sent a text. Perhaps it was a happy birthday message to family or friends.

What about the other lead, the 'something not destroyed' angle? She must have kept and hidden something. But where? If she'd hidden a thing in England, she'd have no concern he'd find it. But he'd seen her tell-tale signs of alarm when she realised she'd made a mistake.

If it was a mistake of real concern, it must be in Australia. The 'where' must be in the NT. It was the only place she'd been before she caught her plane, and her time after she was at the billabong until the plane left was tight. There were a few free hours, but hours were all, particularly based on the report from a witness about someone driving around there in the early evening. That witness statement indicated she'd not departed until after dark. As best he could judge, she'd just driven from the murder site to where she abandoned the car, and she'd done it at night when her view of the surrounding countryside was very limited.

On that basis, whatever she'd hidden must be either at the murder site, along the way, or at location they'd found the car, and it must be holding something important. Rechecking the murder site even more carefully had to be the best place to start. Last time the search had concentrated on finding any physical evidence associated with murder. It hadn't focused on nearby hidey holes where something could be stashed.

It was possible she'd seen another location, a possible landmark, when she'd driven to the billabong with Mark, and that she'd stopped there on the return run. She was clever enough. But seeking that was futile as there were far too many options. He'd begin with the site.

Now the trial was over and the guilty plea was entered, his official work was done. It wasn't for him to make a case for leniency. Tomorrow his bosses would be expecting him back at work and would want to dump a new case on him. He'd be buried by next week. So, how to find the time this investigation required? He'd have to squeeze in the time.

He guessed the media would throw plenty of mud on the police after the verdict appeared in tomorrow's papers. Using that as cover, he'd claim a new lead based on Susan's testimony, say she'd indicated she'd hidden some critical evidence at the site, and therefore they needed to search it again.

Tomorrow he'd scout the area and formulate a search plan. The day after, he'd organise a party of searchers. He reckoned about eight people would do it, and they didn't have to be highly skilled. In fact, it was good if most didn't know the billabong. Searches worked out best if viewed with fresh eyes.

They'd go over the site again with a fine-tooth comb looking for hidey holes, somewhere big enough to hide a box or bag of documents. There was certainly a missing will. While she may have burnt most of Mark's papers, her reaction said she had kept back something. In reality it was needle in the haystack stuff, but he must try.

Early next morning, he drove back out to the Mary River and walked along the billabong. The edge gave a good reference point. There were tree hollows and a couple piles of rocks and crevices which were possibilities. He walked around the campsite, looking again for disturbed earth areas. It was much harder after the wet season's rain. He swept the edges, going out twenty or thirty metres.

There were a few possibilities here too, places to be worked over, but nothing super suspicious or promising.

He looked around at the surrounding area, casting his eye out to a few hundred metres for any landscape features. There was one small hill distinctly visible, perhaps five hundred metres away. That was worth looking at. He walked across to it. It was bigger than he'd first thought. Lots of rocks and boulders lay on its sides, but there were no obvious cracks or crevices.

He walked to the back of the hill and stood on a low flat rock at the edge, surveying the surrounding ground in both directions. This hill was the sort of feature someone might pick, but there were no obvious hiding places.

Should he send a couple people to probe and dig around it tomorrow, look for any loose rocks or soft soil? If he had ten people and a D9 dozer for a week, he'd pull the hill apart and perhaps they would find something. But on balance, it was less likely they'd find something over here than in a place closer to the water. He needed to concentrate the limited resources he had for the one day to searching in the most likely places.

He was back in the office by lunchtime and told his boss of his plans. He could see him look sceptical, but he let it pass. The papers had given the police the expected bullocking.

As he started to walk out his boss called to him. "I thought I should tell you now, though you will see this in an email notification this afternoon.

"Your name's on the list for a special operation next week, out in Eastern Arnhem Land. It runs from Monday to Sunday, with long hours each day. You may want to find some time for a break before then."

Next day, they got to the site early. They set out on a systematic search pattern and worked everywhere but the hill over thoroughly and found nothing.

He walked back to the hill for one last look and tried to lift some of the more promising rocks in case there was something hidden underneath. All those rocks he tried were well embedded in the dirt and did not lift easily. There were hundreds more like them, and he didn't have time to try them all.

Now he wished he'd searched the hill properly as well, but it was too late. By three, the crew were all shagged, and it was a Friday. He ordered them to knockoff and told them he'd shout them a beer at the Bark Hutt Inn, for them to head off, buy a round, and tell the publican he'd pay when he came in a few minutes after them.

The work crew headed off leaving Alan alone by the water. He knew he'd tried and failed with this roll of the dice. He walked right to the edge, to the place where they'd found Mark's footprint beside a little bush. He squatted beside that place, where the indented earth had been carefully dug out to make a plaster cast. Now only a small hole remained. He turned to face the billabong.

The water was incredibly still and seemed placid. It was hard to believe, only months ago, a man was torn apart by crocodiles, just metres from here. He knew he should move back from the edge. The danger was no less acute now than then. But, knowing more about Mark than when he'd first come here, he wanted to imagine himself in his shoes on that fateful day.

He stood again, then squatted down a second time, right alongside where his footprint has been found. He now had the sense of being in Mark's shoes as the squatted here and contemplated his future, knowing he had a choice to make. What was it the Top Springs bartender had said? To choose between himself and the girl.

Maybe Susan believed she was the intended victim of the crocodiles because she knew something awful about Mark, while he, unknown to her, had decided the victim had to be him.

Perhaps he was here, contemplating the end of his life before he joined the crocodiles. If Susan hadn't known his intentions but feared for her life, then perhaps she struck the blow to his head, and only later discovered a message from him telling her otherwise. That would constitute the mistake she talked about.

It was a theory fitting some pieces together. He wasn't convinced, but it might help make sense of these events.

Alan's heel slid sideways into the hole as he went to stand up. He found himself overbalancing into the small bush. His hand went sideways to steady himself, landing on the ground covered by the bush. It lodged on a hard, misshaped object lying amongst the leaves there. His fingers closed around it as he steadied himself. He retrieved his hand still holding the object.

It was a palm sized piece of wood, carved into a crocodile shape, with faded charcoal and ochre markings. This must be the crocodile totem carving the bartender described. It wasn't proof but seemed to confirm his theory and was a further step on a path to understanding.

He looked closely at the carving. At first glance, it seemed small and insignificant, but as you looked more closely, you saw it was a representation of an old and massive crocodile, a being of real power.

He felt a sense of its spirit reaching out, connecting to the other crocodiles of this place, and when he looked out across the water, he saw the unmoving head and eyes of a real crocodile contemplating him from a distance away.

It was not the big one, but it seemed to be sending a message directed specifically to him: *'This totem is for you to take to help you discover its owner.'*

He placed the carving in his pocket. He should submit it as evidence, but it seemed too significant for an exhibit bag. Perhaps going forward from here, it would help him gain understanding, a connection between his mind and Mark's, a link like that between Sandy and Susan. He would log the carving but hold it for now. After months lying in the weather, it wouldn't hold any forensic clues. Maybe it would help align his mind to the real Mark though, a man who he'd only glimpsed in shadowed outline. Perhaps somehow, it could bring him towards a point of truth.

As he drove back into Darwin, he realised he was now down to his last option, the tracking of Susan's phone.

He had only the rest of today, tomorrow and Sunday before he'd have to travel away for his new special operation. He would see what he could do in that time. He decided to start with the obvious thing of asking Susan's family and friends if she'd had a mobile while in Australia, as he needed to trace any calls she might have made while here.

He called Susan's father first who answered promptly and told him, "Yes, she did. I'll read out the number."

Alan called David a minute later who confirmed the same number. It was an English mobile, but it had international roaming, so it was possible she'd used it. It took an hour or two of chasing, but finally he got through to the British company who supplied the service. After getting authority from Scotland Yard, giving identification, and sending verification of his credentials, he got access to the call records.

There were plenty of calls before and after Susan's visit, but nothing during the period of the Australian trip. There was also a gap for a little over a week after Susan got back to England. He asked the operator about this. "Oh, that's because she got a new handset. She told us the previous one had been lost in Australia."

This was interesting; it seemed like more than a coincidence.

He rang her father back and asked if he knew anything about a new handset after Australia. "That sounds right. When she got back, she said her luggage got lost on the bus, and her phone was with it. She bought another phone but got the old number reissued. That way all her friends still had her number."

"Do you know anything about her having a different phone or SIM card while she was in Australia? A local one?"

"Not that I can think of. In fact, while away she barely rang. The only time I recall a phone call was from her cousins in Sydney where she stayed for a few days. But that day they rang on their landline because they all had a bit of a chat to our family, if I remember it right. Of course, you could ring them and check if they had a local number for Susan, or I will, if you like."

"I'd appreciate that please. When you find out leave a message. I'm just on my way home now, but I'll check it out in the morning. And please don't tell Susan about this or ask her."

On Saturday, Susan's father rang back. "They think she had an Australian number she got in Cairns. None of them have been able to find it. I've asked them to find their own phone bills and go through them from the time Susan was there to see if they can find anything. It doesn't sound like I'll be able to get it for you inside a day or two as they were heading off for a weekend of camping when I called, and they'll have set off now."

Alan could feel his frustration rise, but he knew her father was trying to be helpful and didn't really understand what was at stake, so he put his angst aside.

The weekend passed in a blur. He thought he'd have time to follow up Susan's Australian phone number, but he didn't. Then the weekend was gone, and he was away on his new job.

The operation was located out in a remote part of the Top End, watching a deserted stretch of coastline a couple hours' drive east of the town of Gove, where a tip-off of a drug landing was received. They were flown in for the week and would stay until the following Sunday. This operation was a continuation of the drug surveillance operation he'd been involved in previously. Alan could feel time slipping through his fingers, but there was nothing he could do.

On Thursday, he had a flash of inspiration. He was almost sure where to find the phone number. He remembered the Mark Butler phone bill, the one linking him to Vic. There were a handful of calls on it he'd never followed up. He seemed to remember three or four calls from the same number in the few days before Susan had come to Alice Springs.

He'd wondered at the time about that cluster of calls, but with lots of other leads to follow back then he had not paid it much mind, not thinking at that stage this phone had even belonged to their victim. But now he knew it had, and perhaps it was not his only phone. Alan now had a strong feeling those calls could have been to and from Susan, calls making arrangements for their trip.

He could feel his impatience to get back to Darwin and follow it up. He also realised nobody had checked the Katherine mailbox where this phone bill was found since before Christmas, three months ago. He knew because he had the key on his desk.

Getting someone in Katherine to go through any new mail was another job for Monday. Perhaps some new contacts of Mark's would also emerge. He thought of getting a constable to go there now. In the end, he decided there was too much at stake and he should go himself.

He used the radio at their base to get clearance from his boss to go to Katherine for two days next week. There was a delay while the request was relayed, then the approval was duly given.

He breathed a sigh of relief. It was not much, but two days should be enough to get to the bottom of this phone story. And who knew what else he might also discover while in the town where Mark seemed to spend a fair amount of time.

Chapter 21 – The Rat Trap

Susan smelt a rat. She knew the minute she saw Anne's face, two days after the trial, when she came to visit, that something had changed. Anne was no longer in her corner. For a minute, she felt overcome by panic. What could she do? If Anne released the texts, the plans she'd made would be to no avail in hiding the truth. Anne didn't seem to pick up that Susan was on to her, so Susan tried to remain relaxed, though her mind was churning.

Once Anne was gone, she made herself think rationally. What would Anne do with this hidden information? Now she saw her error. It was in asking Anne and David to be godparents. She remembered her final words as they'd left, "I just can't wait for it all to be over and to get out of this place forever. I'm glad it won't be much longer now."

She'd caught a flicker on Anne's face as she said this, and now she turned the words over in her mind again. When she'd said them on that day, it was as though they'd been pre-formed in her mind. They were what she was thinking, but they were words someone else had used, words she'd heard and replayed as they fitted her own life too.

Now she remembered. These were the words Anne had told her almost a year before. They were the words Anne's friend, Beverly, said the day before she committed suicide.

Anne had been pretty broken up by the fact that, if only she'd listened better, she could have acted, and perhaps she could have saved her friend's life.

Now she'd taken those words from her subconscious memory and played them back to Anne with exactly the same meaning. And if there was any doubt before, her bravura acting performance at the trial the day before yesterday was the sort of thing that would only be done by someone who had already planned a no-future end game. With her desire to leave in a blaze of glory, a self-indulgent piece of theatre, she'd pushed Anne to action. Her court acting was yet another mistake. She really was getting careless.

But what would Anne do? When would she act? She was a careful and reasoned person. She wouldn't act impulsively like Susan did. Instead, she'd make a plan and determine the best time for the revelation. Anne would realise the danger would follow the birth of the babies once Susan's responsibility for them ended, so she didn't need to rush. The deadline to act would be before the judge pronounced sentence.

She thought Anne would likely delay for as long as possible before then, probably passing a note to her barrister just before he stood to sum up. As he read the content of the texts, he'd realise the basis of the case had shifted, and he'd bring the texts into evidence before the judge pronounced the sentence.

Yes, that was the most likely time. Anne wouldn't want to open Pandora's Box if there was another option. She'd delay, hoping she wouldn't be the one to betray her friend. She'd hope Alan could dig something up to make her admission unnecessary.

Susan's own plan needed to cover this eventuality too. Sandy had visited this morning before Anne. From her ongoing glimpses into Sandy's mind, she saw Alan was planning to re-search the billabong site today and tomorrow, looking for whatever was hidden. Alan had told Sandy of the hill but decided, with just one day free to search, he would ignore it. He'd walked around it, and it didn't seem promising. Susan knew he'd be away next week and could do nothing further until two days before the trial. Even though she knew they'd gone, she couldn't see anything about the trip they'd made last weekend to the Gulf. The details weren't available to her.

Sandy had got much better at hiding her thoughts now she realised how well Susan could see them. So, while she had no information about their trip, she had a sense that any texts or other communications were part of what they were looking for.

She knew nothing specific had been found. That would have been too big in Sandy's mind for her to keep it hidden. At best, Alan would have one or two days to pursue her phone records before her sentencing date. Anything found would get admitted very late, probably on the day. Alan and Anne's timing would be almost the same should a revelation come. Her feeling was very strong that something would happen, but it was only a guess.

She would have to wait and see rather than act precipitately herself. Even if Anne was planning a reveal, she wasn't entirely sure what she should do. She needed to think of a way to forestall the sentencing. There was a six-week gap after sentencing until her babies were due. What she needed was for her babies to come early, no later than on sentence day. Perhaps if she went into labour on that day it would work. It meant her babies would be premature and later was better for them. But with modern care that risk seemed okay.

If she could induce her labour to start on the date of sentencing, no later than just before the judge stood up to give his decision, that would throw a massive distraction into this circus. It would certainly result in sentencing being delayed until after her babies were born. They'd rush her to hospital to deliver the babies, maybe do a Caesar. While she was in recovery she would act. Potassium into her drip line would be best. Perhaps she could also use anaesthetic, which would be easily accessible as she knew the hospital security was weak. She could easily get her hands on something lethal. The benefit of her medical background was that she knew what all these things were and how they worked. She'd only need a minute to do it. She could feign sleepiness to get her chance before they took her back to prison from recovery. She was better than ninety per cent sure it would work, and that seemed the best odds she could hope for. Once she was gone, the trial and sentencing would be over. No guilty party would remain. Case closed. They might try to dig into Mark, but there was no useful evidence. Vic was gone, so that closed off the diary. Alan might pursue what happened to the missing girls, but Mark had more or less told her he'd covered his tracks too well for anything substantial to be found without other evidence such as the passports or diary, and neither of them would come to light — she was almost certain the search would also come to nought. So that was her plan.

While her plan wasn't ideal, it was the best option she could think of. It was now Friday. On Monday, she would be going to the hospital for her routine pregnancy check-up. It would give her a chance to check out what her opportunities were and put something in place.

The best drug to induce her labour on sentencing day would be Oxytocin. She needed a loaded syringe of it on hand for use that day. It was routinely used in the obstetric ward she was visiting on Monday, and she was confident she could find some on a trolley. No one watched her closely these days. They'd decided she wasn't a risk. The prison guard who went to her appointments with her always read a book or watched TV and barely looked her way. Using her medical knowledge, she would often chat to nurses and doctors doing their medical rounds. She knew the trolleys were often left unattended and was sure a chance to obtain what she needed would present itself.

In court on sentencing day, she'd watch like a hawk. Unless a thing gave her an early alert, either Alan coming into the court or some signal of impending action from Anne, she'd act just before the judge started to sum up. That would create maximum impact and drama. She would have the loaded syringe close at hand. They never body searched her, so she could tape it to her body or upper leg. Only a couple of seconds would be required to inject it and to drop the syringe unseen behind her.

She re-ran the plan through in her mind to make sure she had the script and timing right in her head for what she knew would be her last and best performance.

Unless Anne acted right now, which she was almost sure wouldn't happen, she should win. Once she went into labour other things would be forgotten, and when the babies were safely out, she could end it all.

A hospital was an ideal place. So many alternatives, and she knew about a wide range of things she could use. She'd be on a drip, so running an extra drug into the drip line would be easy-peasy. It would barely take a minute before it was too late.

The next Monday, once she arrived at hospital, she checked with the doctor how her babies were doing.

"Well, I'm happy to report they're doing just fine."

"I've been worried about the stress of the trial sending me into early labour. Would they be okay if that happened?"

"I can assure you that they're already big enough to be delivered by Caesarean. By your sentencing, the odds are better than ninety-nine percent they would both be fine."

Susan decided she could live with that chance.

She found a trolley left parked nearby with two ampoules of oxytocin on it. She secreted these plus an empty syringe and needle on her person.

That was more than enough to bring her into labour. Normally, it went into an IV drip, but an injection into the muscle of her leg would work just fine, although it would take a little longer to act. All she'd need to do was to plunge the needle into her leg and inject. It would take barely a second, and her labour would begin. It might take an hour or two to really work, but she could fake an hour or two until the drug kicked in.

Once her babies had been delivered at the hospital, she'd either load up her IV drip with some potassium or disconnect her alarms and dial up the anaesthetic to a sufficient dose.

In a few minutes, it would be all over, and it would be easy and painless.

She was so tired of all this other stuff and didn't want her ending to be hard too.

After she returned from the hospital, she put away the crocodile stone and returned to her crocodile spirit dreaming, loving being in the presence of Mark.

She felt impatient now for her final day to come so she could be with him always.

Bright and early on the morning of the sentencing hearing, she'd load the syringe, attach it her inner thigh, where she could get to it quickly.

It was good to be in control of some things.

They thought they'd sprung the trap.

Instead, she would open it and set the rat free.

Chapter 22 – Pictures from Long Past

It was now only six days until the sentencing hearing would be held. Sandy could feel time sliding through her fingers like a greasy rope. It seemed like an eternity since Alan had gone away, and yet it was no time as all based on the speed with which the days were passing.

She had a nagging sense that she needed to try and find something more to help. The feeling had been with her and building for days, an anxiety which infected her waking being and her dreams.

She tried not to let Susan into her unconscious mind. She had secrets she didn't want to share, particularly where Alan was concerned. Now she maintained an almost continuous vigil in her mind to stop Susan knowing things she didn't want her to know, and she did her best to suppress that part of her unconscious from looking into her hidden knowledge, to keep it from getting into any dreams and memories which rose to the surface when she was not in full control. It seemed to be working. She had no sense Susan had breached her defences. And yet an ever growing anxiety was there, making her perpetually on edge as if waiting for catastrophe.

When a package arrived in the mail, she thought she knew what was in it before she opened it. It should contain early family photos of Mark and his family sent by his uncle. She'd talked to Antonio, and he'd agreed to help in any way he could. He knew it could not help his nephew or sister, but he wanted to help anyway. Sandy thought these pictures may give an insight into the people behind the story of Mark and his extended family, so she'd asked his uncle to send them.

The package was a brown envelope, two centimetres thick. She opened it and began to flick through pictures of a small boy and girl, dark haired and distant looking, along with an Italian mama and papa with a baby in the woman's arms. The first few were early family photos. They must be Mark's grandparents and their long-ago small children in Italy.

She put these photos aside and turned to the next group, a batch held with a rubber band. The first picture was of big solid man, a picture of strength, but with a hard look about his face, although he was clearly handsome.

Perhaps he was Mark's father. She saw a trace of family resemblance in the few adult pictures she'd seen of Mark, but little resemblance to pictures of his father, seen in later life and as shown in his criminal charge sheets.

She put this photo to one side and looked again. She almost dropped the batch of photos. What was a photo of Susan doing mixed up with these? She was sure none had been sent to Mark's uncle by officials. He could have cut one out of a paper, but this was a real photo on old photographic paper. She looked more closely, and it dawned on her. This wasn't Susan but Mark's mother, a young Rosalie Moretti. Confirming her suspicion, she read the back of the photo where the name Rosalie and a date were written in smudged ink. It looked like it was 1960 something, perhaps six or nine. The girl looked like a teenager.

When she looked more closely some differences were obvious, both in the setting of the photo and some features of her face. But it was the look, a half-turned face in partial profile, cascading dark hair over shoulders part covered by a light dress.

The face had the look.

It was Rosalie's expression more than her facial features that screamed 'Susan' into Sandy's unconscious brain.

It was striking how similar both faces seemed when holding that faraway smile, like a look of pleasure at a thing of beauty seen on a distant horizon.

She flicked through the rest of the photos. They held the same similarity, but no others jumped out at her the way this one had. Sandy wondered whether a mannerism or look of Susan's triggered a barely remembered memory in Mark of his beloved mother, from back in the time of his earliest childhood, a look beaten out of her long before she died, but which he'd held fast to in a deep recess of his mind.

She sensed there was something important in these photos that may trigger a response in Susan. Perhaps, seeing herself in another person from another generation, and seeing Mark with different eyes, may change her perspective on what happened. Could it help ease her guilt and regret from being captured and enraptured by this man.

Sandy went back over the first batch of photos with more care this time, scrutinising each one in detail and checking for any writing on the back. She selected two more, one of Rosalie as a girl holding a baby, with overflowing joy and adoration on her face. 'Rosalie and Marco, 1961' was written on the back. The second photo taken maybe a decade later showed an older teenage Rosalie and her two brothers, one who looked older, the other younger. She recognised them as Antonio and Marco, a picture of happy normality. The resemblance of Marco to pictures of young Mark B was striking. No wonder his mother named him after her lost brother who'd died as a late teenager shortly before she married. The final two photos Sandy selected were a photo of Rosalie with her child, a little Mark around two or three years old. Such intense joy and love was on their faces as they each gazed at each other. It gave Sandy a huge pang of 'if only'. If only their life after had been different and they'd grown up as a happy family unit. Perhaps then what followed would have never happened. She also pulled out a couple of later photos of Rosalie and Mark, one where they stood with the big hard-faced man Vincent, whose name was written on the back. In these photos any essence of joy was gone, as if beaten out of Rosalie and replaced by an apprehensive and timid look. She seemed spaced out and depressed, perhaps because she was drinking or taking pills to escape. The final photo Sandy selected was one of Mark as a boy alongside his Uncle Antonio, proudly holding up a fish he'd caught. He looked to be around ten, so this would have been after his mother died, yet he seemed happy in the moment. Sandy thought Susan may treasure this photo. It would be something good to hold onto of Mark as a once happy child with his uncle on a magic day.

She felt profound sadness as she put the rest of the photos back in the package. She was still consumed by that sense of 'if only', but now it felt much sharper.

If only Rosalie's younger brother hadn't died. If only she'd married a good, kind man. If only Mark had gone to live with his uncle after his mother had died, then maybe Mark would have grown into a normal, happy boy, and whatever monstrosity he'd perpetrated that was now destroying Susan's life would never have come to pass.

She knew Alan was trying his best on the phone angle, and perhaps he would pull something off when he got back from Arnhem Land in two days' time. But she needed to try something of her own.

Maybe showing Susan these photos might crack a hole in her protective shell without pushing her further over the edge. They told the story of the descent of Mark's mother from a happy child, sister and young mother into depressive madness, a cycle of horror and abuse. Perhaps by Susan seeing them, she'd get insight into what was happening to her and seek to avoid it. There was little to lose from trying. She'd pay Susan a last visit. It wouldn't be official. Her work around Mark's identity was complete. But everyone at the jail knew her, and she doubted Susan would refuse to see her. She had to make a last attempt to reach Susan in a way that helped her free herself from a haunted past, to see how it had come to pass with clear eyes.

So here she was at the entrance to the jail at visiting hours, hoping to be admitted. She was here unannounced but didn't think Susan would object, though she'd seemed withdrawn on Sandy's recent visits with her mind in another place.

Soon enough she was sitting in Susan's cell. Susan was spaced out, lost somewhere inside her head. The expression on her face was eerily familiar to that of the battered wife of the final photos of Rosalie, lost in another world, desperately seeking escape. Sandy had a sense of needing to pull her back into the world of hope, to find a way to break her inward-looking cycle.

"I've brought some photos with me today of Mark and his family. His uncle sent them to me. Would you like to see them?"

At this mention of Mark and his family, Susan seemed to slowly come out of her trance. She sat up straight, and her eyes recaptured their intensity. For half an hour, they went over the photos. Susan didn't appear to notice any similarity between herself and Rosalie, but she was enraptured by the photos of Mark and Marco and touched their faces. She held the photo of Mark holding the fish up to the light and smiled at him with happiness in her eyes. It felt joyful but otherworldly to watch her acting as though she was communing with a person who no longer existed.

Sandy felt a pang of doubt about whether coming here today was the right thing. Even though it brought Susan out of an almost catatonic state, the glint of madness in her eyes seemed stronger.

When visiting time was over, Susan asked if she could keep the photo of Mark with the fish, the image of him as an earlier version of the man she'd once known. She asked with such tender longing that Sandy felt powerless to say no.

As she left, Susan thanked her with heartfelt thanks for showing her the photos and brightening up her day.

Chapter 23 – Two Minds of Madness

Susan sat staring at the photo of Mark as a boy for an unknown, uncounted time. The mid-afternoon light softened and faded into a twilight world. Still, she sat and stared. Only when the light was fully gone, and she could no longer see did she rise, turn on the electric light, and shake herself, as if awaking from a trance. The crocodile stone was still in her hand. Alongside it was the photo, and both gave her great comfort.

Seeing Mark as an innocent boy had given her such a yearning for a different life, a life with him where none of the bad had happened. Maybe each would have gone about their own lives, passed the other in the street, unknowing, perhaps to have met as adults, each with children of their own. Would the spark of attraction have sprung forth and burnt brightly if they'd met in that way? She was sure it might have kindled something, but even if they'd never met, they'd have each gone about their own lives, ones both better and fuller than in this desolate wasteland they now inhabited.

Part of her wanted to claim self-defence, fling everything aside, walk outside into bright sunlight, begin a new life where each day belonged to her and her alone, to do as she chose — laugh, sing songs, dance in the rain, let bright sunlight sparkle in her hair and let soft clean air wash over her skin, to leave behind this world on the inside of a mad, empty cage.

Yet at the same time, in another part of her being, she yearned for the man whose picture she held, to again touch his face, feel the roughened skin, stubble and the fuzz on his neck, to sink her face into the hard muscle of chest, feel his steel sinewed arms wrap around her.

She couldn't have both, but she wanted both. Part of her mind was trying to speak above the noise, reminding her she had the power to take control, that she could and must choose.

She'd seen the pictures of Rosalie as she'd surrendered to brutality and abandoned future hope. She'd tried to flee and failed. In the end, she took the only way of escape she could see. Susan recognised the waste of that choice, the waste to Rosalie, the waste to Mark. Yet she was treading the same steps, walking the same path.

Her conflicting thoughts were like two birds that sat perched alongside each other in her head. Each was calling out in a language all its own. One was like the bright winged parrots of a tropical jungle, with glimpsed colour flashes. It called out with raucous squawks and told her of flying free amongst the trees. The other was dark, like ravens and blackbirds of her childhood. It moved amongst shaded spaces, roosting in a dark cavern and spoke in a soft, musical voice of otherworld things, unknown and unseen but yearned for. When she looked up, the voices became muted but remained unceasing. Both were clamouring for the ownership of her soul, saying she must choose them.

She wished Vic was here. He was a loyal friend to Mark. He'd know what to do. She wished he'd wrap his arms around her and still the endless noise of dull screaming filling her mind.

But he was not here, and only she could choose. The great weight of this decision and its consequences rested on her and her alone. She put the photo out of sight even though she longed to look some more. But it was only the palimpsest of a presence, the faintly captured image of a thing long gone, a person whose soul had gone far past this place of innocence, overwritten time and again with violence and its consequences, so only faint traces of the original remained.

Unbidden, a memory of her own childhood came to her. It was a memory of the last time she'd seen her aunt, a person who'd been like an older sister who she'd spent countless hours of her childhood with. She remembered the awful news her mother and father had told her, later confirmed by her aunt who was only twenty-two at the time. Despite this, somehow the dreaded C word was being used. They'd cut her open and tried to take it out, but it failed. Over the following few months, she had faded into a shell, still with a bright smile, but ever weaker until the day they'd stood around her grave and Susan had felt her heart would break.

She remembered their final conversation when her brave aunt had said to her, "Em, you must go out there and live the life I hoped for but can no longer have. It's up to you now."

So she'd taken her Aunt Susan's name and become Susan Emily, and done her best to life a full life in memory of her aunt who she best remembered as an impulsive young woman, game for anything. She'd followed her own impulses, as her aunt would have wanted her to. Now, events beyond her control had allowed her life and choices to unravel. This was not what she'd wanted. Her aunt would not blame her. Maybe when this was over, she'd get to see her again, too.

She turned her mind back to the photos in her hand. She knew she had something more to decide. She needed to choose best way forward. Perhaps she'd allow herself to gaze upon the picture of Mark again, to postpone the choice to when her soul was less troubled, a time when she could just see it for its goodness, not see all that had overtaken it since that long ago time.

She decided she would hold the picture and stone side by side tonight and use their power to drive away crocodile dreams. Rather, she'd hope, in the few days left to her before the final curtain fell, that she'd once again see the world with clear eyes.

For three days, Susan vacillated between a desire for bright freedom and a desire for dark oblivion. She held both the stone and the photo next to her skin and refused to surrender to the call of the crocodile ringing loudly in her ears. She snatched only brief moments of sleep, fearful if she slept too deeply or too long, she would lose control of her ability to choose.

And yet choose she could not. These dual presences sat side by side, calling out in her mind, and neither would yield to the claim of the other.

When her parents, and Anne and David came to visit, she pushed the weight of choice aside, talking to them as if every day was a new tomorrow and her future was an open place. She sought to be her old self, to laugh, tell jokes, to savour each moment as a thing of value.

She could see Anne was full of distrust for this false brightness. Her distress sat more heavily and openly than Susan's did. Her parents masked their discomfort better, but in their minds she sensed their distrust for her furtive and frantic shards of brightness. It was the Susan of old, but not quite.

The weight of her choice made it hard for her to eat or concentrate, and her clothes were loosening despite her swelling belly. The face staring back from the mirror grew gaunter and more haunted as each day passed. All the while these two beings fought for control of her soul.

On the final night, she reached for the picture to look one last time, knowing she must choose. She hoped the image of Mark as a boy would guide her. But the photo was no longer alongside the stone in her pocket. She searched all the places on her person where she could have left it. Still nothing. Next, she searched her cell, moving and putting everything aside, systematic as she checked, sure she could locate it, but still she found nothing.

She remembered having it on the floor next to her chair, alongside the crocodile stone in the visitor's room earlier when her parents came. Perhaps it slipped from her grasp when it was time to return to her cell. She banged door over and over until the warder grumpily appeared. She asked if she could check the visitor's room, believing she'd dropped her photo there.

They went back there together. As she opened the door, she knew in a glance the photo was gone. The bins had been emptied of the paper drink cups, chocolate wrappers and tissues of the visit, the floors were freshly mopped, the benches wiped, and the odour of disinfectant lingered.

She said to the warder, "Can you find the cleaner. He must have picked up the photo of my friend Mark which I left on the floor, next to my chair. I really need to get it back."

The warder looked at her with a stony face and said, "Too late for that. He drove away over half an hour ago with all his bags of rubbish on the back. By now they will all have gone into the tip which he drives past on the way home.

At first, she felt a surge of disappointment, but it was replaced by relief. It was over. Her choice was gone, the bright bird of hope flown away with a last raucous shriek. The noise in her head stilled at last.

It was an omen. The hand of destiny had once again spoken. She returned to her cell, her mind was calm again. She ate dinner with renewed vigour, her mind clear in its empty space. She climbed into bed and set the stone aside, knowing that tomorrow her torture would be ended.

Chapter 24 –Last Roll of the Dice

It was late afternoon on Sunday before Alan was home from the bush. Sandy wanted some of his time after his week away, so he postponed his visit to the office. He'd go there first thing in the morning on the way to Katherine.

Last week, he'd radioed the Katherine police station to let them know he needed to visit. The station had organised an office for him to use for the two days he'd be there.

He was in Katherine before ten o'clock. To begin he went through the phone bill log of calls from Mark's phone. He tried to ring the number from the suspect call cluster but was advised it was disconnected, so he got to work tracing it.

Late that afternoon, he finally got advice that the number had belonged to a SIM card with $30 of credit, purchased in Cairns by a Susan McDonald.

He obtained a log of the calls she'd made on it. There were only about ten, most from when she was in Sydney. A couple of calls were made while she was in Cairns and Melbourne, and just two texts were from the Northern Territory, one from Borroloola and the other received from the same UK number while Susan was in Timber Creek. Alan now he had the times of the texts but not their content. Still, he knew he was on to something when he saw the time of the second text. It was from 9.05 am on the date when Mark and Susan were last seen leaving Timber Creek.

When he'd been there two weeks ago, standing outside the pub where Mark's car had been parked, his phone had been in a dead zone, and he'd to walk along the road for over fifty yards before he got reception. That meant when Susan checked her phone at 8.00am she'd have got nothing. She was probably still asleep at 9.05am when the message was received as they drove away. It would have been on her phone when she woke up.

What if it was something bad about Mark, some record sent from overseas, something terrible, maybe even something to do with a missing girl the way that Mike from Top Springs had hinted. If Mark had found out about the text, he'd have known he must stop Susan talking. Perhaps she was fast asleep when the text came in, and he'd heard the ping, picked up the phone to look, and suddenly he knew.

There were plenty of possibilities, but his police intuition told him this is what really happened and all the rest was window dressing. It fitted too well with what followed later. If she knew and Mark knew she knew, then unless she agreed to keep his secret, and he was sure he could trust her, she was in peril. And if he needed her to disappear, what better way than by a crocodile. It fitted the crocodile symbols which surrounded him.

Perhaps in that moment, she somehow turned the tables, and he had taken her place. Then, knowing that the secret must be hidden, she'd decided to cover all evidence of them being at the billabong. She'd done such a good job her plan had almost worked. If not for Charlie finding the head, and if not for him and Sandy and their little game of one upmanship, Mark's murder would have been missed.

But fate had intervened and, despite all the odds, the head, and with it the murder, and the cover up had been found. Susan hadn't tried to hide her movements until that fateful day. She was not naturally secretive, but in that moment she'd seen it as her only choice. Even so, despite her cleverness, she'd been caught and now convicted. She must have decided not to reveal the truth for the sake of her unborn children. That's what she'd told Buck.

If Mark had killed one or more other girls, as Mike had suggested, that was the kind of secret someone would want to take to the grave if they still loved the other person, as Susan clearly loved him. It all hung together. It was plausible, and most importantly, it made sense of the facts. But it wasn't evidence, just an educated guess.

Well, enough speculation.

Now the UK number needed to be traced. He also needed the content of the texts. He spoke to a woman who told him the UK number was part of UK Vodafone, and he'd have to contact them to get the owner details. She'd put in a request for the content of the texts, but it could take several days.

After some sweet talking and cajoling, she admitted it may be possible inside forty-eight hours. The absolute best case was just over twenty-four hours, so perhaps late tomorrow afternoon. "I'll put it to the top of the pile and mark it of highest priority. Then I'll follow it up tomorrow morning when I'm back on duty."

Alan thanked her. He knew he'd got the best result possible.

Late in the night, Alan got an identity for the owner of the English phone. It was Anne, which didn't surprise him. As a legal secretary in London, she was the sort of person you'd ask to trace missing persons.

About four o'clock the next afternoon, his phone rang. It was the operator from the previous day. "I have the texts. I'll email you the transcripts, although I can also read them out if you like."

He wanted to avoid any chance of the information being broadcast in the office where perhaps others would hear. He also needed a hard copy in front of his eyes, daring not to let his imagination run away, lest he mishear or misunderstand.

"Could you email them through straight away, please."

In a minute, a new email pinged on his phone. His hands shook as he opened it. It was a one-line document with two files attached. Each was a text transcript, the first from Susan's phone.

Message sent from Borroloola, 10.27 am, Central Standard Time.

Anne,

Can you check out two names below?

Saw notice saying missing in a place I stayed.

Are they home now and OK?

Text back soonest.

Will check next town where phone works.

Having a great time in Oz.

Love and see you soon,

Suz

Names:

Fiona Rodgers, Age 25, Aberdeen Scotland

Amanda Sullivan, Age 24, Newark New Jersey USA

The reply was sent the next day but not transmitted until three days later, received at 9.05 am, Central Standard Time.

Dear Suz,

This FREAKS me out, what I found:

Those girls came to Australia but are missing.

USA one came 2 years ago, last seen Airlee, Qld, 6 months later.

UK one came 18 mths ago, last seen Adelaide, SA, 1 month later.

Both listed as missing, but not under current investigation

Investigation summary –

- Girls may have wanted to disappear

- Both withdrew most of their cash before they left

- Both announced they were going on a trip – never seen since

- Did not say where were going or with who

- No current links between cases

- Last contacts followed up, no useful information

- Both girls seen meeting unknown man soon before last seen

- One friend thought man's name Mark – no such person located

- Parents are convinced of abduction or worse

- Re Fiona Rodgers, that was her real name.

But everyone called her Kate – dead sister's name she used from when a little girl – weird

She looks a bit like you -double weird!

This all makes me scared – Be Careful!!!

Take extra care if you meet a Mark.

Love, Anne

This was the smoking gun. This was dynamite. It all made sense, an exact fit to yesterday's speculation. This must be her Mark.

Alan would now confirm the two girls were still missing. That would be a job for tonight when offices on the other side of the world were open. Then he'd get back to Darwin in the morning before the sentencing hearing was finished to give this evidence to both barristers and the judge.

He rang Susan's barrister, a man he knew socially. They had an off the record chat where Alan advised him that by tomorrow, he'd be in possession of evidence that would dramatically change the case, but it might be mid-morning before he had all the information he needed as he was waiting for some final information from the USA tonight.

"Okay, but you'll need to be there by 2.00pm sharp as I'll begin my summing up around then and will need any new information at that time. I can probably stall a bit, but once I'm finished it will be too late. The judge will make his decision, and it'll be very difficult to reopen the case after that.

"Don't come too early either though. Before my summing up, all the different parties' depositions will be made. Let's get all that out of the way before you produce whatever you have. In fact, when you arrive the best thing would be for you to approach the bench directly on your own behalf but send me an advance copy just in case anything happens to delay you."

Alan printed the text. He put it inside in an envelope and wrote *Only to be opened if I don't arrive in time* on the outside. Then he put the envelope into an overnight express bag marked with the barrister's name and address and dispatched it.

Chapter 25 – Sentencing Day

They were all gathered in the court. The only person Susan couldn't see was Alan, but then perhaps he didn't want his nose rubbed in the disappointment of failure. He may still arrive yet, and her plan allowed for that. Anyway, Sandy was there to support her.

The judge ordered the court into session and said, "We're here to rule on the sentence to be given to Susan McDonald after finding her guilty of the murder of Vincent Marco Bassingham."

David and Anne had organised innumerable petitions of support, character references and statements from prison officials as to Susan's behaviour and conduct as a model prisoner. Susan had agreed to them making these submissions on her behalf. They said her life was there for all to see. She'd been the model schoolgirl and university student, a successful laboratory technician, a person who'd made one misstep and admitted to it and was now willing to pay for what she'd done.

They and her barrister would now argue that compassion from the law was required to allow her to have a life with her children, who would soon be born.

Even the prosecution had indicated a willingness to be reasonable, as they saw it. They'd said they'd be happy with a minimum sentence of twenty-five years, and a non-parole period of around twenty years rather than seeking to have Susan spend the rest of her life in jail, never to be released, as would be a reasonable expectation for such a cold and callous murder. Betting seemed to be what this was about right, although the judge was noted for no nonsense sentencing.

Even the judge seemed to feel some sympathy for her, but in reality, his hands were tied too. Sentencing rules for crimes such as Susan's were clear. With a not guilty plea, it would be thirty-plus years, and with a guilty plea, remorse and good behaviour, release was possible in around twenty years. People had assured Susan she'd only be around forty-five and so still have life in front of her when released.

But Susan found herself unable to care.

Tonight, her babies would be delivered. Then all this would end. Whether her sentence was ten, twenty or thirty years, or it was deferred, it would matter little. They would be carrying her away in a box and this awfulness would be over. She had longed for this day to come, the day when she could stop fighting the world and deceiving her friends. She had even worked out how to do end things with minimal discomfort. She didn't feel frightened at the prospect. Ending her life couldn't be that hard after everything else she'd been through since she'd met Mark. It was one last test of character, one she knew she could pass.

She found herself only half listening as the various parties opened sentencing submissions. The prosecution was reasonably short and to the point, saying that in a case like this, they would have normally sought life in jail, but in view of Susan's early guilty plea, her apparent remorse, and otherwise good character, they would be prepared to agree to a sentence of twenty-five to thirty years. Despite sympathy for the plaintiff in some quarters of the community, they could not go agree to anything below this, as a strong deterrent message was also required. Hence, they demanded an absolute minimum non-parole period of twenty years.

After the prosecution had spoken, her legal representative called witness after witness. The judge was limiting the time for people to speak to ensure the sentencing ended today. "Normally, I'd limit this part to a couple hours, but in view of the level of support for Susan, I'm prepared to allow continuation until a maximum time of 2.00 pm, after which both parties will have a short time to sum up before I make my ruling. We will conclude by 3.00 pm, the end of normal court sitting time."

The morning flowed away until a lunch recess was called. She could see support drifting away from her side. After lunch, only Anne and her parents remained to be called. They would be hard to watch. It had been hard enough when David had taken the stand, but she had to bear it. She would do her best to close her mind and emotions.

It was funny. Normally without the crocodile stone in court, she found herself very distant, like someone watching proceedings from on high. But despite her lack of interest in the first part of the day, this final part of the trial captured her attention. This was her life they were talking about. Slowly, as they talked, her life started to flash before her eyes like a fast-running movie. With it came a huge sense of loss. Was this all the life she would get to live? It seemed such a waste.

After lunch was much worse than she had imagined. Anne had to stop herself from crying on several occasions. Susan's mum was the same, and her father, even though he didn't shed any tears, had been even more excruciating as she watched him put everything he had into this fight for his daughter. She even noticed prosecution team members dabbing their eyes a couple times as they watched and listened, though their senior counsel sat stony faced.

The closing submissions of the prosecution took five minutes and were merely a quick reiteration of their previous points.

As her counsel was standing up to speak, an orderly passed him a sheet of paper, signalling he needed to give it his urgent attention. He looked annoyed at the interruption and looked around as if waiting for something. Not seeing whatever he was looking for, he picked up the piece of paper as if to start reading it. She looked at Anne whose face was white with tension, and in that instant, she knew. The paper was a transcript of the texts, but her barrister didn't know their contents. He looked like he was about to start reading it but was still distracted as if waiting for something else to happen.

Susan felt for the syringe strapped to the inside of her upper leg. She fumbled as she pulled it clear and removed the needle cap. She was hidden from sight where she sat on her own. Her prison warder sat behind her. She only needed another two or three seconds to plunge it into her thigh and inject it. She glanced down. Yes, it was all in place and ready.

Once she'd injected it, she'd let out a scream to draw attention to herself and clutch her belly, saying her contractions had come.

She looked up and took a deep breath to steel herself for the last roll of the dice. As she did so, the back court door opened and two people walked in, one she recognised as Sergeant Alan Richards. Why had he arrived so late? Of course. He'd come here for the same purpose as Anne, so nothing was changed there.

She turned her attention to the second man. He was so thin and emaciated he was almost skeletal, and he hobbled with a severe limp. His hair was long, ragged, and unwashed, and his beard was long and straggly. His clothes were clean but hung on him like bags. There was something fierce and uncompromising in his face and eyes.

At first Susan couldn't comprehend what him being here meant. Then recognition came.

The man's eyes turned towards hers and looked at her with knowledge and penetrating intensity, and she knew. This walking skeleton was Vic, returned from the dead, yet so obviously alive. She put her hand to her mouth and let out a muffled gasp, and the syringe fell from her hand to the floor. Susan spoke his name, loudly and clearly so all could hear her. "Vic, is it you?"

Vic raised his hand in acknowledgment and gave her his trademark grin.

She wanted to run to him and hold him, but she was restrained by a handcuff which attached her left hand to the rail.

Alan glanced at her and nodded but then immediately turned his attention to the bench.

"Your Honour, I'm sorry to interrupt. I'm not normally in the habit of barging into a court in session, but something extremely significant has happened in this case. I've obtained information today that I consider has a vital bearing on this case and any sentence you impose. I ask that you order a short recess to allow me to inform Your Honour of it on a one-to-one basis."

She saw the prosecution barrister start to rise to object. Her defence team seemed less surprised, but then perhaps they'd already known something.

Alan approached and spoke briefly to the prosecution counsel. This barrister nodded then said, "Your Honour, I would agree to a short recess as I accept this is relevant and of great importance."

The judge looked at the defence barrister and nodded his assent. He ordered a fifteen-minute adjournment.

Then he, Alan and the senior counsels left the courtroom.

Everyone else stood there dumbfounded.

PART 2

ESCAPE FROM AN EMPTY PLACE

Chapter 26 –Crocodile Watcher

Vic had a vague sense of being still alive and hurting, really hurting. His mind seemed unable to focus, but he had a sense of being wet and cold, and one of his legs felt like it was on fire. He seemed to drift in and out of awareness over and over again. He had a woolly memory of his helicopter refusing to respond to the controls, then flashes of a smashing and tearing impact as it hit the cliffs.

Based on this memory, his mind said he should be dead. People did not survive crashes like that. But his leg hurt like hell, and the rest of his body and head hurt in lots of places too, so it sure felt like he must be alive. Now his mind formed a muddled thought. He hoped this wasn't hell and this was him damned to endless pain. That would be a seriously bad place to end up in if he'd died. And he was so thirsty. He badly needed a drink and soon. Apart from the pain in his leg, his thirst was the thing forcing him to wake up.

At last, his mind gathered enough clarity to open his eyes so he could look around. He was lying tipped back and half on his side. His body was held against something behind him. He tried to look up, but his vision was blocked by a huge wall of rock and a thing on his head. He looked down towards where the pain in his leg was coming from. His leg seemed bent back at a funny angle under whatever he was lying on. It did not look good. No wonder it hurt so much.

As his mind cleared further, he tried to feel his hands. He brought one hand up to his face. With it, he felt for the other, which was squashed under him at his side. He pulled it free with his good hand. It seemed to work too. He looked at them both.

Yes, they were both there and neither looked too bad. A few cuts on the knuckles of his left hand, but his right looked just fine and didn't hurt when he moved it. His left hand transmitted pain to his shoulder when he moved it.

Using his good hand, he started to explore his surroundings. First, he felt his face to try work out what was blocking part of his view. It was his helmet, still on his head. As he felt around towards the helmet's left side, he realised his head was resting up against an uneven rock, and there were a series of cracks and fissures running through this side of his helmet, which was like a broken egg still held together with sticky tape. He felt under his chin, and sure enough, the strap that held the helmet on his head was still closed. It took a few goes before he finally managed to click it free.

Now he needed to try and take the helmet off his head so he could see properly. He tried with just his right hand. That brought pounding pain into his head as the helmet twisted sideways while staying in place. There was nothing for it but to bring his left hand into action too. His left hand seemed to move okay, but Christ his shoulder hurt as he tried to grip the other side of the helmet at the same time. It felt like something had pulverised the muscles of that shoulder. He touched rock below this shoulder. He was lying pushed into it and had probably landed hard that way, bruising lots of muscles. But he could move it, so he didn't think anything was broken.

He took a deep breath. This was going to hurt, whatever he did, so might as well get on with it. He gritted his teeth and with both hands together managed to pull the helmet free. His head and left shoulder felt like they were on fire, and waves of fog and surges of pain flowed through his brain. He lay still for a minute, willing the pain to stop. As it receded, the thirst and pain in his leg came flooding back. Part of him wanted to close his eyes, give up, but he knew he had to keep going.

Now he explored his head with his fingers. There was sticky stuff that felt like dried blood on the side of his head next to the rock, and some parts of his scalp really hurt to touch. But nothing felt broken there either. Perhaps the now broken helmet had saved a busted skull and instant death.

He felt around to work out what was behind and under him. It was flat, smooth and slippery. His brain slowly processed this touch information. He was still strapped into the helicopter seat. He and the seat were lying on a rocky shelf at the base of a huge rocky cliff.

Realisation dawned on him that the helicopter seat, with him strapped into it, had torn free from the rest of the helicopter and fallen down the side of the cliff until it hit this rocky base. He made himself lift his head and look around. Now he could begin to get his bearings. As his eyes travelled upwards, they followed the line of a huge rising cliff, going almost directly up for what looked like hundreds of feet. The only things that could get up there would be birds and ants. It was beyond ordinary animals to climb this rock face, beyond a rock wallaby, even a cat. He tried to look over his shoulder and behind him. His view was blocked by something that must be the seat.

The roaring and gurgling noise from behind him must be the river, bare metres away. His body was wet and cold, his clothes drenched. Had he been in the river at some point? It seemed unlikely if he was still strapped in and the seat had landed here. More likely falling rain had drenched him.

As he had this thought, a huge flash of light followed by an almost instantaneous crash bang told him he was in the middle of a great thunderstorm. As the flash died away, he realised it was approaching dark. Only a small amount of light remained in the sky. He must have been unconscious since mid-morning, probably eight hours ago. No wonder he was thirsty, despite the rain. Lying in this valley for most of a hot wet season's day would have baked and desiccated his body.

Suddenly, huge cold splashes of rain came cascading onto his face. He turned his head towards the downpour and drank in the large wet drops. It wasn't enough to quench his thirst, but the moisture cleared his mouth and mind, and helped him to think more clearly.

He needed to unstrap himself from the seat and then try to extricate and attend to his leg. After doing that, he would get a proper drink and try work out what else to do.

He felt for the belt release by his waist and pressed the release mechanism. It popped free, and his body slumped sideways, coming to rest hard against the rock, sending spasms of pain through his injured leg and his shoulder.

He felt towards his foot, trying to determine the source of the excruciating pain. He realised his leg was twisted at a strange angle and trapped under part of the seat. He discovered that, by turning his body further to the side and facing down, the pain in his leg was eased. In this position, he could get both his hands underneath him. He pushed himself upwards. As his weight came fully off the seat, a spasm of pain shot through his leg, like boiling water had tipped onto it. His body dropped back towards the hard rock, but that set off another even worse pain in his leg. On his second attempt, he cautiously lifted himself, inch by inch. It eased the pain up to a certain place and then it started to increase again. He watched what happened. Initially, his lower leg straightened, which reduced the pain. But then it started to twist the other way bringing the pain surging back.

What he needed was a way to lift the seat base clear of his leg so he could get his leg out from underneath it and straighten it straight. The bones in his lower leg must have broken for it to twist as it was.

He moved into a half kneeling position on his opposite hand and knee. With the other hand he gradually levered the seat out of the way. At last, its weight took over and it fell sideways away from his leg. As it moved it, another pain spasm came, but now his leg was free.

He moved his body to bring his leg into line with his foot. Using a half kneeling gait, he slowly dragged his body away from the edge of the cliff, heading towards the roaring water. This was visible as a phosphorescent glow in the near dark as it thundered down the gorge. At its edge, he used his good arm to scoop handfuls of water into his mouth. He was tempted to shove his face into the water to quench his thirst, but knew it was best to drink slowly. After a few minutes of sucking handfuls of water his thirst eased.

He lifted his head to gaze out across the wild white water. It was an endless thundering cascade. It stretched to the other side of the gorge where another similarly sheer cliff rose, maybe three hundred metres away. His place by the water was sheltered by a protruding rock, a couple of body lengths in front of him. It was three times his height and about two metres wide, and it jutted out into the cascading water and offered a relatively calm edge for him to access.

A movement at the periphery of his vision caused him to look to his side, downriver. Barely a metre away, two eyes sat in the water watching him. It was an enormous crocodile. With one swish of its tail, it could have lunged forward and grabbed him, finishing off the work of the crash. But it didn't move. It just stared, remaining motionless in the water. It seemed to be watching him with purpose but not with malicious intent. He almost felt it was guarding him. Perhaps it was not hungry just now and would look to feed later.

As imperceptibly as he was able to, he eased back from the water. His leg protested, but that was secondary to survival. The silent watcher's position remained unchanged.

Now he'd drunk and relieved some of the pain in his leg he could barely move. Every muscle and bone in his body felt bruised. Each crawled step took great effort. It was barely five metres from the edge of the water to the cliff face, and the back of the rock ledge was little more that a metre above the flow. If the crocodile decided to come after him, there was nowhere he could go.

Slowly, he dragged his body back as close to the cliff edge as he could. It was still raining hard, and he was shivering with cold. He pulled up the remains of the seat and propped it against the rock wall forming a roof and barrier of sorts from the river. This gave him a tiny shelter from the torrential sky. He curled his body under it as best he could and tried to take his mind away from where he was.

He slept fitfully. Every time he moved spasms of pain shot through his leg. His shoulder throbbed continuously, and hard rock dug into the tender parts of his body. But he needed rest, and this was his best option for now. He woke in the early predawn light.

The sky was still a heavy grey, but the rain had stopped. In the night, the river had risen, and half his rock shelf was now gone. He couldn't stay here. If the water rose two more feet, all his dry land would be gone.

He eyed off his options as the light slowly brightened. The cliff on the other side of the river seemed slightly less forbidding. But even if his leg wasn't broken, there was no way he could cross over three hundred metres of thundering water with only one leg to kick with. It was totally hopeless.

If his dry land was taken by the river, it would claim him anyway, and if it did, he would let it wash him where it willed until rocks smashed him apart.

But, for now, he was alive. As he contemplated his survival, it felt miraculous to have landed in a way where his seat and helmet protected him from death and to have found shelter on a tiny rock ledge just beyond the water. It seemed remarkable, despite everything else about his circumstances looking grim.

It reminded him of the story Mark had told him of the bullet wound to his arm, how he had to patch himself up and make the best of it for many days without medical attention, apart from a bandage and a few antibiotic tablets. Though he didn't understand why, he felt a kinship to Mark in this place. As he thought about it, he remembered the crocodile from last night. He felt as if it was sent by Mark to guard and protect him, perhaps to help him find a way out of this mess.

He looked around the water's edge, wondering where the crocodile had gone while he slept. At first, he saw nothing. Then he made out a shadowy outline in the stiller water. It was still there, sheltered by the jutting rock. As he watched, a few scales along the back and tail broke the surface, and then more of the head and body emerged. This animal was truly monstrous in size. He had nothing to measure it, but when he thought about the length of his helicopter from tail rotor to nose, it didn't seem to be much different. That was well over twenty feet in length, way bigger than any crocodile he'd ever seen before.

Funnily enough, the crocodile's head was now facing the other way from last night, facing downriver. Vic was tempted to try and head upriver. Heading in the direction of civilisation seemed the most logical way to go. There was a rock ledge that started a few metres above him. It ran upstream from where the sheltering rock joined the cliff. He looked at it, wondering if he could scale it. It would bring him higher above the water, which seemed extremely desirable with a rising river. But as he surveyed it, he could see no way up its smooth edge. He may have managed to climb it with two legs and two properly working arms, but with one good arm and leg he couldn't.

He looked at the crocodile again. Was it his imagination, or did it seem to be waving its head and tail in a way that pointed downriver? It must be his crazy imagination, but there did seem to be something of Mark in it which was trying to direct him, sending a whispered message from Mark's crocodile brother saying, "Come this way. Come this way. Follow me."

He tossed up what to do. In the end, he decided to defer his decision while he checked the helicopter seat properly in case it held something useful. Then he needed to examine his broken leg carefully and see if he could find something to splint it with.

His glance in the half-light showed a massive area of purple bruising six inches above his ankle, and along with stabs of shooting pain, he could feel the bone ends move and his foot flop around when he moved his leg. It was clearly broken, but his foot seemed to have feeling, and the skin wasn't broken, so those were good signs.

He decided to watch the level of the river for a few minutes to see whether it was still rising, while also looking for a way to support this broken leg. It would be very difficult to travel far the way it was, and the continual movement of the bone ends would be causing further damage, not to mention pain.

He carefully examined the seat. Apart from a few jagged bits of metal which had come with it when it was torn from its mountings, that was all it was, a single vinyl covered pilot's seat along with a piece of the floor, around two feet square. It ended at the edge of the bubble doorway on his side. There was also a small piece of metal attached above the seat's left side where the seat belt mounting had torn away from the rest of the helicopter body, and his belt was still attached to it. He looked more carefully at the piece of floor. This is what had landed on the side of his leg and trapped it, breaking the bone, somewhere in his fall down the cliff to the ground. It was lucky he'd remained strapped to the seat as he fell. It had protected him from being smashed apart on the rocks. He was also lucky his leg had been struck by the rounded edge of the floor piece, where the door met the floor, and not by some of the other jagged pieces of metal. His luck had left the skin on his lower leg to be bruised but not torn open. His shoe also seemed to have protected his foot from serious damage. He was wearing just shorts and a T-shirt. He'd put his other clothes into a small overnight bag which went in the space behind the seats before he left Wyndham yesterday. That was gone. He felt his front pockets, wondering if his wallet was there with that infernal memory card, cash, and ID. No sign of it. It must have fallen out too. Not that those things were useful now. At least he had his boots on. They were a good solid pair. He'd need them to try and walk to reach help, if he could escape from the river first.

He resumed his search. In the back pocket of the seat, he found his plastic covered flight map of this part of the NT. With it was something of much more value, a multi tool pocket knife. He vaguely remembered having it a couple years ago when he'd bought this helicopter. But he couldn't remember having seen it in over a year. Here it was. This discovery was very timely now.

He looked around the rock shelf to see if anything else useful was in sight. There was no vegetation, but there were a few small pieces of timber and one reasonable sized stick that he could see, maybe four or five feet long and one to two inches thick. It was a bit knobbly but fairly straight.

Perhaps he could use it as a splint for his leg. If there was some wiry grass or bark handy, he could use that to wrap around his leg and then tie it to the timber.

He wondered what else he could use. He knew he needed to support and protect his leg to give it a chance to heal if he was to find his way out of here. If he cut up his map, maybe the plastic would be strong enough to use to tie the splint together. Then it came to him. He had all he needed right here with the seat itself. He could use part of the foam lining to provide padding, and he could cut the seatbelt and vinyl cover into strips to tie it all in place.

He worked away for an hour dismembering the seat with his little pocket knife. Now he had a pile of foam rubber pieces, seatbelt strapping and about twenty vinyl strips in various sizes up to few feet in length. He also had a few pieces of cording and wire from the seat's internal contents. His pocket knife even had pliers with a cutting edge he could cut wire with.

He set to work binding his leg. First, he padded it with foam tied into place with some of the thinner strips of vinyl. Then he broke the long stick into two lengths, each about two feet long, one of which was placed on each side of his leg, running from knee to ankle. He took the stronger and longer seatbelt and vinyl pieces, and with them he tied the whole contraption together in several places. Finally, he wrapped the cord and wire around as well, for good measure. It wasn't perfect, but it kept his foot and leg straight, and it felt like it wouldn't fall apart when he moved.

As he worked, he watched the water level. Now barely a foot of clearance remained from his workspace to the water's edge, and it was still rising steadily. The storm further up the catchment last night must have been a serious one. He suspected there was lots more water to come through yet.

Well, there was nothing for it but to follow the crocodile's lead and head downriver. He looked out and then up and down the river. It was funny; even though the water was continuing to rise, it felt as if the flow had slowed. Last night's foaming and thundering white-water river seemed to have eased into something still fast and dangerous but less wild. The tumbling whitecaps were gone. The level was now almost a metre higher than when he'd gone to sleep, and the volume flowing was huge, but the broken surface had smoothed to a tea coloured, swirling, running tide.

He looked up the river. The cloud overhead had broken into threads and patches, one of which obscured a weak sun. Sitting below it and between the cliffs was a thin crescent moon, palely visible in the morning light. Something in his brain clicked. New moon, running tide – that was it. At least part of the rising water and slowing flow was due to an in-running tide pushing back against the storm flow.

He remembered yesterday morning at this time as he'd flown across the coast from Wyndham, it was high tide in the big estuaries, and it was still running in. It was one of those king tides that came up twenty feet. Around mid-morning, the tide was full. Today high tide would be an hour later. It was acting like a huge dam, holding back the new water pouring into the river and forcing it to rise. The tide was slowing the flow to something more manageable than last night's thundering rapid. That would have smashed him to bits, but maybe he could swim or float in this. He chucked a piece of stick out beyond the protruding rock. It moved downstream at a fast-running place, tricky but manageable.

Slowly his mind absorbed the implications of this. He couldn't stay here, that much was apparent. The tide still had another hour or two of rise, and this water would flood his rock shelf completely within the hour. But it was now possible he could float downstream in this river, at least until he came to a place where there was a break in the cliffs, which would give him a place to drag himself out. Rather than fleeing the rising water, he needed to use it to help him escape. If only he had a boat or raft, something that would give him buoyancy as he went downriver. He looked around. There were not enough pieces of dead wood to make a raft. Could he tie some smaller pieces together? It would help a little, but there wasn't enough to add much flotation. He glanced again at the seat, and the solution came to him with a flash of clarity. The seat was full of foam rubber, lots of tiny bubbles of air. While the seat would probably float, the metal parts would weight it down, and it would be cumbersome to hold on to it and swim with. No, what he would do was cut out pieces to use. Even though he'd already cut out foam to pad his leg, the vast majority remained in two big lumps, one at the bottom and one at the back. He'd cut these out in the largest pieces he could manage, and then he'd would tie them together with more strips of vinyl. The strips would give him something to hang on to. If he managed it right, he could largely float as he was carried along by the flow of the water.

He realised he'd left the huge crocodile out of his consideration. Sharing the water with it gave him a pang of fear. But it'd had plenty of opportunity to harm him before and done nothing. And it was not like he had any choice. If the water kept rising, he'd be forced into it soon enough. Then he and the crocodile would be in it together anyway. Better to do it with control. Perhaps he could break off a piece of metal from the seat and use this to push it away if it came too close.

He looked at the size of this enormous animal and realised that idea was ludicrous. It could swallow him in entirety in a single mouthful. Even so, he felt better with the idea of some protection, if only token. Plus, a piece of metal might come in useful somewhere else in his trip. Come to think of it, he should pull the entire seat apart and look for anything else useful in it before he left. The seat was the only potentially helpful object he could see in his surroundings.

Vic set to work again. First, he cut out two large pieces of foam, which he tied together. They were nice and light, so the buoyancy would be good. Then he stripped what remained of the vinyl, which he cut into long strips for future ties. It was hard work with the little knife, and his bad shoulder pained him.

At the back of the seat was an elastic mesh holder, with gaps of about a centimetre between the threads. If he could make up a frame, perhaps this could be used as a fish net. He packed all these pieces into his broken helmet, which served as a useful basket, and then he stripped out all other pieces of cord and wire, along with any metal fittings he could remove.

Now there was little more than the metal frame remaining. He cut it free of the seat remnants and looked closely at it. It was light aluminium. It should be brittle if he could find a way to break it. A fissure ran into the cliff face behind him. He jammed one end into that. Then he found a rock to bash into the middle where the metal curved around. After several blows, he cracked it through. He worked on the other end and broke it through.

That gave him two curved pieces of aluminium, each about four feet long. As gently as he could, he bent each one into a reasonably straight shape, though one had a hook like bit at the end. The pieces didn't break or buckle, so that was good. They looked strong and could be used as poles to push off rocks and otherwise guide his passage.

Now only the broken shell of seat remnants remained. He poked around at it to see if anything useful was left. He picked it up to look underneath. As he did, he saw a small object fall from a crack between the upright portion of the seat and the base, which were still held together with fragments of fabric. He looked at it in amazement. It was a transparent plastic cigarette lighter, not something he'd ever use as a non-smoker himself. Someone else must have. Perhaps the previous owner of the machine was a smoker. It must have sat there for at least a couple years, fallen out of a pocket into that gap unnoticed.

Remarkably, he could see it was still half full of what looked like lighter fluid. It seemed too good to be true. If he could think of one single extra thing he'd need to survive, as well as his knife, this was it. He felt almost scared to use it, but he flicked it open. Sure enough, a spark and flame came. Quickly, he shut it off, knowing its precious contents must be preserved.

Chapter 27 – Swimming with River God Baru

Vic looked at the sky and the sun, part seen through cloud. His mind clock and belly said mid-morning. The tide was getting close to full. Perhaps an hour or two remained until the peak. The water was starting to bubble around his feet. Ready or not, he must take to it. But he had one last thing he needed to do. He still had his plastic flight map of the area. He needed to determine where he might find a way to get out of this river valley. Even though it was at a large scale, the detail was surprisingly good.

He located the Fitzmaurice River, following his route of yesterday up the course of the river until the tight bend and the fatal cliff. He remembered a big creek on his side a few miles back and another on to the other side a bit closer. That one looked most promising. If he got to that side, it was an obvious way out. But despite his float, there was no way he could cross to the other side of this huge torrent.

His best bet was to stay close to this edge, where rocks and ledges slowed the flow a little. He followed the valley on the map. He had a vague memory of a steep, jagged gully cutting down a couple miles back. Not much more than a crack in the cliff, really. He found what looked like it on the map. This showed it running back into the hills for a way, so it looked like a creek ran down it in the rain. He made a quick decision that this would be his destination to aim for.

The water almost completely covered the rock shelf now. He clipped his helmet to a strap around the foam float, pushed the metal poles into the straps where they would not fall out, and pushed the lighter into the smallest pocket of his shorts and zipped it closed. He half stumbled and half crawled to where the rock shelf fell away into the deep water and deliberately avoided looking towards the crocodile lest his nerve fail. Holding his float, he eased himself off the rock shelf.

The current quickly picked him up. He was floating down the river about five metres out from the edge. He decided to go out a bit further. It gave him a better view forward along the cliff, and he was also less likely to be bashed into rocks on the edge. He looked around. The crocodile was nowhere in sight.

He tried to estimate the distance he was covering and his speed by taking reference points along the cliff, estimating their distance away and counting how long it took to reach them. It was far from accurate, but his estimate was he was doing something around ten kilometres an hour. He barely kicked or paddled, deciding to save his energy and keep watch as the cliff faces swept past him.

At this rate, he estimated it would take between twenty and thirty minutes to reach the place he wanted to try and climb out. It was only a guess, but it was good to have something to occupy his mind as he felt very vulnerable floating down this large river knowing at least one crocodile was somewhere nearby. He just hoped the place he was heading for would have somewhere to climb out of the water. Where he was travelling now, the cliffs rose sheer from the water for more than a hundred feet.

After what seemed like about fifteen minutes, he noticed a thin crack visible high on the cliff line, a few hundred yards in front of him. He wondered if this was what he was looking for, but there was nothing further down the cliff. As he reached and passed under this place, he realised this must be a creek which ended in a waterfall. He watched a thin line of water fall a hundred feet into the river below. He moved a bit further out into the river as he passed below it, both to avoid its spray and to widen his angle of view. Another green line in the cliff was visible in a few hundred yards. This one seemed to track all the way to the bottom. He began to paddle and kick his way towards the edge. It was slow work with only one good leg. Each time the broken leg was jerked by the current, pain shot through his body.

Now he could see the crack clearly. There was no obvious rock shelf, but a ribbon of green ran all the way to the water's edge. A couple trees at the bottom appeared to have their trunks partly covered by water. If he could get to those, it would give him something to hang on to and stop his passage.

Now the gap to the trees was closing, and he could see better. One tree looked like it had two trunks about a foot apart. He'd try to aim for the point where the water ran between them and jam himself tightly into the gap while he grabbed on to one side. He looped his arm through the strap between the bundles, trying to maintain his line.

As the gap closed, the trees seemed to be rushing towards him very fast. His body slammed into part of the trunk with a huge weight of water behind him. His broken leg bashed into the trunk lower down, and he almost screamed aloud with the pain. He wondered if the still rising water would tear his body through the gap, but he jammed firm. However, the weight of the water was too strong to get out of the gap. He couldn't push himself free. He could only hang on and hope that either the water slowed further on the incoming tide or it fell low enough later in the day for him to get out of the tree and climb up the bank. That would be easier said than done.

From here, he could see no way out up the creek. The crack in the cliffs vanished into gloom behind a wall of trees and creepers. He heard the noise of running water rushing down the hillside coming from behind the trees.

He forced himself to relax and stay calm, to savour the pleasure of having made it this far. His tired body craved rest. It was caused mostly hunger. It was over a day since he'd eaten anything. In this cold water, he was burning energy fast. A light-headed, dreamy feeling stole over him. He thought of bars of chocolate, bowls of steaming stew, and slices of bread and butter as his stomach growled. He let the fantasy take him to block out the reality and pass the time.

The sun sat in a mid-morning position. He thought of yesterday's breakfast, a large plate of fried eggs and bacon on thick toast slices, washed down with steaming coffee. Then he thought of his mother's cooking, her light and fluffy cakes served with cream or ice cream. He deliberately followed the food trail in his mind, great slabs of steak, hot buttered potatoes, bowls of pasta and rice.

He may have dozed off in this dreamy state. He came to when he realised his body was being lifted up the tree, the gap widening between the two trunks. He had risen at least a foot, maybe more, and in about another foot the gap would let him pass through. He needed to turn his attention to what to do next. The force of the water had definitely eased.

He measured the distance to the edge where other trees grew and where the flow was most slack. There was a batch of trees about five metres downstream and a similar distance across from where he was.

If he could reach them, they may allow him to get to the bank, the rock face edge, or whatever lay out of view beyond the trees. He thought about how best to do it. When his body was high enough to pass between the trunks, he'd use his good leg to push off from this tree trunk as far as he could go towards the next destination. Then kicking with his good leg, he'd put out the hooked aluminium pole and try to catch a tree before the current carried him past.

It didn't quite work out that way. The flow was still strong, and he wasn't yet high enough to pass through. But the current had eased enough to let him slide around the side of the trunk, away from the centre. Inch by inch, he pushed his way around, his injured shoulder hurting as he used that arm to help force himself back against the current. At last, he got himself free, and then he also freed his float.

He rested for a minute holding tightly to one trunk. The exertion had taken a big part of his reserve of strength. When he felt his tiredness ease, he bunched himself up with his good leg against the trunk, took a deep breath, pushed, and struck out.

The current was far stronger than it looked. He was rapidly swept along the bank, back towards the main river. He only had two more metres to cross but was fast coming to the edge of the treed place, just a bare rock cliff again.

With all his effort, he paddled and kicked for the edge, missing the last tree but managing to grab hold of the protruding cliff rock where the fissure ended. He realised the creek running from the gap in the cliff had a strong flow. It pushed him back into the main channel. He'd stopped right where the creek met the main river.

There was a slight back eddy where he was, which allowed him to hold on. He worked his way around until he had a good grip of the edge then set about pulling himself back along the rock ledge following the creek up into the fissure.

He had to do this by inches to bring himself around the rock edge into the side channel and then along its side. The hand holds at water level looked few and far between, and he was terrified that if he lost his grip, he'd be swept back into the river. He needed to stop and think before he did something stupid.

He looked upwards. There was a broken slope rising above him for about five metres which he thought he could climb using hand holds and the occasional foothold. It looked like there was a ledge running back along the side of the fissure up there that he could follow.

Climbing with only one leg and with one shoulder, which hurt to move and lacked strength, was extraordinarily hard, particularly carrying his gear. But he was determined not to surrender to the river, and he carried his future survival in that small bundle. His bruised shoulder screamed loudly in protest and a jab of pain came from his leg with every movement. He'd grown soft from days of sitting on a seat in a helicopter.

At last, he pulled himself clear of the water. He rested for a minute before slowly beginning to climb the rock face, little by little. It looked to be about a sixty-degree angle, not sheer, but mostly a dead lift with his arms.

It seemed to take forever, but he persisted, and at last, he came to a clear flat ledge about a foot wide. He lifted his bottom onto this and turned to sit, facing out to the river, arms feeling like jelly, his whole body trembling with fatigue.

As he sat there, he looked below at the raging river. The tide had started to fall away. While the river level hadn't fallen appreciably, the rate of flow had increased again, a white broken surface returning.

The sun was now at its highest, telling him this river trip had taken two or three hours. If he hadn't got out of the water, he'd have been taken again and smashed by this it. It was again too strong to swim against.

Next to the edge below him, its tail waving steadily to hold it against the current, he saw a shape emerge from the water. It surfaced, exposing almost its full length, raised its head as if to nod to him, and opened and closed its nearest eye. He could have sworn it winked.

He felt a sense of Mark speaking to him. "I've got you here. Now you must get on and do your part. Susan needs your help. You must return."

Vic couldn't help himself. He knew it was ridiculous, but he grinned, raised his hand and waved back. "Message received. Over and out," he called out at the top of his voice.

With that, the crocodile rolled its body over and slid sideways into the water, disappearing with the flow.

From here, it was all up to him.

He didn't give a damn whether others called it superstitious claptrap. He was certain his mate had returned and given him something he must do. It was the least he could do for his brother of the crocodile spirit.

Forever after, Vic remembered this strange being as the River God Baru, an ancient crocodile creature of the dreamtime, or perhaps an Egyptian deity who held power over this river and all things within it.

And through his connections to these river creatures Vic too shared part of this heritage, following in the path of his river brother, who had swum beside him.

Chapter 28 – Climbing a Small Mountain

Vic looked at his walking stick. He'd carved thirty notches into it. That meant thirty days had passed since Crash Day. He'd gone perhaps five kilometres from that place, as the crow flies, but he felt he'd walked a hundred miles and climbed Mount Everest.

He could feel the long hair on his face, now past itchy. He looked down at his one set of clothes, his T-shirt and shorts. They were falling apart, with several holes in the shirt and the threadbare shorts almost worn through in several places. He noticed his skinny arms and legs and wondered where the muscle had gone.

That was the trouble with mostly eating things he caught with his hands — lizards, frogs, an occasional bird, and bush rat. Except ants, he ate insects of any shape or size he found. He'd tried a wide range of plants, seeds and fruits, testing them slowly and carefully after early stomach cramps, but only a handful passed the real food test.

He should feel depressed. It had been extraordinarily hard, and his journey had barely begun. But he'd made it to the top, and he still had both legs and feet, and his injured leg was only a bit crooked. He still couldn't put weight on it, but at least it had mostly stopped hurting, except when he banged it.

He looked out across the barren stony landscape in front of him. As best he could tell from his map, it was something around three hundred kilometres in a fairly straight line to either of the two main roads he could head for, either the Stuart Highway, somewhere around the Edith River Crossing fifty kilometres north of Katherine on the road to Darwin, or the Katherine-Timber Creek road, somewhere around the Flora River crossing and a similar distance west of Katherine. The way he'd go, up and down hills, following creeks and ridge lines, it was probably really a four hundred kilometre walk.

If he could manage five kilometres a day, it would be eighty days of walking. If he could up it to ten kilometres a day, then perhaps a bit over a month, as long as there were no major setbacks. He figured it was about the end of January. Assuming sixty more days of walking, he may see civilisation about the end of March. He could get lucky and strike someone out here, but his chances during the wet season were low. It was a big one with a lot of flooding and water yet to run away.

He refused to consider the fact he may not make it. His survival so far felt miraculous, so this didn't bear thinking about. Still, it seemed like a bloody long way to walk.

What he wouldn't give now for a cold beer, big steak, and a plate of chips was hard to imagine. That would be his motivation to keep driving on. That plus seeing the surprised looks on the many faces who would have given him up for dead, along with a big hug from his mum and sister. That would be reward enough.

But his first destination was to get to Darwin and talk some sense into that silly girl of Mark's. Stop her sacrificing herself to honour Mark's imaginary memory. The real story, whatever it was, must come out. That surely was the purpose of Mark's message to him.

A day after he got off the river, he realised he still had his wallet in a back pocket of his shorts. He hadn't lost it. There was not much in it, just a license ID, credit card and about $100. But the memory chip Susan gave him was still there. Even if he'd yet to read it, soon enough he would. Once he did, he'd know the real story, the one he knew Mark wanted told. He'd put it out there for all to know. He was past hiding secrets.

He looked at his meagre possessions, a makeshift backpack made out of strips of vinyl and bark, padded with foam to make it soft to carry; a spear with a harpoon like head, cut and ground out of a piece of the aluminium seat frame from the helicopter; a knife blade made of similar material bound to a wooden handle; his stone cooking bowl; his fire kit – some smouldering embers wrapped in damp bark; a timber water scoop; a fishnet on a pole; an instant paperbark humpy, really just sheets of paperbark to sleep under to keep the rain off him, with a couple sticks to support it; and a few other odds and ends, penknife, cigarette lighter, bits of metal, twine and wire.

He wrapped his paperbark shirt over his shoulders to minimise the sunburn and insects. He put on his bark and vinyl hat and adjusted his makeshift pack so it sat in balance on his good shoulder and took the weight off his gammy leg. He put his walking stick to the ground next to his bad leg and stepped out.

He'd picked a ridge line on the horizon to head towards, due east for now, though he would adjust between north-east and south-east depending on the lie of the land. He'd decided to break his journey into manageable sections, like this one to that next ridge line. After each bit he'd stop, rest, and see what he could find to eat. He'd also stop whenever he came to something promising like a little swamp with frogs; several frogs on a stick made a tasty barbeque. But he couldn't just hang around in this empty place and catch food. He had a destination he must reach, and sooner was better.

That plate of steak and chips beckoned real loud!

As he walked, he relived the events of the last month. It had begun when he'd made it to that little ledge and said goodbye to the river and to that strange crocodile in which Mark seemed to reside. River God Baru he'd named it then, based on a half memory of an Egyptian story of that name with big crocodiles in it. In his mind, it almost seemed to have a human face — Mark's face. It certainly conveyed a presence beyond a mindless predator. At other times, he called it just Baru, the word Mark used for his East Arnhem crocodile totem, symbolised by the carved miniature version he often carried. Now in his mind this being was a fused version of the two identities, one a totem and one a real crocodile, which he mostly called River God Baru.

Sometimes he wondered whether his memory of his escape down the river was a hallucination, invented in his imagination in that time of pain and no food.

He only half remembered how he'd crawled along that ledge, the weather steadily worsening as the early morning sunshine was covered over by ever thickening clouds and gusts of wind blowing in from the north. They got ever stronger as the afternoon progressed. Weak with hunger, he'd edged his way up and away from the river, climbing above the gully with its own thundering creek. As the heavy rain started to set in, he knew he needed to find shelter. Along with the hunger, he was getting really chilled with the cold wet wind.

He scoured the hillside for openings. Finally, he found a reasonable sized crack in the rock, dry with a sandy floor and sheltered from wind. He'd dragged himself into it and curled up, too exhausted to move, although hunger was eating into his belly.

As best he could now remember, he'd barely moved for the next three days. The wind and rain surrounded him, and water poured down the hillside. He came outside only occasionally to drink water, pee, and look at rain streaming down and wind lashing the trees.

Finally, on the afternoon of the third day, it started to blow itself out. By this time, he was almost delirious with hunger. The pains came and went, but a constant belly ache remained. He had to eat soon to allow his body to repair. Late that afternoon, clouds broke into high streamers, with occasional light showers and patches of sunshine.

He'd set out to survey his locale for food. It wasn't promising around the cave, but beyond it, the ledge opened out onto a rocky slope, extending up into a barren hillside. He found a stick for support and half crawled, half walked, as he worked his way around, looking for something edible. Anything would do. The best chance would be a reptile sunning itself.

At last, he spotted a fat bluetongue sitting on a rock in the afternoon sun, ten yards away. With all the patience he could muster, he slowly crawled towards it until it was in reach of his stick. A well-directed blow gave him his first meal.

He was tempted to rip into it and eat it raw, but the grass and leaves on the rocks were drying, and he thought he could light a fire. He'd gathered a few dry twigs and leaves from his cave. From these, he slowly built his fire, adding drier bits from nearby. After ten minutes, it was burning steadily and large enough to dry out and burn bigger sticks, which were scattered around the hillside.

When he had a good bed of coals, he'd dropped his lizard on and let it cook. The taste of that meat, with the juice and fat dribbling down his chin, was one of the most exquisite things he could ever remember. He finished it way too soon, but that was good with his stomach so shrunken.

Since then, he'd shepherded his fire, bringing it to his cave that night and keeping it continuously burning for thirty days by wrapping embers in sheets of damp paperbark and carrying this in his helmet. In that way, he could keep it alive for many hours, ready to spring back into life when he stopped and blew on it. He had his lighter, but that was only a reserve. It would be gone in no time if he used it to make a fresh fire each day.

The day after he caught the lizard, he'd set to work creating things he could use to aid his survival. He used the mesh from the seat along with some wire and a pole to make a hand net. With that, he caught tadpoles and frogs in the streams, and sometimes little fish. He'd found a flattish hollowed out piece of stone and worked on it to grind it out further until it held about a cup of liquid. If he slowly heated it in a fire, he could make an acceptable tadpole soup. Various insects made tasty additions, grubs, termites, caterpillars, even the odd cockroach. He'd have loved salt to flavour the soup, but it still gave him a nourishing feeling as he swallowed it. To this soup base, he added various plant foods like the starchy roots of water lilies.

He laughed thinking what his mother would say. "You become proper bushman, Vic. What happened to that takeaway hamburger?" But hell, while barbequed frogs on a stick didn't quite equal a good chicken satay, beggars couldn't be choosers.

For two days after the weather broke, he'd concentrated on feeding himself and rebuilding his strength. He'd made a better splint for his leg, which was starting to set at a slightly crooked angle. It was beyond him to fix properly, but he set it as straight as he could in the splint, using pressure on the bent side to pull it back. He would tighten the binding until it hurt a little, and then do something to block the hurt out. After an hour or two, the pain would ease. While he'd not got it fully straight over the last month, it had improved. With the bone ends pushed together, the pain was now mostly just a dull ache. He'd also made a good walking stick with a shoulder support, padded with some seat foam, so he could walk effectively, just lightly tipping the foot on the ground as he swung along.

He'd used his knife to cut strips of tree bark and pandanus leaves and twisted these together into heavy and light twine he could use to tie things together. He made simple spears out of lengths of wood, some with fire hardened tips, others using jagged metal pieces from the floor of the helicopter wreck. As his leg and balance got better, he tried to spear larger fish or small animals. A couple of times, he succeeded, though nothing was big enough for a feast. So he made better weapons. He broke one of his metal poles into shorter lengths and used one piece to fashion a strong knife to use for better for cutting and digging. With the second piece, he fashioned a harpoon like spear head with a tip that wouldn't slip back out of a big fish or other animal. He tied light but strong twine to the back of the timber shaft and carried it with the end tied to his pack. His logic was that if he hit something big, that would stop it getting away. No creature could run or swim fast or far dragging his pack. Even so, he'd caught nothing more than a couple of good-sized fish, but he'd keep trying for a big wallaby or kangaroo.

The idea of a whole wallaby roasting in the fire grew large in his imagination, although, as yet, he'd only glimpsed these in the far distance. He also made a couple of shorter throwing sticks, slightly curved, that he could use to try and bring down low flying birds.

He wished he'd paid more attention when his grandfather tried to teach him desert bush craft. He could surely use those survival skills now. They were foreign to a town camp boy, but he was learning, self-taught.

He'd kept an eye out for a hollow branch, which he could block at one end to carry water, and finally found a piece burnt in an old bushfire. Now he used that to hold water. He'd also searched for soft clay he could use to make an eating or cooking pot, removing the need to carry his heavy stone, but that had not materialised so far.

On the third day, when he had made all the urgent things he needed and started to rebuild his strength, he set out to explore his surroundings. His cave was on a shoulder of the hill with the creek to one side. It still flowed steadily but had fallen to a level where he could cross it in knee deep water.

The hill shoulder continued for a few hundred yards at a moderate slope before it came up against a huge cliff, hundreds of feet high. At one end, it curved around making an impenetrable barrier up against the river, a place where the gully cliff merged with the river cliff. At the other end, he could see the hill shoulder with the cliff behind it narrowing in towards the gully from which the creek flowed out of the higher hills. It followed this path as it curved out of sight. That direction, away from the river, was the best area to look for a path that would bring him to the top.

It sounded easy, and he tried to trace it on his map. But his map gave him no detail at this scale; it simply showed a broken place running in the rock and going back for several kilometres before it vanished towards the top of the mountains. He knew he needed to get to the top of these mountains before he could head cross country.

By his figuring, he had to climb up several hundred feet to reach the flat land at the top. He'd used a process of trial and error to work out a way. Hillside valleys were treacherous places, with many areas of loose sliding rock and never-ending sheer cliffs, places where an apparent path suddenly vanished into thin air, and a chasm of hundreds of feet lay before him.

He'd planned to set off and carry his gear to the top, then head overland, but it was much more difficult than that. With his level of incapacity, he couldn't explore safely and carry his gear at the same time, so he'd evolved an approach where he would explore alternate days and shift his base camp on the other days. The exploration was to find a safe path higher and further away from the river, as well as a place with enough food, water, and shelter to let him stop and rest.

The day after he found each new campsite, he'd first shift his gear and then spend the rest of the day fixing and improving his equipment and building up his stores of food. He experimented with cooking and drying the animals he caught. At the start, frogs were plentiful, then he caught a couple of fish big enough to smoke. One night at dusk, he managed to bring down a fruit bat with a throwing stick.

He'd also worked out how to make a cake with a starchy plant root that grew in the soft dirt in gullies. He'd pound this into a paste, shape it into palm sized flat cakes, and cook them on a hot stone. Their flavour was close to disgusting, but they didn't upset his stomach, and after he'd eaten a couple, he'd feel better for a while, as if real food had part satisfied the hunger which always sat inside him.

He soon figured he needed a reserve of food and tried to achieve this while he could, sensing the going was likely to get harder in some places. If he could catch a wallaby, he could dry a large amount of meat in one sitting, as well as fully satisfy his craving for meat. He experimented with making snares fashioned out of wire and bark twice, which he set on likely looking trails along rock edges. He succeeded in catching a couple of bush rats in them, but the bigger game eluded him.

The search for an escape from the maze of cliff valleys had also been so much harder than he expected. The first creek soon broke into several branches, each climbing along its own valley gorge. He would follow one's winding passage along a rocky creek bed, clambering up and down over boulders, only to find it ended in a fifty-foot waterfall with no way to get to the top. He also tried the hillsides to see if they gave ways to come around the sides of steeper cliffs, but again he usually struck dead ends.

In the end, the most promising valley system seemed to be a large secondary creek which ran off the main creek about a kilometre up from the main river. It climbed steadily following a relatively open valley, with steep but not sheer hills flanking it.

Twenty notches had been cut into his stick by the time he got to a place he reckoned was about five kilometres along it. At this point, it turned suddenly hard right. As he came around this bend, he saw towering cliffs all around and no way up. He began to think it was impossible to get to the top. This place was a maze with no exits.

At that point, he contemplated returning to the river to try and fashion a raft which would allow him to float down to the mouth, and from there, he could use the tide to bring him up the Victoria River until he came to somewhere like Bulloo River where he could get help. He decided to give it another week to make it to the top before he retreated and sought an escape that way.

He backtracked along this valley for about a kilometre to where he remembered a significant branch to the right. The country to the right seemed steeper, and it had seemed counter intuitive to go up there. But he had no choice but to try.

By now, despite limited food, his body was getting much stronger. He was using his broken leg, not to take real weight, but to give him an extra hold and counterbalance as he climbed. He remembered movies where mountaineers used pegs driven into rock crevices for hand holds and thought that was worth a try. Early on, there were a couple places where he'd had to retreat from ten-foot cliffs which, if he was fully able, he could have scaled but were beyond him then. He'd reasoned wooden pegs could be driven into rock cracks to surmount these, and twine used to lift his pack up after him.

He found a place by the creek where several large saplings grew. He bent and broke these into lengths which he put in the fire and burnt them through in their middles into increasingly smaller lengths. When it was done, he had twelve solid wooden sticks, each one to two feet in length with a fire hardened point at one end. That plus about ten metres of bark twine which could hold his weight became his climbing equipment.

As he worked along this new valley, he'd begun looking at it with different eyes, searching for parts where the sides might be scalable with his new climbing gear. About a kilometre along this new creek, he came to a waterfall of about twenty feet where a rock ledge blocked him. But at the sides were cracks in the rock which he thought he could scale. It took several hours, and many goes, but his technique improved with practice. Eventually, he mastered a sideways, crab style climb where his strong arm and leg pulled him to the next level while his weaker side gave him an anchor. By nightfall that day, using three pegs left in key locations, he made it to the top of this waterfall.

He rested there and the next morning replenished his stores. To his great delight, he caught two fish of eating size in his dip net. He set off again in the late morning, and by about lunchtime, he came to another similarly sized cliff. This time his climbing technique was better, and it only took an hour to scale before he pushed on again.

From there on, the creek bed was covered in large boulders, taller than his height. His progress was incredibly slow. The valley sides became much too steep to climb. He advanced slowly, only making a few hundred feet a day. He followed this narrow valley for three days. It twisted and turned like a corkscrew, but he climbed steadily.

At the end of that time, he felt he must be nearing the top of the mountain. In the late afternoon, he rounded another twist in the valley, conscious of a noise ahead. In front of him was a beautiful waterfall flowing over cliffs into a lovely circular pool of water. Above this waterfall it had looked like the hillside ended, at least from his view from below, he could see no more hills rising behind. But all the cliffs in front of him and to the sides were sheer. He could see nowhere that a mountain goat or rock wallaby could scale, let alone a half-crippled man.

He'd felt burning disappointment to be trapped there despite the majestic waterfall. The beauty of the scene took his breath away, but he'd wanted to scream in frustration at being so near and yet so far.

He made himself rest for two hours. He swam in the waterfall pool, luxuriating in its crystal clarity, and speared a fat catfish, the best meat he had found so far. With this food in his belly, he knew he couldn't let himself give up.

*＊＊

Using the application of a different logic, it took another five days to reach the top. He backed up to the first useful looking side valley. Rather than trying to think as a person, this time, he tried to think as a rock wallaby would.

He sat and watched these elusive creatures, looked for places where they left their dung and places where they rested, but he particularly looked for their trails. If there was a place where they could get up and down the side of these hills, then he would do so too, even if he had to crawl.

After a couple of blind tries which left him exhausted and still at the bottom of the valley, he cracked it. The route was an unobtrusive place that, at a glance, looked like a fissure and crack in the rock. As he watched and learned, he realised the rock wallabies were following this path from the high sides of the hill down to the water.

He worked his way up, leaving his gear on the valley floor. The climb was surprisingly easy. A couple of times he'd had to worm around narrow gaps sliding over smooth rocks on his belly, but he suddenly found himself on a gently rising rock scree slope that continued for a few hundred yards to a low ridge.

At the top he came out into an open valley, a sort of grassy woodland, with rich deep soil. A creek meandering along it, opening into clear rocky pools and passing through swampy glades, before it plunged over the cliff edge. Behind it were only the low ridges of upland hills.

That was two days ago. He'd felt so elated. He had made it to the top, and at the top was food aplenty.

It had taken the rest of the day to bring his things up with him, but it was easy labour knowing the way ahead was open. That night he'd caught a large fish in the creek, and a duck, both of which he roasted and fed on until he could eat no more. After he's smoked and dried the leftover meat.

He'd rested more yesterday and replenished his larder, making a good batch of his flat cakes. He'd even found a native bee nest in a low branch and broke out a piece of hive. The sugary bush honey gave him a wonderful energy lift, and he used some as flavouring to hide the bitter taste of his cakes.

He'd thought of setting a snare on this narrow path to catch one of the wallabies. It was the perfect place, and he was sure it would have succeeded.

But within a minute of thinking this, he changed his mind. Like the River God Baru crocodile, the wallabies had helped his escape. In return, he would do them no harm. Instead, he ascribed them their own special, dreamtime ancestor totem in thanks.

Now on his thirtieth day, he was finally leaving nowhere, and really was on the way to somewhere.

Despite the pain in his shoulders and an already aching leg, he walked on with purpose. As he crested his first ridge, he thought, one kilometre down, only three hundred and ninety-nine to go.

GRAHAM WILSON

250

250

Chapter 29 – The Long Walk

Dawn of day thirty-one was cold and cloudy, although the rain had stopped. Big thunderstorms had swept over Vic in the night, and despite his paperbark shelter, which kept most of the cold rain off his skin, the wetness still found ways through. For the last two hours before he arose, in the predawn light, he'd shivered almost uncontrollably and considered getting up and walking to warm himself that way. But with thick cloud the night was dark and walking while injured would be fraught with danger when he couldn't see his way. He couldn't afford another broken leg or to re-injure the damaged one. That would make walking out of here impossible.

In the first pale dawn he dug deep in the covered coal bed of the fire and found still glowing embers. He didn't plan to cook but wanted to feel warmth creep into his chilled skin and bones before he set out on another long day of walking. On thinking more he soon realised that while it would be comforting to sit by a burning fire and soak it up, he'd warm just as fast by walking, and with everything so wet, it would take at least half an hour to get the fire burning well enough to offer much comfort. Now it was light enough to see he could make his next half kilometre in that half hour.

He reckoned he'd made six kilometres yesterday. It was only an educated guess, but it fitted with the geography he could read from his map. Six kilometres didn't sound like much. Hell, if he was fit with two good legs, he could have done that in an hour. But he still couldn't step on his injured leg, only lightly touch it to the ground. That meant that every second step, he had to swing his body forward on the walking stick, with it taking the place of his bad leg. It wasn't too bad to go a hundred steps like that, even two or three hundred. But after five hundred, his shoulder, which was still tender from the crash, was burning like fire from supporting his body with each alternate step. Five hundred steps was his limit before his body needed to be rested.

If he pushed it further, he started to make mistakes. Once, he'd missed seeing a hole, and his stick had gone into it, upending him. Another time, when he flinched from the pain in his shoulder, he'd not made the step properly and had landed badly. In his attempt to correct, he'd tried to take full weight on his bad leg. Christ, it had hurt, but worse, it had seemed to give a little like he was starting to tear at the weak joining of the bones. After that, he knew he must be extra careful. But he couldn't sit and wait here for another month until his leg was strong enough to take his full weight.

He'd spent enough of daydreaming huddled around the non-existent fire. He quickly packed embers to make a fire around midday when there would be enough dryness for the wood lying around to catch fire and burn properly. He loaded his pack and other items and walked on. Slowly, he made his steps, counting as he went. In time, the steps added into tens, hundreds, and thousands.

The routine was similar and each day merged into the next.

Walk two hundred steps, rest as he counted to fifty, walk another two hundred, rest, walk, rest, walk, rest, until a thousand steps were passed. Then he'd sit on a flat rock or log for ten or fifteen minutes, chew a honey cake or a piece of dried fish, and let his muscles get their energy back to do it all over again. At four thousand steps, he'd stop for lunch, reckoning that was four kilometres and time for a big break.

He would light a fire, heat his cooking stone, and make a soup with whatever was to hand, including things already part drunk and part eaten. Then he'd look for midday food opportunities, a reptile in the sun, a fish in the shallows, perhaps hit a low flying bird with a stick, or find some bush apples or plums, before walking two more kilometres in the afternoon, before searching out a stopping place while the sun was still high enough. He always searched out a place near a creek or waterhole, where frogs and other water creatures promised easy food. Snares were set for a bush rat or other likely meal. Then time was spent digging for yams and roots, lily bulbs or whatever was to hand, fresh cakes for dinner and cold cakes for breakfast. Any excess meat was dried and smoked over the fire.

He always ate yesterday's food first unless it was fully dried. It was safer than keeping food for longer and seeing it go mouldy, and he didn't want to get food poisoning. Sometimes, when his evening preparations were done, he'd allow himself an hour to lie and sleep in the falling sun. It helped give his exhausted body the strength to hunt and prepare a proper evening meal, and at that time, there were less mosquitoes to disturb his sleep than in the night.

He didn't know what was worse, the chronic tiredness or the chronic hunger. Both were always present, even when his belly felt full or he'd just slept for the night. He knew he really needed better nutrition for both his strength and stamina. He craved fat and sugar along with fresh fruit and vegetables. But his mind was in a positive place. He was slowly making forward progress, and each day his bad leg grew a little bit stronger, and his body continued to heal its injuries.

In the late afternoon, he'd get a good fire going, waiting for a hoped evening meal to appear. That hour, just on dusk, was his hunting hour. He'd watch where birds landed, so he could sneak up as they roosted. He'd watch for fish movements in the shallows, a chance to use his spear. Sometimes, he'd stake out a track to a waterhole and wait patiently for an animal to come past to drink. Twice in his first two weeks, he got a wallaby that way and spent all the next morning smoking and drying the surplus meat. He now had several pounds of dried meat and about twenty yam cakes as a food reserve.

With the added energy from his extra calorie intake, he decided he'd try and walk further each day, increasing the distance to eight kilometres, or eight thousand steps. His progress on the map seemed to line up with these distances pretty well. Maybe it was a bit less, although it was hard to judge with the ups and downs and detours. The extra two thousand steps felt hard for the next week, then it got easier, so he went to nine thousand and then ten.

His need for food increased as he walked further, and he started to use his reserve. The muscles on his body had started to fall away further, and he realised he was losing strength. He decided he'd look for a good place to stop for a couple of rest days, to build up his reserves, and then try to maintain a steady eight to ten thousand steps per day from there.

He now saw ten thousand steps was falling short of ten kilometres on his map. Perhaps eight kilometres was closer, but if he could do eight or nine thousand steps, that was still around seven kilometres.

He found a good cave in a low rocky hill near a big waterhole. This would be his rest place.

Each day while there, he let himself sleep until the mid-morning, then he hunted, fished, and dug roots for the rest of the day. Those early cool morning hours gave him the best rest. During his days in the cave, he caught two fat magpie geese, two good sized catfish, speared in the clear water, and one wallaby. He also had as many yam cakes as he could carry. His stick now had over fifty notches. He wanted to be out of here before he got to one hundred.

His leg could now bear the weight for a half shuffling step, though he still used his stick to stop himself stumbling and doing more damage to it. Day followed day. Sixty days passed, and then he was at seventy. That meant he'd been walking for forty days now, making it early March by his calculations. Most days he did between eight and ten thousand steps, although there were places where the country grew very rough, and he only made five of six thousand. There were also places where the hills and gullies forced him to detour from his intended path or even backtrack. He realised he was going as well as possible, but he was also burning out his body and slowly destroying it. He needed more starch and fatty foods. Dried meat was good, but the chewing now took effort, and his vegetable diet was limited and also hard to chew.

He was now in the very top of the Fitzmaurice catchment. His map showed a place called Wombungi Outstation was somewhere near here. If he could find it, perhaps there would be someone there, perhaps some food. On his seventy second day, his mind was wandering as he walked, ever returning to steak and chips, alternating with pictures of his mother.

And then there was the image of Susan. She was always in his mind, or nearby now, as he walked. She was his purpose, the thing that most strongly drove him on. He had a sharp etched memory of her face that day when he last saw her, bold and challenging, and yet with a quiet hopeless desperation that was mostly hidden but there to read for those who looked right in. He knew she really needed him.

He kept on walking, one step, and then a second, with the partial support of his stick, repeated a thousand times before he needed to lie down, rest, and often fall asleep. It was all he could manage now. Then he would wake and make himself repeat it, perhaps two or three times in a day. He knew his body would continue to weaken and start to fail him, but he just had to force himself to keep going.

Suddenly, he found his way stopped. He looked down at what was in his path. It was a four strand, barbwire cattle fence. In the last week, he'd seen an occasional scrub bull in the distance or a track, but he and they had kept away from each other. Now this was a sign of real cattle, and with real cattle, maybe food and people.

He followed the fence. It was easier than walking blindly through the bush, and it had a graded track along the edge, so walking was easier. Just on dusk, he reached a corner with another fence and followed this. In the last light, he saw station buildings in the distance. He hoped it was Wombungi. It must surely be Wombungi.

He didn't know this place or its people. He had a memory it was a cattle station that had been sold to the aborigines, although he a vague idea it had an outside manager and ran cattle. But that was only second-hand hearsay.

Whether it was a cattle station or an aboriginal camp, he hoped there would be other people there who would help him. He wished he could hear a generator or see some lights, but there was nothing.

He came to the front door and banged, but it was closed. He tried the door. It was locked. He walked around outside. There was no easy way in. He wondered if there was a car or other vehicle he could drive, or maybe something else useful. Maybe even a store of food.

He checked the outbuildings and found not much on offer there. He found a tin to serve as a billy can and a half packet of biscuits on a shelf in a shed. He ate the packet of biscuits and, exhausted, lay down on the shed floor to sleep. He woke to thunder and lightning in the early morning, then the sound of rain on the tin roof, but rolled over and slept on, pleased to be dry and out of the rain.

In the morning light, he better explored his surroundings. It was clear the station was used, at least in the dry season, but it appeared to have been abandoned over the wet. There were no cattle in the close in yards, although he'd seen fresh tracks in the big paddock he'd walked around. The house was locked up tight. He knew he could break in if he tried and would probably find more food. But unless there was a phone, which was uncertain, it was of limited use. The one thing he found which was useful was a big map hanging on the wall of the shed. It showed the paddocks and roads.

There was a road to Dorisvale Station, which looked like it was thirty of forty kilometres away, and there was a road to Innesvale Station, which looked like it was seventy or eighty kilometres.

Dorsivale Station was closer, but he didn't know the people there, and he was far from sure it would have any people there in the wet season. If not, it was a long way further to walk to the main Darwin road.

He knew Innesvale was now an aboriginal owned station but with a manager. He'd not done work there, but he'd met the manager and his family in Katherine at last year's Show. He was almost sure there would be someone there over the wet season, and it wasn't too far from there to the Katherine-Timber Creek Road should he be wrong.

He decided to walk to Innesvale, no longer stopping to find food. Instead, he'd eat the remaining food that he carried and walk as far and fast as he could each day.

He abandoned his pack and other possessions except for the walking stick and billycan, which he filled with his food. He found an old piece of canvas, which he wrapped around his shoulders to replace the paperbark. If he was fit, he could have walked it in two days. He hoped he could do it in three.

It was an hour after dawn on the fourth day when he stumbled up to the station house to find a caretaker eating breakfast. The man didn't know him, but he took one look at him and pulled out an extra chair. "Reckon you could do with a feed," he said. "You look a bit hollowed out."

The kettle was hot. A cup of tea was poured and loaded with sugar. In a few minutes, there was a plate of toast and eggs in front of him. As he took in the food, he could feel the sugar give him strength and his mind begin to clear. The caretaker didn't seem to know about him and the helicopter crash. Some people lived in their own world and left the outside world behind.

But the caretaker had a car and could drive him to Katherine, and there was a phone, so he could ring ahead. He tried the number for the police. For while, he went around in circles, trying to talk to someone who could help. When asked who he was he said he was Mr Campbell, but that didn't mean anything at the other end of the phone. He recalled the name he needed was Sergeant Alan Richards.

It took three calls to locate him. He happened to be working in Katherine that day. At first, he sounded impatient when he got put on the line. Vic suspected he had no idea who a Mr Campbell was. But Sergeant Richards put on his polite voice and said, "Yes, Mr Campbell, how can I help you?"

Vic tried to find his own polished voice. "I understand you're the detective who led the investigation into Susan McDonald, the lady charged with Mark Bennet's murder. I have important evidence in relation to this. I thought you should know about it. I hope it's important enough to change what happens in her trial."

Silence came from the other end of the line, then eventually, "What did you say your name was?"

"Vic Campbell. You and your partner, Sandy, met me at the Paraway Hotel last December."

Now he heard the penny drop. "Vic, helicopter pilot. But you're supposed to be dead. They told me your helicopter crashed out west, somewhere near the mouth of the Victoria River. They found wreckage floating in the water. Where are you, and what's going on?"

"Best I can tell, I'm not dead. Bit skinny and hungry looking. I had a long walk to get here. Took me upwards of seventy-five days, or at least I have seventy-six notches on my walking stick without one for today.

"I've just arrived at Innesvale station, which, as I'm told, is a couple hours' drive west of Katherine. The caretaker has offered to drive me to Katherine. Thought maybe we could meet, and I could fill you in."

"I imagine you've not heard any news for a bit," Sergeant Richard said. "I can fill you in as we drive. But you need to know that Susan has been found guilty of Mark's murder at a trial two weeks ago. She'll be sentenced today.

"I've been frantically working my butt off, right here in Katherine, looking for any information that might change the outcome of that. Within two hours, I hope to have all I need. Then I was going to hop in the car and drive non-stop to Darwin to ask the judge to take it into consideration before he makes his sentencing decision this afternoon. That'll be at soon after two o'clock. It's why I sounded a bit rushed.

"If you could get to Katherine no later than ten thirty this morning, then you could come with me to Darwin. We can talk on the way. What I have now will certainly help her, but anything you add will make it better. I know she doesn't want my help, but I'm determined to give it anyway. You're the one person I think she'll listen to."

Soon they were on their way. Vic decided to skip a shower in the interests of time, but the caretaker found him a clean pair of shorts and T-shirt even if they were a couple sizes too large. He also gave him clean socks to put on his feet and returned them to his battered boots.

He double checked he had his wallet with the SIM card in his pocket. With that done, they left.

Chapter 30 – Deliverance

It was a crazy rushed drive to Darwin, even though they stuck more or less to the speed limits. As they drove, they talked. They both felt in a great hurry, but with three hours of driving, there was no rush to talk.

Alan gave Vic a muesli bar to eat, saying he looked like a starved Ethiopian and, as they couldn't afford the time to stop for a proper meal, he'd have to make do with that. Vic chewed it slowly, savouring every delicious morsel. It was real food, and he felt more of his strength returning and his mind sharpening with each little bite.

As he ate, Vic filled Alan in on his miraculous escape. He even told him about the crocodile and how it seemed to be giving him a message from Mark about helping Susan and at the same time protecting him. Alan looked at Vic quizzically a couple times as he talked about the crocodile, but Vic stuck to his guns.

Alan told him his own story about the huge crocodile at the Mary River and how it appeared to be grieving as they took away the parts of Mark's body. "Sandy and I both saw it. We told Charlie, the fisherman who found the head, about it. He gets it. But we've not told others because we don't want to be thought of as crazy.

"So, don't worry. I believe you. I don't know so much about Mark, your friend, but it's clear he and crocodiles have a longstanding and deep affinity."

Vic laughed. "Did you know he has a crocodile skin totem from east Arnhem Land? Says the blackfellas out there kinda adopted him when he first went there to work. Now he carries a little carved crocodile as his totem crocodile wherever he goes. Baru he calls it.

Alan dug in his pocket and pulled out the carved crocodile he'd found at the billabong. "It doesn't look like this I suppose. I found this on the bank of the Mary River about a week ago. I feel like it's guiding me forward too."

Vic nodded and laughed. "I suppose neither of us should admit it to the rest of the world, or they'll all call us nuts. But somehow, it seems like Mark is out there pushing and pulling the levers, the clever bastard. It feels like he and his crocodile friends are helping us.

"I suppose I should say that in a past tense, but somehow, since I met that crocodile out on the Fitzmaurice River, deep down, I think of Mark as still being alive.

"I know the truth will be bad for what people say about Mark. But I'm sure he wants the truth out. He doesn't want Susan to carry the can for what he did. That's the message he gave me out on the river and entrusted me to deliver. So, I made myself keep on walking, step after step, even when my body wanted to lie down and give up.

"When we used to work in the bush together, most mornings, Mark would go off early and write into a diary. Once or twice, he read stuff out aloud to me. Once, he described me and my helicopter as a metal bird which the real birds laughed at for its clumsiness. It was very funny. He had a gift to tell a good story.

"Back then, I asked if I could read it. He said no because it told all the bad stuff about him as well as the good, and that he didn't want me to know the bad stuff. I knew he was a mercenary in Africa, killed people there. That's how he took the bullet in the arm, but there was obviously more bad stuff as well he didn't want me to know about.

"But he told me when he died, I'd have his diary, and could read it all, that I'd know both the good and bad, like a brother should. Then, if I wanted, I could tell the world his secrets.

"It was like he had a kind of death wish. He knew he wouldn't live to be an old man. He said he was like a cat with nine lives, but one day all his lives would run out, and he thought it would be soon. He wasn't afraid, just determined to live life until it was over and that would be that. He was completely fearless, you know. Something must have happened to take away all his fear and put a hard, dangerous thing in its place. All of us, all his friends, sensed the dangerous bit though we pretended not to notice.

"But there was a good side too. He was kind and generous to his friends, good to bush people. He really got on with my mother. She told him she'd adopted him, even though he didn't ask to be adopted. He said he was pleased to have her as a mother as it really made me his brother. She said having a brother was not so important. What he needed was a mother to take the place of the one he never had, most of all, to give him some love inside, and that was her job. I think she thought, if only he was given enough love to replace what he'd missed when he was little, the bad part would go away. But it never did.

"Instead, I think Mark looked to the girls to fill that space. There were lots of girls over the years, but most of them never stuck. If they tried to hold on too tight, he pushed them away. Once or twice, I thought he really liked one, but a lot were just good time girls, out for their own pleasure too, and soon they went on their way.

"He didn't seem to mind a lot. "Easy come, easy go," he used to say. It was like he was never prepared to invest much in them emotionally. So, when they left, it proved they weren't worthwhile. Some were gorgeous, and he could really charm them, but none seemed to go anywhere.

"Deep down, I think he was looking for someone special, sort of like the mother he never had. The girl he needed had to be strong enough to stand up to him but not too pushy. Any girl who liked him and wanted to stay there couldn't hang on too tight. He really hated people who tried to bully him, either physically or with emotion.

"From the first minute Susan came along, it was different. He told me he first saw her standing on the beach at Cairns before she saw him. Right from then, she'd captured him, like by magic. He went on a dive with her, made friends and the next thing they were lovers.

"By the time he left Cairns, he'd pretty much made up his mind she was the one. But then there was all this bad stuff he'd done, and he didn't want her to see it. It was like he was trying to charm her, be open with her, yet something inside him kept closing her out.

"She was as captivated by him as he was by her. She was determined to find out who he was. I don't know what the bad stuff was, but she must have found out something, something really bad. She as good as told me that. And that's when it went all wrong. Before that he made a will, which I witnessed, giving all he owned to her, not that she knew. And he made me an executor to the will, making me promise, no matter what happened, that I'd look after her.

"But when I found out what she'd done, that day you told me at the Paraway Hotel, I felt real mad at her. I went and saw her in prison and made her tell me what she'd done. At first, she tried to pretend, but I slapped her, told her I needed to know if she'd killed my best friend and brother.

"After that she said she had and she'd made a mistake and wished now she hadn't. She wouldn't tell me why, but I knew, deep down, she'd discovered something terrible about him.

"I asked her for the diary. I said Mark had promised it to me. So, she gave it to me. Not the full-sized thing. But she'd made a copy, photographed it onto a tiny memory chip that fits in a phone. It was hidden in her shoe in prison. She said it was given to me to respect Mark's promise to me.

"She told me it was mine to read but to be careful with what I did about it, that it had bad stuff inside it about Mark, and she didn't want to poison his memory through this, particularly so their child wouldn't have to know this about his father.

"Deep inside, I think I knew about Mark's bad stuff before she said it, but then it was in my face. It made me responsible too. I knew as I read his diary I'd share her secret and I must share the decision about Mark's future, to decide along with her what the world should know.

"I still have the chip. It's almost the only thing I still have from the crash. It was wrapped in sticky tape, and I put it in my wallet, which is still in my pocket. The chip may be wrecked from the water for all I know, but even if it is, the original diary will be somewhere, and the story will be in it.

"When Susan gave it to me, just before Christmas, I didn't want to read it straight away. I didn't want to know the bad things Mark had done. I knew they must be very bad for Susan to hide them away like she did. All I can think of is that perhaps he did something bad to some of those girls I met.

"So, I never tried to read his diary before I crashed. But when I got out of the water, and I knew Mark was helping me survive, I also knew that this tale had to be told and Susan would never tell it. It would mean destroying his memory, and she won't do that.

"Susan thinks her silence will protect him, but she'd wrong. It will only harm her without helping him, and that's an even greater wrong. Even if she locks this secret away inside herself so she can never tell, someone will still find it out one day.

"If I can't read the diary on the chip, I'll make her tell me where the original diary is. I know that's what Mark wanted. Even she can't be allowed to stop him from having his story told."

Alan nodded as Vic talked. His words made sense and fitted with what he'd uncovered himself. He saw too this truth about Mark had been in front of Vic for many years past, but loyalty had made him blind. Instead, it was left to this slip of an English woman to summon the courage to search and find. But now her own courage was destroying her. If she stayed locked up, or worse, her blood would be on Vic's head too, as it would be on his and Sandy's for their role in her destruction.

Alan told Vic about his own discoveries, first about Mark's real name and childhood, and then about the suspicion of Mark's role in a couple of deaths when he was a teenager, but with no evidence that hadn't gone anywhere.

Next, that Mark had just vanished when he was eighteen, except for a single record when he was twenty, leaving on a plane going to London. They'd been unable to find him overseas and assumed he must have taken another identity.

Then he came to the final piece of the puzzle, the text message from Susan to Anne asking her to investigate two names, and Anne's reply. "That message was picked up in Timber Creek at 9.05 am on the last day anyone had saw Susan and Mark together, just at the time when Mark was seen driving out of town with Susan asleep in the passenger seat. I only found out this morning that the two girls are still missing. The American girl took a while to trace, and the final phone call about her from the USA only came in at ten this morning."

Now it was Vic who was nodding. "Yes, she must have found out later that day when she woke up. Mark must have found out what she knew. It fits with what she told me, that she was frightened when she killed him, believing he would kill her."

Alan continued, "Yes, she must have believed he'd do the same to her as what he did to the others.

"On the basis of the evidence of the text messages, I intend to ask the judge to delay sentencing until I can undertake an investigation about what happened to these other girls. There's clear grounds for self-defence or a greatly reduced sentence, regardless of what Susan has admitted to. I don't have anything directly against Mark, but I have good grounds for a further investigation and more importantly to uncover a story that makes sense.

"I've been in Katherine because I was allowed a couple of days to work on chasing up any leads to Mark Butler's identity, which seems to be centred in Katherine. I'd convinced my boss it's important now we've uncovered the Vincent Bassingham identity. It's luck I was still here this morning gathering some final pieces of information before I go to the court in Darwin.

"I've deliberately avoided telling my superiors what I've found out in the last day because I know they'd want to do it all officially using lawyers and media management and being super careful. But there isn't time, and any publicity would be very dangerous. I'm fearful Susan has become suicidal, and after the sentencing, she'll find some way to end it all. The best chance to prevent that is to break it all open in court, ask the judge to delay sentencing, even release her on bail while my own investigation proceeds."

"I'll help by giving this evidence of the diary," Vic said. "I'll ask for copies to be made for you or whoever's given the job of doing the investigation. It'll support your story and give a further and better explanation of who Mark was and what he's done"

They were both confident this would be enough to at least suspend if not change the court decision. "My real worry is Susan," Alan confided. "I'm terrified of what she might do when the truth she's so desperately been trying to hide comes out."

Vic turned to Alan and said, "You worry about convincing the judge. Let me worry about Susan. That's my real purpose in walking all this way, to help her see the real truth. She's become blinded to what Mark wants her to see. She'll only further betray him and his legacy if she seeks to harm herself or deprive their children of their mother, as Mark was deprived of his."

"By the time my mother found him and adopted him, it was too late to rescue him from himself. Susan sees danger if her children know their father and the evil he did. Much greater is the danger to her children if they never know their mother's love for them, if they never know the joy of being held in her arms and comforted.

"That's what I need to make her see; that of all the people here she's the one who most deserves to live, the one who still has the most critical role to preserve the good parts of Mark's legacy, particularly for their own children.

"I was lost in an empty place, but I escaped with the help of my brother Mark. Now she too must escape from her own soul's empty place. I'll lead her out, as Mark has led me. It'll be enough to bring her to the place where she holds her own children. Once she holds them, as my mother held me, she'll know an even better love than what she had for Mark, and that love will hold her fast.

"So don't fear from here. In that moment of truth, she'll hate us both, and she'll fight to keep her secret. But there is a power in this truth that even all her will can't stop. As the crocodile spirit protected me, his brother, from the river, so too will the power of this crocodile brother's spirit protect her in her moment of danger".

When they arrived outside the Supreme Court building in Mitchell Street, Darwin, the time was 2.05 pm.

Chapter 31 – Judgement

They walked into court just as a barrister was standing to start speaking. He and Alan gave each other a subtle nod. Vic remembered the communication between himself and Alan about the importance of timing of their arrival.

The court was jam packed. There were so many people that it was hard to separate familiar faces amongst the sea. But Vic's eyes weren't for the court at large. He was looking for Susan, searching towards the front of the field of faces, looking to the central place where she should be, awaiting the courts judgement. He kept looking from face to face until he found her. Despite his words of surety to Alan a bare minute before, he now felt uncertain at how his mission would be received. Not that he would be turned aside. His purpose was both to meet a promise to Mark and to help Susan, whether his help was wanted or not. But it mattered to him what she thought.

Suddenly, his eyes found her, and in a split second, their gazes were locked on each other. He realised in the first instant she hadn't recognised him. Hardly surprising when he imagined what he must look like. But as their eyes locked, he felt her recognition like an electric shock. She called out his name loudly and with joy across the silent court room, and then smiled towards him, an overwhelming and radiant smile. He could tell she wanted to run towards him, to fling her arms around him, and he wanted that too, so much.

He felt his heart skip a beat. She was more beautiful in person than the image in his mind. He smiled back, basking in her warm smile, and he waved his arm towards her in acknowledgement, needing to do something to signal his affection to her. Her face lit up even more. She looked so delighted to see him, perhaps unable to believe he really was still alive and right there.

It was hard to think straight at a time like this. He mustn't let himself get distracted. He had a job to do and couldn't let her distract or influence him away from that.

He realised Alan was speaking to him. "Would you just wait here for a second while I approach the judge and seek his permission to talk to him directly?"

Vic stayed where he was and watched as Alan walked forward and made his request. Initially, the judge looked unsure, but then he looked towards the two barristers for a reaction. Alan approached the barrister for the prosecution and said something quietly to him. This person obviously already knew Alan. After a few seconds of speaking, he saw the barrister nod his head in agreement, and Alan and the barristers followed the judge from the court.

Vic turned his attention back to Susan. She was sitting with her hand over her mouth looking stunned. Her eyes bored into him, intense and pleading. He gave her another quick and intense smile, trying to convey comfort and certainty. Then he found himself unable to meet her gaze, knowing he must do something she was fighting with the whole world to prevent — tell the truth about Mark.

He looked away from her and saw Sandy, who he recognised from the meeting in Katherine, sitting next to Buck and his wife. Buck was trying to greet him with a delighted wave, and at the same time he whispered to Sandy who was now waving too.

He walked over to join them. They made space between them for him to sit down. They were both speaking at once, trying to ask the same questions about what had happened to him and where he'd been.

He and Alan had decided to tell no one, en route, of his return. They'd let the news spread from here. They didn't want a media pack waiting for them and interfering with what they'd come here to do.

Vic could feel a rising murmur of gossip spread behind him, people trying to work out who he was, mostly clueless both as to his identity and as to why he'd come. He saw a tight knit group of people extending to the side and behind Buck all looking at him intently, seeking an introduction or explanation. Everyone clamouring for him. It was all too much. He felt faint and dizzy, needing to grasp at the side of the rail as he sat. He realised it was a long time since he had eaten, and his reserves were running low.

Buck looked at him with concern. Vic had still not found any words. Buck reached into his pocket and found a chocolate bar. "I think you need this. You were always built like a greyhound, now you look like a greyhound starved for three months."

Vic took it with thanks. He tore of the wrapper and took a big bite, letting sugary sweetness fill his mouth and lift his brain into action. "Thank you, my friend. You have no idea how much I needed that. Not quite the steak, chips, and beer I've dreamed of over the last seventy-five days as I walked across that Godforsaken Empty Place from where I decided to park my chopper, but it still tastes so good. Now, what were you saying? Oh yes, where have I come from? Well, as best I can now remember, it's a gorge about ten miles upstream from the mouth of the Fitzmaurice River.

"I was lucky to run into your bloke in Katherine," he said, turning to Sandy. "He offered me a lift to this establishment to join in the entertainment, otherwise known as the hanging of our good friend Susan. Alan and I, we think we've a thing or two to say which may upset the well laid plans to bury her in a cell for a couple of decades."

He suddenly realised that everyone else had stopped talking and whispering, and his voice was resonating across this part of the court. Now he felt embarrassed. "Just a private conversation between me and my very good friend Buck here. I'll stop talking and keep eating now, if it's okay."

Buck's wife, Julie, broke into delighted giggles. "Oh, Vic, it's just so good to see you alive and well if a bit thin. Like a scarecrow, really. And still with the ability to make a joke about the worst of things."

Her words were like a circuit breaker. Vic felt he was home, and he slumped back in the seat, surrounded by his friends.

Around him, the conversation rose from a murmur to an almost roar, everyone clamouring to spread their part of the story they were only just starting to understand.

Suddenly, the judge's gavel rapped on the bench. The noise soon subsided into stunned silence. The judge's assistant spoke in a loud voice. "His honour has requested Mr Vickram Campbell join him now in his chambers."

Vic stood and followed the man from the court. A couple times he wobbled, feeling lightheaded and not quite used to walking on his leg without a stick to support him.

He found himself seated in the centre of a group of four men. Alan, he knew. The other three he realised were the judge and two barristers, all minus wigs. They looked at him expectantly as brief introductions were made.

The judge asked Vic to briefly tell him about his meeting with Susan and the object he'd been given. He reached into his pocket and removed the small chip wrapped in plastic from his wallet and gave it to the judge. "When I saw her in jail, I asked Susan for Mark's diary, which he'd promised me when he was alive, to let me read. I think it'll explain the real reason for what happened between her and Mark that led to his murder.

"Susan told me a copy of Mark's diary was on this memory card. I didn't get to read it before I crashed. It's been in and out of the water many times since, so I don't know if it'll work. But I believe the truth about Mark and why she was frightened of him is told here."

The judge passed the memory chip to Alan. "I assume you can get this transcribed and provide me with some analysis of what it means within a few days. That's if it is not damaged. Even without it, there's a clear inference from the texts as to why she was afraid. On this basis, I'm prepared to make a ruling to suspend sentencing until your investigation has a chance to gather sufficient further information.

"I'm also inclined to make a ruling that this lady, this remarkable lady, I would say, is released on bail forthwith.

"It's clear she had a real fear of this man. I consider that there are good grounds for a retrial with this new evidence, even a dismissal of the charge, though her past guilty plea makes it more problematic.

"Because of the way this evidence involves other parties, where there is grave concern about their fate, I'll also impose a ruling that all the evidence I've heard here is to be held in total confidence to the parties present here now until the investigation has concluded. Do I have the agreement of all of you to what I propose?"

They all nodded.

"With your permission, I should like to speak briefly to Susan's friend Anne before I announce my ruling, just to confirm from her own mouth about the text in question. After I announce my ruling, I'll talk to Susan McDonald and ask for her cooperation, if she's willing to give it. Not that it will change my ruling if she doesn't. She's been through more than enough."

Anne was called in. The judge briefly confirmed, in the presence of the others, that she'd received and sent the texts which were referred to. Anne nodded and then smiled her grateful thanks to Alan.

"Your honour, I promised her I'd keep her secret until such time as she was able to tell it. I still don't know what it means, but I've been so conflicted keeping this hidden, knowing how it would go for her if it wasn't revealed. Yet I was bound by my promise to her. Today, I decided that regardless of my promise, I must reveal it. But it would have still been a betrayal to her, so I'm glad this didn't come from me."

The judge nodded and gave her a fatherly look. "I would feel lucky to have a friend as good as you. We both know your duty to the court, but friends are always friends, and promises remain promises."

Vic followed Anne her back into the court room, with the others trailing behind.

When all were seated, the judge started his ruling. "Ladies and gentlemen. As you may gather, some very significant evidence has just been brought before this court. It raises serious questions about whether the original guilty plea made by Ms Susan McDonald should, in the interests of justice, be allowed to stand.

"I have therefore suspended my judgement as to passing sentence until this new material is investigated. As this material appears highly favourable to Ms McDonald's ultimate exoneration from these charges, I have also ruled she should be released on bail of ten thousand dollars, to apply forthwith.

"In addition, while I do not require it, I seek her cooperation to assist us with the new investigations we need to pursue to resolve this matter.

"Until this investigation is complete, I'm not prepared to disclose further information as to the nature of the new evidence. In addition, I make a suppression order, effective immediately, on all parties who hold the information. to which I refer. That has just been laid before the court. None of it is to be disclosed without the specific approval of this court. Its premature release has the potential to harm this inquiry.

"I permit the release of my ruling today, but all other evidence I have heard today about Mr Vincent Marco Bassingham is hereby suppressed until I rule otherwise."

With that, he rapped his gavel and stated the court was dismissed, and then he left the court for his chambers.

For a minute, there was total stunned silence as people tried to grasp the meaning of what they'd heard. Slowly, people started talking amongst themselves, though still nobody moved.

A minute later, the judge's associate returned and asked that Susan accompany Sergeant Alan Richards and Vikram Campbell to the judge's chambers.

Susan was accompanied by a prison guard. The judge waved to him and to Susan's handcuffs. "You can take them off now. I've ordered her release, and I'm assured that bail will be posted before she leaves the court."

The handcuffs were removed, and the judge indicated to the prison officer to leave, suggesting he may wait in the main court building if he needed further instruction.

The judge looked at Susan in a kindly way. "I think you've had a rough few months. You can stop fighting us all now.

"We now know enough to know that while you've told us the truth about what you did, it is far from a full and satisfactory explanation of what happened. We may not know a full answer as to why, but we now have additional evidence, thanks to Sergeant Richards here.

"For instance, the key evidence, which was brought before me and led to this ruling, was the transcript of the text sent by you to your friend Anne and her reply to you. It makes it clear there were deep suspicions, held by you, about the role of the man you knew as Mark Bennet in the disappearance of two other backpackers.

"I've ordered an investigation into these matters by the NT police, to which Sergeant Richards will give his urgent attention. As you've already heard, I've suppressed all information relating to this out of my respect for the potential victims and their families.

"In addition, Mr Vikram Campell has informed me he holds a copy of Mark's diary, given to him by you. I've instructed this be provided to the NT police to assist in their investigation. Mr Campbell has already done so, though we're unsure whether it sustained water damage during the last three months.

"Now, Ms McDonald, many people have tried to compel you to do things over the last few months. All we can say is your strength of will has been extraordinary. With this new knowledge, we at least begin to understand the reasons why.

Now I ask you, most earnestly, to please assist us with this investigation. You hold a detailed understanding about these events. I could order you to do so, but I see no point. You are clearly not someone to be intimidated by any punishment I have at my disposal.

"So, instead, I simply ask you, for the sake of the many people who fought for your freedom and for the sake of these missing girls, whatever their story may be, to assist us all.

Susan struggled to find words to say. She'd fought so long and so hard, and it had all been futile. Now the truth was out anyway. Nothing she could do could put the genie back in the bottle. Even her thoughts of suicide seemed empty now that Vic had been returned to her. She wouldn't waste that gift of life restored by what she saw now was a selfish act. Mostly, she just felt exhausted and stunned, so she just looked up and nodded and then covered her face in her hands and tried to stop her shoulders from shaking. She sat there crying quietly at first, then sobbing as if her heart would break.

After a minute, Vic walked over to her and put his thin arms around her shoulders, brought her to her feet, and led her outside. He realised the main job for which he had been returned, was not to find her justice, not even to protect her from herself, but to hold and comfort her and bring her beyond this place of desolation.

He grieved for Mark; she grieved for Mark and for so much more — the loss of joy and innocence, the destruction of a belief in human goodness. Together, they'd share and let go of their void of empty places and find new meaning beyond it.

As they reached the corridor outside, she reached out and hugged herself tightly to him. "I'm so glad you came back. I'm so tired of being alone. When you were gone too, I felt I'd lost every last friend in the world. Now you're back, I don't want to ever let you go. I want you to stay here with me and hold me like this forever."

Vic pulled her head into his bony shoulder, stroked it, and kissed away her tears. "We are together. We'll each make the other strong again."

Suddenly, Susan started laughing. "We're such an odd couple, aren't we? The fat pregnant prisoner with the huge belly who waddles when she walks, and the crippled wild man fresh from the jungle, one who looks like he hasn't washed or eaten a proper meal in three months, and who is mostly skin, hair and poking out bones."

Vic laughed too. "Well, you have me described to a T, but you were a bit kind to yourself. You forgot your tear-stained face with mascara all down your cheeks, and the fact that now that I've hugged you, you're starting to look and smell like me, with smears of bush dirt added to your pretty dress."

Susan screwed up her face in a mock grimace. "Vic, hug me again. I want more of your smell and feel on me. It's more real and better than anything else I can think of."

He pulled her too him again, and they wrapped their arms around each other and held close for a long time. This time, it was more than a hug. It was a promise.

Susan thought of the syringe lying on the courtroom floor. She was glad it was there, and she was here. She saw, suddenly and clearly, that a great madness had possessed her mind.

Chapter 32 – Release

At last, they separated and returned to the courtroom. A handful of people had left, but most were still sitting there, all looking stunned.

As she and Vic walked in together, holding hands, all eyes turned to them. A spontaneous cheer erupted. People started to clap for her, perhaps for Vic too, but it seemed mostly for her.

It came to her then. She'd thought of most of these people as her enemies, wanting to see her locked away. In previous days, she'd thought they'd been calling for her blood. But most of these people were actually on her side.

It was a big room with over a hundred people packed in. Most of them were clapping and cheering for her, celebrating her freedom.

She looked around and saw Anne, David, her family, her cousins from Sydney, Buck and other station people, Sandy, Charlie and Rosie. There were lots she didn't know, people who had no reason to care what happened to her. Yet here they all were, come to support her. She stopped in the middle of the empty courtroom floor, tears running down her face, and she smiled and waved to her family and friends.

"Thank you, everybody. Thank you with all my heart."

She turned to Vic and said loudly and clearly, so all could hear, "And most of all, thank you to this man. For those of you who don't know him, his name is Vikram. He's the pilot of the helicopter which crashed on the Fitzmaurice River just before New Year's Day.

"He's walked without stopping for the last seventy-five days with a broken leg to get here today. He tells me that now he's made it, all he wants to do is go to the pub for a cold beer and a big plate of steak and chips. So, if you'll excuse us, that's where we're headed."

As the clapping and cheering continued, she gave him another hug and walked across to her family and friends to say thanks to them.

It was far from over, but she had hope again.

About the Author

Graham Wilson lives in Sydney, Australia. He has written and published twelve novels and a memoir.

They comprise two standalone novels, *Mysteries* and *Risk Free*.

He's also written two book series:

1. The Old Balmain House Series – three novels

2 The Crocodile Dreaming Series – seven novels

Arnhem's Kaleidoscope Children is a family memoir.

The *Old Balmain House Series* starts with the novel, *Little Lost Girl.* Its setting is an old weatherboard cottage in Sydney, where the author lived for seven years. Here a photo was discovered of a small girl who lived and died one hundred years ago. The book imagines the story of her life and family, based in the real Balmain, an early inner Sydney suburb, with its locations and historical events providing part of the story background. The second novel in this series, *Lizzie's Tale*, builds on the Balmain house setting. It's the story of a working-class teenage girl who lives in this same house in the 1950s and 1960s. She falls pregnant and is determined not to surrender her baby for adoption, and the novel follows her struggle to survive in this unforgiving society. The third novel in this series, *Devil's Choice*, follows the next generation of the family in *Lizzie's Tale*. Lizzie's daughter is faced with the awful choice of whether to seek the help of one of her mother's rapists' in trying to save the life of her own daughter, who is inflicted with an incurable disease.

The Crocodile Dreaming Series is based in Outback Australia. It starts with the first novel, *Visitor*, which tells the story of Susan, an English backpacker, who visits the Northern Territory and becomes captivated and in great danger from a man who loves crocodiles. The second book in the series, *Victim*, follows the consequences of the first book based around the discovery of this man's remains. This third book, *Void*, is about Susan's struggle to retain her sanity in jail while her family and friends desperately try to find out what really happened on that fateful day before it is too late and she's jailed. In *Vanished,* Susan disappears, and the novel follows the story of the search for her and four other lost girls whose passports were found in the possession of the man she killed. The final book in the series, *inVisible,* is the story of a girl who appears in a remote aboriginal community in North Queensland without any memory except for a name. As she rebuilds her life from an empty shell, fragments of the past return and, with them come dark shadows that threaten to overwhelm her.

The book *Arnhem's Kaleidoscope Children* recounts the author's life in the Australia's Northern Territory, his childhood in an aboriginal community in Arnhem Land, and explores the people, the danger and the beauty of the place, and of its transformation over the last half century with the coming of aboriginal rights and the discovery of uranium. It also tells of his survival after an attack by a large crocodile and of his work in the outback of the NT.

All books are available as both as eBooks and in print.

Graham is planning a memoir about his family's connections with Ireland called *Memories Only Remain* and is also compiling information for a book about the early NT cattle industry, its people, and its stories.

Graham writes for the creative pleasure it brings him. He's particularly gratified each time an unknown person chooses to download and read something he's written and particularly when they write a review, good or bad, as this gives him an insight into what readers enjoy and helps him make ongoing improvements to his writing.

In his other life, Graham is a veterinarian who works in wildlife conservation and for rural landholders. He lived a large part of his life in the Northern Territory, and his books reflect this experience.

More information about Graham and his books and writing is available from the following sites:

Graham Wilson – Australian Author on Facebook and Goodreads

Graham Wilson's Author Web Page

www.grahamwilsonbooks.com

If you wish to contact Graham directly please use the email: grahamwilsonbooks@gmail.com

291